Secrets of a
FORMER
MAYOR

*What really happens
behind the Chamber doors!*

RYMA BEPHALAN

BALBOA.PRESS
A DIVISION OF HAY HOUSE

Balboa Press books may be ordered through booksellers or by contacting:

Balboa Press
A Division of Hay House
1663 Liberty Drive
Bloomington, IN 47403
www.balboapress.com.au
AU TFN: 1 800 844 925 (Toll Free inside Australia)
AU Local: (02) 8310 7086 (+61 2 8310 7086 from outside Australia)

Print information available on the last page.

ISBN: 978-1-9822-9219-5 (sc)
ISBN: 978-1-9822-9220-1 (e)

Balboa Press rev. date: 10/11/2021

I dedicate this book to my beautiful sister Julie for making me finally put pen to paper. Love you, Sis. Xx

PROLOGUE

I WAS A GOOD MAYOR, ONE THAT CARED ABOUT THE CITY. I HAD NO other agenda other than to see the city flourish into a great place to live. I had no dreams of being a politician or using the mayoral position as a stepping stone to further my career.

As a qualified lawyer, mother of three amazing daughters, with a devoted and loving husband, I really couldn't have wanted for anything more in life.

When I decided to run for councillor of our city council, it was a huge decision. People were friendly and encouraging. I ran a good campaign with an excellent platform. From start to finish, the election campaign was a great experience. I had beautiful friends around me that put in a massive effort to help me with my ads and mailouts.

It was a big step going from councillor to mayor. An important job to do, and I have a new respect for anyone who stands for election to take on the role of mayor.

What goes on in local government? I have decided to share a few stories with you because I believe that people need to know.

I share stories from my childhood through my last election and some of the juicy stuff during that time.

You would have to question the people that you vote onto your local council. What are they like? Would you vote for someone that has a party trick of poking his penis in a Corona bottle? Trust me; there are some absolute dickheads voted onto local government. So take a good look at your local government elected members. I bet there are a few stories to be told there too!

CHAPTER ONE

Do you think it is a good idea to run for public office? To put yourself out there for all and sundry, to lay crap on you, comment on everything you wear, say and do!

If only I had known what was install for me in the future, I never would have put myself in that position. My name is Elizabeth Valenti, everyone calls me Liz, and I wanted to share what happened during my term as the mayor of Wanjup.

Have you ever sat there wondering what on earth local councillors are thinking when they make decisions that negatively affect so many people! Back in 2008, the Dim Wits on the council decided to close the traffic on a major shopping road. The main road in the city. It didn't work, it crippled small businesses, and most of the small shops along the strip closed. Why would any city need another mall where drunks, druggies and homeless people can hang out? Just bloody stupid! The council paid for a traffic consultant to give them ideas on making the city traffic flow better. Unfortunately, the people conducting the review did not consult with the local business owners or those that live in the precinct. Instead, they sat at their desks and did a review from another city.

After the council spent over $1m on closing the road and its subsequent failure, I decided to stand for the next council election. I believed that I could make a difference and set these idiots straight. I have lived here for nearly my entire life, raised my family and watched Wanjup grow from a population of 25,000 to over 45,000 and seen firsthand the ridiculous waste of money that the city has spent.

My election platform was to bring good governance to the city and stop the waste of rate payers' money. I am a qualified lawyer and had my law firm in Wanjup. My campaign was relatively straightforward. Once I had my meeting with the Returning officer from the SA Election commission and paid my $100 nomination fee, I put my profile together, organised newspaper advertisements, and organised a mail out to my ward area. Our council has four wards, with each ward having three councillors to represent it, together with the mayor. It is a council of 13 elected members, way too many councillors for a small city.

I had terrific backing from everyone at my tennis club and the local sailing club that I and my husband sponsored through our company. People were genuinely happy to support me and encouraged me to stand up to the absolute idiots that were currently running our city. Little did I know that being a councillor gave me very little power to make changes.

Being a lawyer and owning my own business earned me respect because I am a professional person with high integrity. I also think that the reason that I have lived in the area for over 25 years and raised my family here showed my commitment and knowledge of Wanjup.

I won my seat on council with an easy victory over the other three candidates. It is quite an honour to have your fellow citizens believe in you enough to give you their vote. Councillor Elizabeth Valenti has a nice ring to it!

I learnt a lot in my first year on the council. It is incredible how much goes on in your town, of which you have no idea. We tend to surround ourselves with like-minded people, people who hold similar beliefs and morals.

Finding out about the homelessness problem, the abuse of drugs and domestic violence and unemployment are all areas that have never, thankfully, affected my family or anyone else I know. These things were happening right under my nose, and I never saw it.

As a councillor, I would listen to people's requests and do my best to help them, generally, like tree removal, building approvals, road modifications, etc. Usually, I would meet them on site, take notes and photos and be their conduit with the city's staff. That part is so important as most people don't know who the right person is to talk to in the city.

Getting past the reception desk can be the biggest hurdle. It can be impossible and extremely frustrating, trying to speak to the right person in the city. That is why having the help of a councillor is essential.

The first two years on council flew by very fast, and I felt comfortable in my role. I guess this is why I believed running for the position of mayor was achievable.

The mix of males and females was even with six males and six females. I got along well with everyone and found them all friendly and very helpful.

On the night of the council election, when I was running for councillor, I was quietly confident, three candidates were running for one position, and I was the clear winner by nearly 300 votes. My family were incredibly proud of me, especially my parents. I was giving my mum some serious bragging material at their retirement village.

My husband and parents attended my first council meeting and took lots of photos. I had a name plaque with my name and councillor written under it. I felt pretty overwhelmed at my first meeting, having to vote on matters I wasn't familiar with, speaking into a microphone with the public present and the local press.

Everyone was so helpful and kind to me, making the transition onto council very pleasant. If only I knew what was to come in the following years!!

I was accepted as an equal, well regarded by my peers and felt like I was a part of something exceptional. On the other hand, I felt guilty calling them a bunch of idiots for making dumb decisions in the past. There is a lot that people don't know about how things happen behind closed doors.

Every month a council meeting is held and is open to the public, where they can ask questions and listen in on what city decisions get made on their behalf.

We are sent our council minutes, usually seven days before the meetings. So there is a lot of information to absorb to enable you to make an educated and well-informed decision when deciding on which way to vote.

City officers always end the reports with their opinion on what recommendation they want. But, unfortunately, these recommendations are usually what the CEO, Paul Aldman, wants us to choose.

For a basic run down, the staff at the city are the ones who generally put reports forward to the councillors to consider. The staff always put their recommendation at the end of the report. After that, it is up to the councillors to question the report and decide whether to recommend or oppose it.

The CEO generally tries to manipulate the decision in favour of the officers/staff recommendation. The reports can have big holes in them, and it is up to the elected members to ask the right questions. The officers will go out and get an independent review on something, and these reviews tend to fall towards the outcome that the CEO wants. Yes, the CEO is extremely manipulative. He ensures that the debate in the council chambers goes in the direction that he orchestrates.

Before every council meeting, there is an hour meeting behind closed doors with the elected members and the officers who have put the report forward and the executive team and CEO. Decisions are made in the backroom and not the actual chambers. Citizens are welcome to come and make a deputation in favour of or against any agenda item during the council meeting. However, it is a waste of time as the councillors already have their mind made up. They generally make all the right noises to ensure that the public thinks they are being listened to and ask the right questions of the officers.

If you want to get your opinion heard, you need to meet one-on-one with the councillors in the ward where the agenda item is located. Separate and divide the council and get heard by the strongest and most opinionated councillor, who will make your point behind closed doors before it hits the public chamber.

CHAPTER TWO

Let me tell you a little about the council I joined. The mayor, Ron Yag, is a large man and ex-army in his late 70's. A kind man who gives his all to help people. Then there is the deputy mayor, Derwent Peabody, a shoe repairman; he works at the local shopping centre. Scrawny and one of the most unattractive men I have ever met. His salt and pepper hair is greasy and needs a good wash; his face is covered in old pimple craters, probably due to teenage acne, that never fully cleared up. He constantly supports a sizeable cold sore on his top swollen lip. He speaks with a terrible lisp and constantly wheezes with his lousy asthma. This man is someone I would never trust; he would talk to you with a smile and agree with what you say, only to turn around and vote against you and say awful things behind your back. Derwent got married during my term as mayor to a cleaner called Patricia. Not a match made in Heaven. You would hope that Derwent got on top because if he were lying under her, she would crush every bone in his body! She was obese and a nasty woman. You know the type of person who would say snarly comments to you like "how would you know, you have never worked a hard day in your life"! or "it's ok for people like you, you've got daddy's money", dismissing the fact that I have worked my arse off my entire life.

Patricia worked for a special needs centre that looked after adults with disabilities and couldn't look after themselves. However, Patricia lost this job. A good friend of mine, Meagan, who does the catering for this centre, came to my office to tell me. Meagan also informed me that Patricia was fondling the older men for money while cleaning their rooms. One of the patient's family members became suspicious when they noticed money missing and set her up. They left a cheap necklace and a $50 note in their dad's top drawer and told the head of staff and a couple of staff members when they left. They also took a photo with their phone and sent it to the centre's management as proof, to try and catch the culprit.

After Patricia finished her shift, the head of staff went into the room to check on the necklace and cash; sure enough, the money and necklace had disappeared. He called Patricia into his office before she had a chance to leave the building and asked her to empty her pockets. She refused and got quite offensive at the request. He threatened to call the police if she didn't comply with his request, so Patricia finally pulled the money and necklace out of her pocket. Her boss was shocked to see over $500 with the necklace he recognised from the sent photo. She certainly had been busy. It is funny how none of the male patients complained.

He had received complaints over the past few months from patient's families regarding missing money but struggled to pinpoint who was responsible and how to catch the crook. It is never pleasant having to sack someone, especially when you trusted them.

Meagan did the right thing by me and came to my office to let me know what had happened and that things were about to get horrid in council because of it. But, unfortunately, the head of staff never pressed charges against Patricia because he believed sacking her was enough. He would never give her a reference, though.

I personally never liked Patricia; she gave me bad vibes when I was near her. She was a 'User". Patricia married Derwent shortly after I came on the council. She moved her tribe of teenage children into his house and begun bludging off him. The former mayor was invited to America to do a "Sister city" agreement. He asked the deputy mayor to join him. Ron brought his partner Sylvia and allowed Derwent to invite Patricia. The ratepayers of Wanjup fully funded this trip. Patricia took full advantage of this and attended dinners and events with no formal invite and clocked up the expenses. To note that Sylvia didn't participate in the events and was very respectful of her place, she was just so pleased to travel with Ron.

As deputy mayor, Derwent attended many dinners and events. Patricia went to every event that included free food and drinks. She wasn't going to miss out on anything. Patricia was very proud to hold the title of the deputy mayor's wife.

I do believe in Karma; Patricia left Derwent two years after they were married. She kicked Derwent out of his own home and forced him to move in with one of his sons. She then went about screwing him for everything he owned, including his superannuation. Patricia left the poor bastard with nothing. Not a bad wage for only a few years of work. This woman, although she has Derwent's money, will never find true happiness or love. She is a miserable bitch who will spend the rest of her life trying to scam another poor soul.

Derwent was always two-faced with me; he would act kind and agree with our conversations, then turn on me behind my back. I believe Karma is the true leveller in life. The shit that he gave me came back in buckets when he married Patricia.

Then there is the councillor, who is a total sleaze, Donald Geary. He is the typical used car salesman. This guy is everyone's friend but no one's friend. You would never want to go to war with this guy thinking he has your back! He would run away at the first sound of gunfire. He stinks of alcohol at most council meetings and is constantly screaming poor, even though he lives in a mansion and wears designer clothes. I am reasonably sure he never read the council reports that he was voting on because the questions asked were clearly stated in the paperwork. He likes to ask lots of questions, relevant or not because the local press would print his name in the paper saying he asked questions and have it recorded in the minutes of the meetings.

Donald was very much a "look at me" type of guy. Not that he was attractive! Standing five foot six inches and weighing close to 120kgs, able to kill councillor Derwent if he accidentally sat on him! Donald lost all his hair young and has massive bags under his eyes. Donald always misses council meetings but makes sure he attends every third one, so he can't be kicked off the council. The cheeky bastard still runs for re-election on the council, and people believe his bullshit and vote for him. He is even considering running for federal politics. This man is delusional. Oh! Fun fact, this same councillor publicly pulled his pants down and poked his penis into a Corona beer bottle at the local football club, in front of a crowd of men, to prove how small his penis is!! Yep, there is top-notch talent on council!!

Donald would call me asking for crayfish because he had a hot date coming over for dinner. My husband Mike loved cray fishing and would often bag out his daily catch limit. Being Italian, our family also made its own wine. So, Mike would generously give Donald a couple of crayfish and a bottle of red to enjoy with his date. Happening regularly, Donald never had the same woman over twice. I think we all know the reason for this!

He would attend charity rallies and events, be the big showman and talk the talk, but he didn't walk the walk. People who volunteer in the various charities around town would comment on what a nice guy he is, but he never actually did anything. He wouldn't get his hands dirty helping out but would post photos on social media about being at all these different places pretending that he was helping people. However, Donald had the right contacts to put various charities in touch with, which is the only way to see where he helped them.

To describe Donald's personality, he is always smiling, always acting the fool, knows everybody, even if they don't know him, and is not shy in speaking out about any subject matter. My mother always said, "empty vessels make the most noise"!

On the flip side, Donald is an alcoholic and smokes like a chimney, and the smell is quite overwhelming when he enters a room. As an elected member chosen to make decisions on the running of our city, it concerns me that people voted him into office. He sells second-hand cars, knows nothing about economics or how to run a business, let alone read a balance sheet, and is making decisions that affect thousands of people who live here.

Donald would ring me at night for a chat about what was going on in council; we would confide in each other and generally have a bitch about what the other councillors were doing. When I first came onto the council, he was there straight away to give me guidance and help. I truly appreciated this as there is a lot to learn about the role and the politics behind closed doors. However, these conversations stopped when I became the mayor. By this stage, I had learnt so much more about the person he was, more than what people saw. It was too dangerous to confide in a loose circuit like Donald once I held such an important position. He would turn on me in such a cruel way I was shocked and highly disappointed. Stupid because I should have seen it coming. Some people are born without a backbone.

Another councillor, Lincoln Harvey, has blonde hair, pasty white skin and is very skinny. He looks like he needs a good feed and a gym membership. Lincoln had big aspirations to become the mayor one day, and I am sure he is looking at taking over the local state seat. But, seriously, why would such a wealthy man want to give up his time, to sit on council meetings and not be out enjoying life? It became clear to me, after a few months, that the current mayor Ron, wanted Lincoln to take over his seat when he retired.

Lincoln spoke very well and was raised in Wanjup; he knows the area and the people. He loves the theatre and has been in many plays. He also loves to dress up; he makes a better-looking woman than most women in town when he is all dolled up in Drag! A very confident man. He only achieved education to the end of year ten. His work history was purely volunteer work. Never actually having applied for any position in a paying job, he lacked the experience of real-world employment and experience. Lincoln received a large fortune from his grandparents and never had to get a job. Lincoln is a lot of fun, though, as most gay guys are. He doesn't walk but prances and jumps around like he has Red Bull for breakfast.

Another councillor who is a real piece of work is Sharon Day, who thinks she is more intelligent than everyone else; Sharon works on analysing people's faecal matter, "poop," so she has some intelligence with her microbiology degree. Her intelligence, unfortunately, is misguided. To supplement her income, she is a casual sex worker. Sharon is against anything that could be profitable to a ratepayer. She would rather see the city overrun with homeless people and vermin than back a new business idea for any growth in the city. Sharon is fortunate not to have to work out for her incredible body. A tidy size 10 with a large bust and long blonde wavey hair. Sharon is married with one child and is the type of woman who speaks to you while turned side-on, with her shoulder to your face, like she can't wait to get away from you. I never trust anyone who can't look you in the eye. She is one of those stuck up bitches who pretends that her shit doesn't stink. Her clothing was always creased like she just picked it up off the floor from throwing it down there the night before. She was also extremely jealous of me. Sharon was friendly to me when I was just a councillor, but when I became the mayor, her kindness disappeared overnight, and her fangs came out dripping with resentment for me.

Sharon is a Lincoln fan and told me I had no right to run against him because I hadn't been on council long enough. What an idiotic comment from a stupid woman. Sharon loves the fact that Lincoln splashes his family money around, and she is there to help him spend it.

When we both came to the council, I dressed in a suit or a dress and jacket. Normal wear for a lawyer. Sharon turned up to meetings wearing clothing that was not business-like at all. Something you would wear to do gardening or clothes to lounge around the house on a Sunday afternoon. It was interesting to see how she started to morph into my style over the coming months. Suddenly, Sharon wore dress pants and nice tops; then the jackets began rolling in, even dresses teamed with a coat on occasions. They do say that imitating someone is the highest form of flattery.

It made me feel proud that I influenced how people dressed to attend the council meetings, even as a councillor.

Sharon was so jealous when I became the mayor that she scrutinised everything I did. She didn't have enough poop to analyse or men to find her attractive in her secret part-time business. She would rant on social media about anything that she perceived I did wrong, and people would believe her. I started receiving emails and social media comments on how I was wasting the rate payers' money.

She didn't stop there either; she would run to the CEO to complain about the fact that I got a new mobile, briefcase, scarf or another part of my uniform. These items were all above board and were well within my budget. She just couldn't stand to see me receive anything.

Sharon would vote against my motions put forward at council just to spite me. She would have a snarly comment on any matters I raised and generally be a complete bitch to me. I noticed that Sharon and the

CEO Paul were very close, always having private meetings and sharing private jokes when in my presence.

Councillor Pauline Ashley runs a catering business and gives leftover food to the homeless. The city employs her company to cater for most of their functions. Pauline is ancient, with greasy thin grey hair, like Donald; she is an alcoholic and chain smoker. Another stinker, why is it that people who smoke don't realise how much they smell of smoke when they enter a room! And I call bullshit on the conflict of interest that constantly happens with her catering business. How can a sitting councillor be allowed to vote on events we have when her company directly gets hired and paid for by the city. Pauline is another turncoat when it comes to loyalty. As long as you are hiring her catering business, you are a friend. Employ another catering business; then you are dead to her.

I had heard rumours that the mayor would not stand at the next election, but when I asked mayor Yag, he would lie to my face and say he wasn't sure what he would do. Ron Yag wants to retire, is overweight, and his health is not good either. The role of mayor is quite demanding and gives very little time to relax and look after your health. So he left it until the absolute last minute to publicly announce he was retiring and would not stand again for election. He had told quite a few fellow councillors of his intention to stand down but somehow felt threatened to say it to me.

When I decided to run my campaign for mayor, it met with mixed emotions from my fellow councillors. Some were encouraging, while some were perturbed. Lincoln was the favourite person within the councillors to take over being the mayor, as he quite often paid for expensive dinners and gifts for the whole council. The current retiring mayor groomed Lincoln to take over his role.

Lincoln, the man he was grooming, knew Ron would retire and had already started his campaign. Credit to Lincoln, his campaign was very professional and well run. His boyfriend's father was the brains behind his operation, and I was impressed with how they ran the campaign.

CHAPTER THREE

To give you a bit more background on the other elected members of the council. There is another, less exciting councillor called Belinda Stump, who worked for the caravan park. This woman was in her early thirties, quite skinny and vertically challenged. She looked a bit like a broom handle with dark hair. Belinda's background was in sales, and we all thought she would bring an intelligent conversation to the table. Instead, Belinda would turn up late to council meetings or not turn up at all. She never commented or had an opinion on any reports and waited to see which way the vote was going before raising her hand. She was fast to accept the meeting sitting allowance and clothing allowance, would put in her weekly travel claim and be quick to take up any overseas or out of state conference attendance. Belinda was an actual waste of space in the council chamber. She lasted her term and lost the next election.

Then there is councillor Jack Piper, tall with a good build, friendly face and very sincere. He is Jewish with strong beliefs. Jack's wife, Monique, is so beautiful, you would never doubt that she was a Victoria's Secret model and a gorgeous and kind lady, the perfect couple. Jack always brought up interesting questions on the tabled reports at the council meetings and was fair and never judgemental towards anyone. Jack also decided to run for the mayor position when Lincoln and I were running; councillor Donald Geary also ran for the role and came in last. Jack was one person who I could trust; there weren't many I would put in that category. He spoke slowly with eloquence and with knowledge. You would stop and listen to him because he generally made sense and wasn't going off on a tangent that would lead to his benefit. Councillor Jack would read the agenda and highlight areas of concern to bring up relevant questions. There is nothing worse than sitting in a meeting listening to someone talk absolute crap and wasting everyone's time so that they can hear themselves speak. Jack is a good councillor, and I wish people elected more on to council like him. He was on the council to do his role and do it well; he had no side agenda for self-benefit.

Councillor Lucy Meadow is a beautiful soul! Lucy was elected to council two years before I was elected. Lucy is the typical earth-loving hippy, no jacket or suits for this lady. She loves to wear overalls, baggy dresses with flowers in her hair. She often wore large broaches made out of gum nuts or other flora, and never dressed in a business-like manner, even if I approached her and asked that she dress up for an occasion. Lucy had her style, and if you didn't like it, then too bad!!

Lucy ran her fruit and vegetable business locally and loved everyone. No matter what age, colour, sex or religion. She was at peace with the earth and her surroundings. As Lucy ran her own business, she understood the challenges that small businesses faced and was an excellent advocate for business. Lucy was able to understand the balance between progress and caring for our fragile environment.

Lucy became close friends with councillor Sharon Day and became a strong voice for all matters to do with the environment. Unfortunately, Sharon had blinkers on when it comes to understanding the local business community's needs. She would happily sabotage the city's future growth to protect a weed. Sharon was a bully and forced her ideas onto poor Lucy, who sometimes found it hard to stand up to her. Sharon believed herself to be most righteous on everything she had an opinion. She put herself on a pedestal and looked down her nose at everyone.

Then there is councillor Barney Jones; this guy is a retired policeman. A unionist believing that anyone who owns a business should give money to those who don't want to work. Increase the unemployment benefits and increase company taxes. Barney is another councillor who loves to hear the sound of his voice in the council chambers and asks obvious questions where he already knows the answers. He has an alliance with councillor Sharon Day, and together they plot and scam the reports to go in their favour. They badger the city officers to include their point of view in reports that come to the council for consideration. I would quite often see them leaving the CEO's office, and they would refuse to tell me what they were discussing. Bloody rude really, they think they are clever doing their secret squirrel crap.

Barney was diagnosed with cancer last year, which took him away from the council for about six months. Instead of standing down at the next election, he was re-nominated and was again elected back into the council. He has been away from the meetings more than he has attended due to his poor health. Why do older people hang onto a position of power when so many other people in the community can step up and do a better job if given the opportunity? I think they are just highly selfish. Barney would sit in the chamber and constantly mutter under his breath, slagging off other councillors after commenting on a subject. He was loud enough so you could make out what he said, things like "Wow, that was intelligent", "he obviously has no idea", or other demeaning comments. Full of self-importance and arrogant mannerisms, he is a very unpleasant man to be around.

Alex Smith is a councillor who tends to slide under the radar. He is pint-sized, pushing five feet tall, and a generally nice fellow who works at the local shopping centre with Derwent. They do look out for each other, but Alex is nothing like Derwent. Alex has a caring nature and works hard at looking after the needs of his ward ratepayers. It is not all about him, but rather what he can do for you. Alex takes pride in his elected role, always turns up to meetings on time, and is well prepared. He doesn't have a wife or any children. He suffers from Post-Traumatic Stress since he left the Navy.

Alex is another councillor that I would feel comfortable confiding in, even with his allegiance with Derwent. He is not someone that handles conflict well and will always try to be a peacemaker. He would be the diamond in the rough.

Then there is John Driver; this guy is your typical sweet man that doesn't want to rock the boat. He has his opinions but generally will curve towards the popular vote. He is of average build for a sixty-plus-year-old, belly only just starting to protrude and hair receding beyond his ear lobes. Not a big drinker, doesn't smoke or swear and is a good listener. John has a family of four girls and a loving wife. He also works at the local shopping centre with Derwent and Alex but in a very different area. His role is the property manager of the shopping centre.

There are some people you meet in your life that don't have any impact or significance. Whether you met them or not, your life doesn't change; then, others have a pretty profound shift in your life's journey, for better or worse. John is one of those people I have enjoyed meeting and getting to know him and his family, but with no impact on my life.

CHAPTER FOUR

COUNCILLOR LINCOLN WAS CHARMING TO BE AROUND AND ALWAYS HAD a smile. The former mayor Ron Yag took quite a shine to him, and he would mentor him through council proceedings. But, unfortunately, Lincoln's parents had nothing to do with him; his mother raised him as a sole parent until he was five, then dropped him off at her parent's house, never to be seen or heard of again.

When mayor Ron Yag knew he was retiring from his role as mayor, he starting bringing Lincoln along to all his events, functions and presentations so that Lincoln could learn the ropes. As a result, you would often see the two of them having coffees in town, discussing various things in the city.

The following two years flew by, and the election was looming. I still had two years of my councillor term, and Lincoln's time was up. But he wasn't going to be re-elected as a councillor; he nominated only for the role of mayor, as he believed no one would beat him. Lincoln was so overconfident that he would win the mayor's election; he never considered losing. He never thought that he would lose his place on the council if he lost the mayoral race.

Lincoln volunteers at the local gym, which doubles as a dance studio; you can hire a room to carry out dance classes. The city fully funds this building. Mayor Ron Yag was a significant influence here, to give Lincoln a platform to run for mayor. Lincoln did not have a job and had never worked for anyone, apart from helping out his friend's dad's business washing cars, and this was so that he had something to put on a resume. Not having any tertiary education or business experience,

Ron knew he had to help Lincoln be a serious contender for the mayoral position. The gym receives sponsorship from local philanthropists and fees from hiring out the space for dancing. Mayor Ron Yag decided that the gym needed a CEO! So, he selected Lincoln for the position. He might have no CEO experience or business education, but Lincoln is sitting in his purpose-made CEO position. It looks good on a business card.

One day out of the blue, Lincoln asked me, "Liz! You aren't thinking of nominating for the mayoral position at the next election, are you?"

"I have no idea Lincoln." And that was the truth. I was still getting my head around the whole councillor position and the inside politics that ran with it.

"You will let me know if you are going to run, Liz? I have this in the bag, and you will be wasting your time and money if you decide to run against me!"

Ballsy little shit! I thought. "Sure, Lincoln, if I decide to run, I can guarantee you will be the first to know!"

My husband Mike and I travelled east to Broken Hill for a Caravan getaway with many local 'Grey nomads'. These guys always know how to have fun.

One night, a few older gentlemen approached me to inquire about the upcoming election for mayor in Wanjup.

"Good evening, councillor Valenti." "Stop!" I laughed, "I am on holiday with my husband, and you must call me Liz."

"Apologies, Liz. We were just showing you the respect you have earned." "We won't take much of your time; we just wanted to know if you have considered running for mayor of Wanjup?"

"No, I haven't; I know that Lincoln is fairly sure he has it in the bag. He has a massive following around town, and I reckon he will be impossible to beat."

"You have our full support Liz, and I can assure you, there are plenty of funds available to support you if you are willing to run against this imprudent man!"

I thanked these beautiful supporters and agreed I would consider it.

On the other hand, Mike wasn't a fan of me putting myself out there for the mayoral position.

"Are you seriously considering this, Liz?" Mike asked. "The opposition will tear you to shreds, and I'm not sure you are ready for it!"

"I agree, Mike, but someone has to stand against Lincoln, and even if I just dilute his votes, it will be worth it."

"Not a good enough reason Liz, I am not supporting this madness, and you need to think about what you are putting your hand up for!"

"I know, you are right. I am happy just being a councillor, and I am busy with my girls; they come first."

As the time passed and the election came closer, I received more and more pressure to run against Lincoln. So many people had no respect for his foolish mannerisms or misguided confidence. People could see through his political alliance and his mentorship with the retiring mayor.

Mike had to go away for a week for a business meeting to sort out another family business section. It was during this time that my supporters pounced on me.

They organised a meeting at my home office and spoke of the readily available funding to start my campaign. They had organised support staff to guide me through every aspect of the campaign, and all I had to do was say yes, l will run.

They were very good at stroking my ego and my confidence. I could take on the world after my supporters left my office! But I was happy to start with Wanjup. So, I agreed to run against Lincoln.

So, as promised, the first person I called was Lincoln. "Hi Lincoln, it's Liz," Lincoln replied, "Don't tell me you are calling to say you are running for the seat of mayor?"

Wow, he was on to it already; word had spread quickly. "Yes, I have decided to run. It wasn't an easy decision, but I can't have you running unopposed! I don't believe I will win but thought we could have some fun campaigning against each other."

"I am disappointed you have decided to run Liz, you know you won't win!"

"True, Lincoln, but there is no law against me giving it a go. I might learn a few things during the campaign process. I do wish you all the best, and may the best man win."

For the remainder of our time together on council, I would often see Lincoln in mayor Ron's office and see him meeting with the CEO Paul.

This man had many influential people pushing him to run for mayor's seat, and I am sure the mayoral position was a stepping stone into state politics, if not the federal government.

Leading up to the election, Ron would bring Lincoln along to many of his appointments and ensure that Lincoln had his photo taken with him for publication in the local newspapers.

Ron even had Lincoln do a few of his presentations. The deputy mayor should have done these presentations, not a councillor. It was apparent that Ron was preparing Lincoln for his role as mayor.

I formed my campaign team and started working out my platform, advertisements, postal flyers etc. It was pretty exciting, and we all had a lot of fun. The questions asked through my webpage and other social media were relevant and intelligent. People were respectful and kind.

One day, my campaign crew and I walked through town handing out flyers for my upcoming election, and Lincoln's team was doing the same. Lincoln and I even walked for a while together, having a bit of friendly banter with each other. It was a nice and pleasant campaign.

The campaign was fun and an overall great experience. However, Lincoln truly did not take me as a serious contender for the position of mayor. I had pink tee shirts made up, and he had purple-coloured shirts.

During my campaign, the tone in council started to change towards me. I had only been on council for two years, and many councillors didn't believe I had a right to contend for the seat. Although three of the seven candidates had never been on council, that didn't matter because they weren't a severe threat like I was.

My campaign only went for a short time compared to Lincoln's, who had more warning to get organised. However, we did have fun campaigning, and the whole experience was enjoyable.

I didn't think I would win as Lincoln's campaign was all about the youth and underprivileged in the city, and I was pushing for the people who paid rates and getting better facilities for them and boosting local business.

On the night of the election vote count, the first count came in with Lincoln winning by nine votes, and the returning officer said it was too close to call, so ordered a recount. They recounted nearly 25,000 votes. When Lincoln rang me that election night, I was having dinner with Mike and his friends. Lincoln's voice was very excited as he yelled, "Liz! I've won! You need to get over here now because they are doing a recount, and you need to be here." I didn't believe what he was saying; how could a vote be that close.

I had decided not to attend the vote count on Saturday night, firstly because I didn't think I would win, and secondly because Mike had just returned from a car rally and I wanted to spend the evening with him.

It was a balmy Saturday evening in October. I was eating dinner with Mike and the crew he had just returned from a car rally with, raising money for the Royal Flying Doctor Service. I hadn't seen Mike in seven days. I gave myself no chance of winning the count to become the mayor. Don't get me wrong, I wanted the position but knew what I was up against, youth and politics.

When Lincoln rang me, I was shocked to hear that I had lost by only a few votes, which triggered the recount. Lincoln exclaimed, "The returning officer, officiating the count, decided that it was too close to call, so has ordered a recount. So you need to be here in case you win. But, again, it's too close to call; I'm so excited, Liz, get your arse over here now!"

I left my dinner half-eaten and dragged my poor husband across the road to the Townhall, where the vote count took place. It felt like it took forever to count the votes. It was hot in the room, and the poor staff looked exhausted. The general murmuring in the room was unsettling, with eyes constantly darting my way.

The Scrutineers were on high alert and checked every pile to ensure that staff put the votes in the right pile. As this election was purely a postal vote, it was a hands-on affair. I didn't want to be there and just wanted it all over and done. Finally, after another two hours, the poor election counters had finished and had concluded who the official winner was!

Then the returning officer finally announced who the winner was, and I nearly fainted.

The returning officer took the microphone and announced, "The new mayor-elect of the city of Wanjup is Elizabeth Valenti". Holy crap! I thought, this is for real, I'm the mayor! "Congratulation's mayor-elect Valenti." I had won by a total of seven votes. People were screaming for a third count, but the officer in charge would not budge on the final count.

I watched Lincoln's face as he left the building with tears in his eyes. He wanted and needed this position more than I gave him credit. As a wealthy man, he needed to enjoy his money and life before being under the microscope of every critic that ever lived. I think I did him a favour by taking on this role.

A lot of people came to congratulate me, and the press were snapping photos. Lincoln graciously congratulated me then went back outside to cry. He was shocked that I took the mayoral role away from him. It blindsided him. His supporters surrounded him with chants of it not being fair that a third count wasn't done. We both had our scrutineers watching every voting slip counted, and they were also satisfied that the vote was correct and final.

My husband Mike gave me the biggest cuddle and kiss; he is my biggest fan! I then went to thank Lincoln for running such a good campaign, but he had gone outside. Although Lincoln was honestly not expecting to lose this mayoral race, the result shattered him. However, after a while, he regained his composure came into the room to congratulate me. That would have been one of the hardest things he has ever done!

It was a weird feeling winning under these circumstances. I won fair and square; the victory wasn't as sweet with people making me feel I had somehow stolen it from Lincoln! Some people were insulting and believed there should have been another count. Someone had to win, and someone had to lose. I ran a fair campaign, and people who believed in me voted for me. It just so happened that I had a few more people than Lincoln vote for me.

How a few votes can change someone's life forever? I couldn't wait to call my super proud parents. I think everyone in their retirement village knew the next day. My three daughters thought it was great; my eldest daughter Carla posted on social media, "I am now officially the

Princess of Wanjup". My husband was labelled as The Stud (because he was servicing the mayor!)

I woke up the following day thinking, wow, did last night happen! Then the phone rang, 6.30 am from an Adelaide radio station wanting an interview. I asked if I could have 10 minutes to down a coffee and get my head around what happened. While sculling my morning coffee, the phone rang again, and it was The South Australian newspaper wanting a photo and interview. That Sunday was a blur; I had to organise the kids for the picture, they are young adults, but as any mother will tell you, teenagers don't always know how to dress appropriately. For example, my second daughter Michelle had a tee-shirt with a picture of a guy holding his fingers over his mouth in the shape of a V; yep, the caliginous sign, really not appropriate for a family photo. Changed Michelle's shirt, and we were ready for the newspaper photographer.

My phone rang all day with people congratulating me and wishing me all the best for my new role. I don't think it hit me, the enormous role I had just taken on, until the evening when I could gather my thoughts. I felt like I would have a panic attack, but Mike reassured me that I had got this.

It was clear to me on that hot October night that many of the councillors wanted Lincoln to win. I can understand why they would want someone inexperienced to manipulate and mould into what was needed to have their way with future decisions, and I have just put a stop to that dream.

It is incredible how life-change just a few votes can be. I have had so many people tell me that it was their votes that gave me the winning edge. I heard stories of how people forgot to post their vote and drove that afternoon to the polling booth to vote in person, and it was because of them that I became the mayor. And, of course, I agree with them that it was their votes that made the difference.

CHAPTER FIVE

Before I go any further, I should give some background information on myself.

I was born in Port Pirie, South Australia, in 1969 to a German father and Welsh mother. My parents moved to Port Pirie from Fremantle, Western Australia, in 1960, to a beautiful home that my father designed and owner-built. I have an older sister Lisa and younger brother Patrick, so I am the middle child who gave my poor parents the most grief.

I was a terrible eater and suffered from malnutrition due to my fussy eating; my mum's cooking wasn't the greatest either! When I was six years old, I weighed 19kgs and attended the Woman and Children's Hospital every fortnight to have a glucose drip to help increase my weight. The hospital was a two-and-a-half-hour drive to Adelaide from Port Pirie. My mother fed me this awful medicine to increase my appetite; I remember it had a Giraffe on the box that the bottle came in. I also attended speech therapy because I had a terrible stutter and spoke so fast no one could understand me. I remember how much I hated people commenting on my body and putting their fingers around my arm. If someone is fat, you don't walk up to them and go, "wow, you are so fat, I can't fit my hand around your arm", so why do people think it's ok to mention how thin you are!

I attended the local catholic primary school in Port Pirie, St Marks, and did not want to be there. So as soon as Mum or Dad dropped me off at school, I would high tail it back home and hide out the back for the day. Hence at the end of year one, the school made me repeat the year.

Some of my fondest memories were at this school, where I met some great friends and had lots of fun. But, too much, my report card would say, "Elizabeth needs to apply herself to the job at hand" and "Elizabeth needs to stop talking during class", and my grades reflected this. The polar opposite is my older sister, whose report card was always perfect. My parents pulled their hair out, trying to work out where they went wrong with me.

If I had to say what the worst moment at primary school was, it would have to be when I caught head lice. Bloody horrible Nits that only seem to thrive in primary schools. I have the thickest hair, and my poor mother would be sitting there for hours trying to pull the lice comb through my long hair and washing it in everything the chemist recommended. When I caught head lice for the second time in one year, my dad was angry and frustrated watching mum delouse me that he got out the shaver and shaved my head. I was devastated and wouldn't go to school the next day. Being so thin and now with no hair, I looked like a victim from a POW camp. Everyone thought I was a little boy. The kids gave me shit at school, and it was a miserable way to finish off the year. Thank God my hair grows fast.

Another thing I struggled with at school was because I was one year older than all the other kids. As a result, I always felt stupid, dumb, weird, didn't fit in, and always misbehaved on my birthday. Feeling stupid because of repeating a year at school followed me through my entire schooling life. If I can recommend one thing to parents now, it is to get extra tutoring rather than make your child carry this stigma with them. It certainly didn't make me smarter the following year.

My parents worked at schools, my dad was a lecturer in Engineering, and my mum was a primary school teacher, so we had them all to ourselves every school holiday. My mum's best friend lives in Rose Park, and we would house swap for many years. John and Margaret and their three sons would stay at our house on the coast, and we would travel to Rose Park and stay at their house, which was close to the city.

Something about enjoying the big city would make me eat! I was always hungry when we stayed at Rose Park; mum didn't need to force this horrible Giraffe medicine down my throat to give me an appetite. Dad and mum would take us to the Botanic Gardens, Museum and Art

Gallery, the Zoo and the Markets. The local hotel had a beer garden which quite often had live music, and we kids could run around and dance. Great memories.

One year, Dad brought a new station wagon Holden Kingswood. The 1979 Christmas school holidays and my parents decided it was good to drive across the Nullarbor to visit relatives in Perth. This was our first car with air conditioning!! My dad was a heavy smoker who loved the Wee William brand of cigars. He smoked in the car with us kids in the back seat, and we weren't allowed to wind the windows down because the air conditioner was on. My brother's nose bled most of the way, and my sister got terribly car sick. We would fight and annoy the crap out of each other because it was too long to have three kids in the back of a vehicle for that length of time.

Dad allowed mum to have a turn at driving his precious new car, and she had only driven a manual before. She went to overtake a large road train doing 110kms and put her foot flat to the metal, somehow the car clicked back a gear into 3rd, and we lost the gearbox. We spent a week at Ceduna caravan park while we waited for a new gearbox to arrive. My sister fell out of the top bunk during this time and went face first, breaking her jaw. It just happened to be on her 13th Birthday. This was starting to be the trip from hell. I swore that day never to take my future family on a long road trip, even if the car has air conditioning.

So my parents could have a break, they would send us on camps during the school holidays, and my favourite was the YMCA camp at Weeroona Island. You got to meet kids you never saw again, stayed up late to play spotlight at the lighthouse and swam in the beautiful bays; of course, there is always the local shop with jam doughnuts too.

When mum was teaching at John Pirie high school, she went to help supervise a group of 15-year old's on a trip to Singapore. She invited me to join her, and this was my first trip in an aeroplane at the age of 16. We had a lot of fun. One day we were taken out on this old fishing vessel to stay the night on an island off the coast of Singapore. The look on my mum's face when we arrived was priceless. The tide was out so that the boat couldn't use the jetty; we had to jump into the ocean and swim to shore with our belongings in a garbage bag. Mum can't swim, so they put a floating ring in the sea for her to jump in. Finally, after a lot of coaxing, she jumped in, the floatation device disappeared, as did my mum! They threw a second one in, and I managed to get one on each arm and pushed her into shore. That night the people looking after us cooked up a feast of Morton Bay bugs and other seafood freshly caught. I am such a fussy eater, and seafood is not something that I would eat. Everything else they prepared, I wouldn't even try. I had a packet of smarties in my bag that was still dry, so I survived the night on smartie rations and my breakfast. We camped under a shelter and were picked up on the jetty the following day.

When arriving back at the hotel in Singapore, our busload of teenage girls caught the attention of a group of men at the bar, drinking before lunch, I might add! They were Australian submariners and had just taken leave and were staying at the same hotel. The adults' job of supervision just went up a notch. They had to work out a roster to patrol the hallways during the night. My mum got her first watch at 6 pm. One girl came out into the hallway and saw mum and said she had lost a friend. Mum panicked because it was obvious these girls were drunk and had cleaned out the mini-bar in the room. We checked the room then had the other teachers start to check all the other rooms. The hotel staff joined the search, and after an hour, they were deciding to call the police when mum went back to the missing girl's room to check she hadn't snuck back in when she noticed the curtains didn't look right. On inspection, she discovered the girl, passed out and standing upright wrapped in the curtain. Phew! Close call; however, some of the other girls took the opportunity of us all being distracted to join the navy guys at the bar. They were drinking with the guys who were doing a new sailor's initiation. They were handing a bucket around to the new sailors only, filled with a cocktail of alcohol, and they all had to drink until someone threw up. Then they made him drink the bucket again! Disgusting. The girls were quickly marched back up to their rooms, and the sailors received a stern talking about the fact they were only 15 years old.

My parents decided to take long service leave and travel around Europe for three months. I was sixteen at the time and had been dating my boyfriend for about five months. My Aunt Greta came to stay with us to keep an eye on three teenagers. This Aunt was something else! She dressed like a man, even had spurs on the back of her boots. She was a state champion for pistol shooting, which scared the shit out of me. In addition, she had a short German temper which led to us having a few words when I disagreed. However, my parents knew my boyfriend and had no issue with us going out on dates.

On the other hand, Greta told me that I couldn't see my boyfriend while my parents were away. That was never going to be ok with me. I proved too much for her one night, and we had a bit of a nasty fight. The next day I took my mum's "emergency" credit card that she left for us and caught the bus down the road to the local car yard. I purchased an automatic Datsun 120y in burnt orange, then drove to a friend's house and moved in with her until my parents returned.

Greta managed to make up stories about why I couldn't come to the phone when my parents called from overseas. This was before mobile phones were a part of our life. My parents were getting a bit suss when they rang early in the morning, and I still couldn't chat with them. Greta eventually gave them my friend's number so they could call me. They were not happy with me, but they couldn't do much from overseas. I purchased the Datsun but didn't have a driver's licence, so my boyfriend Mike taught me how to drive a manual. He was only 17 and was extremely brave. One lesson I remember, we were going down a very steep hill, and he told me to put the brakes on gently; instead, I hit the accelerator and was racing towards a dead-end with large limestone rocks around it. I panicked and let go of everything, and screamed. Mike had to grab the steering wheel and the handbrake, which stopped the car centimetres from the rocks. He couldn't open his car door, so he had to climb over to the driver's seat. I got professional driving lessons after that and passed my driver's licence. When Mum and Dad returned from Europe, I was in a lot of trouble! The credit card had an interest rate of 26%, and my dad didn't even know my mum had the sneaky credit card. She wasn't pleased with me either as she used that card for spoiling herself. I paid back every cent, including the interest.

CHAPTER SIX

YOU HAVE PROBABLY GUESSED THAT THE YOUNG MAN, WHO BRAVED getting in a car with me, and teaching me how to drive, ended up asking me to marry him!

I got a job at the local television station and worked in the accounts section. Because my parents made me go to finishing school, after I left high school, my typing and stenography skills were very high. As a result, I became a very valued member of the Channel Ten network. I would work in the accounts department during the day and then literally run down the hallways to the news department. You would walk into the smoke haze; the air-conditioning would keep it at a level you could see as you walked in. During the '80s and early '90s, everyone smoked at their desk. It was the norm and acceptable.

I would type up the Porta Prompt for the news presenters. There were seven carbon copies to type on, so you had to be correct on every letter you typed, or you would be going through seven colours of Tipp-ex to correct your errors. By the way, Tipp-ex was a miracle worker back then; they were tiny tubes of coloured paint to match the paper you were typing. Now, it's crazy to think that every newsreader, station manager, floor crew etc., had to have a copy of the news reader's script, all manually typed. It was hell! You had less than the time needed to type up the news and then run every copy to every department before going live. I loved every minute.

After I finished my shift in the accounting department and then the news department, I would run downstairs to reception to welcome the tour groups. I would take the groups of people through the media station and show them how the news was produced. The 'green room', the producer's area upstairs, the newsroom and any other room I could gain access to. I realised that I had the power to entertain the crowds that came through the station, and I loved it.

Then I was offered a position as Executive Marketing Secretary to a prominent bank. I was the executive secretary, who was able to wear the very cool clothes of the nineties. However, ladies much senior to me wore burgundy uniforms that I ditched at high school. They hated me from the minute I walked in wearing a black leather tight skirt. The bank sponsored the state basketball team, so I always had VIP tickets to share with my friends. Being a senior member of the marketing team of one of the most important banks in Adelaide was very cool. I had invites to all the VIP events and loved it. But then my beloved wog boy wanted to move closer to his family! The reason why I didn't want to move took more pages than a book can fill to explain. But as you know, I love this guy, and I moved.

Mike's parents recruited me to run their fruit and vegetable business from their family home. We had recently moved there, and I felt it was an excellent opportunity to spend time with my in-laws. So I would put my baby daughter in my bike's baby seat and ride ten kilometres to the family farm.

Years have since passed, and we have raised a beautiful family together. We have run our own business and enjoyed a very blessed life.

I attended that same university that my whole family graduated from and have worked in various jobs over my career. One exciting role I had, was teaching boxing. A new form of exercise popped up in the early nineties, called boxercise. I had to get my certificate in Aerobics instruction, then attend a boxing school in Adelaide. An interesting fact is, I was the only female in the class. Women's boxing was illegal in the early '90s, and I wasn't allowed to be in the ring with men and actually box; what a joke. The instructor held up a boxing bag, and I had to demonstrate that I knew the correct technique. Then I would leave the ring and watch the other guys beat the crap out of each other. I was a little bit happy; I wasn't on the receiving end of some of those blows.

The other men training for their Level one boxing accreditation had no respect for me. They treated me with disdain for slowing their class because I needed special, one-on-one treatment from the coach. However, I still turned up every week and beat the shit out of that boxing bag. I was better at the speedball than the guys too. I put this down to the fact that as a drummer, I had natural timing. They hated me for this. However, I kept up with them physically on the training track and passed with flying colours. I understand that the guys were upset because my training was under a different system, but it wasn't my fault. I passed my exam and achieved my Level One Boxing accreditation. The Institute of Sport in Canberra even sent me a cloth badge with 'Level 1' written on it. I sewed it onto my training tracksuit jacket.

I have always handled myself well. I don't take bullshit from anyone and am fiercely protective of my family.

When I moved from Port Pirie to Wanjup, I decided to start teaching Aeroboxing. The Police and Citizens Youth Club employed me straight away. They gave me the room for free if I could bring numbers to the venue. I agreed to provide them with 10% of the takings to give back to the club.

I went downstairs to the boxing area, and it stank! Man, No one had hygienically cleaned this place in a long time. So I opened the doors to the neighbouring football field, sanitised the equipment with the most potent alcohol-based products and set about marking my course for the first Aeroboxing class in Wanjup.

The first night that I opened my class, the people kept coming downstairs. My mistake was I never gave a limit to the reception upstairs. The class could have coped with 30 people, but I ended up with 84. My husband Mike was there to help out on the first night. He ended up having to run a circuit outside on the football field to cope with the numbers.

I did run upstairs and say, "Stop" we are full. I had no idea that Wanjup was screaming for something different. I ended up doing nine classes a week while working at my family's fruit and vegetable business, raising three daughters, and helping my husband with our family business. Women are strong and can multi-task, but sometimes we need to nurture ourselves a bit. It's ok not to cope and to fail at things. I certainly did not fail at Aero boxing, I worked until I was six months pregnant with my last daughter, but no one followed in teaching my classes. Boxing was very much a Man's business back in the early '90s.

When I started teaching boxing, no man held back; I can tell you that straight! It was like they had something to prove! To hit me harder than they would a man in the same situation, or it could have just been that I was the fairer sex. It was a great workout. To mix it up a bit, I added a bit of Muay Thai techniques to the class. I would hold the body pad up against my side to take the full brunt of their kicks, which would push me sideways. Unfortunately, I didn't have enough weight behind me to take the force. Hence the kicking part of the class didn't last long and was removed.

I continued to work in the family fruit business until my last daughter went to school. Then I attended university. I had achieved my diploma in accounting which gave me the passion for studying law, and now I wanted to go to university and do my Bachelor of Law.

Our truck hire company took off; we were now employing 30 people; I was doing the book work for that company while still working with the family fruit business and doing their book work. Running nine Aero boxing classes a week, raising three kids and attending university. I would be up to 2 am studying. Mike would walk into our home office and look at me like I was a crazed alien.

I had the most fantastic housekeeper called Susan; she would pick up the kids from school for me. Do their homework with them, entertain them until I got home. She cleaned, washed and ironed our clothes and even cooked us dinner. This woman was my saviour. I was never going to be the mother who stayed at home and did play-doh with the kids. But Susan stepped up and was always there for me. The girls just loved her, but if they couldn't find their homework, clothes, toys etc., they would yell, "Susan took it!" For over 25 years, Susan has stood by my family and me and cared for us, and yes, I did buy her a gold watch because she deserved it!

CHAPTER SEVEN

When I was a child, I was so painfully thin. It wasn't until the first pregnancy that I got an appetite and started gaining weight. I beefed up! Twenty Kilos through the pregnancy, and my daughter only weighed 3.5 kilos. It was all me.

I had post-natal depression, and my weight gain didn't help. It finally started coming off after my daughter was nine months old, only to find out that I was pregnant again! After that, I gained back everything I had lost!

After my second daughter was born, I started to teach Aero boxing, running nine classes a week. I became toned and very fit. I taught these boxing classes until I was six months pregnant with my third and last daughter. I hardly put on any weight with her, only 7 kilos, and she also weighed around 3.5 kilos.

I went back to work as a lawyer, sat on my bum behind a desk, and worked long hours. Food choices were not always that good either. The weight started to creep back on slowly.

One day your favourite jeans fit you well, and the next day, you find yourself lying on your back on your bed, trying to flatten your belly so you can haul that zip up, as the excess fat spills over the edges of your jeans. It's what we call a Muffin Top!

Then to make things worse, I became the mayor, with no time for exercise or any routine. Every day is different and can change in an instant. When you get home, you are so tired; there is no motivation to do anything other than sit in front of the television and have that well-earned drink, and maybe a few chips, biscuits, or anything else you can find to treat yourself.

There were many breakfast meetings and events that all served up the fully cooked breakfast, including bacon and eggs, hash browns and all the trimmings. Then to finish off breakfast, there is always the choice of French pastries with hot coffee.

I could attend up to five events in one day; it was exhausting. Most of the evening events served Tapas style finger food, and nearly everything was deep-fried.

The former mayor had health issues due to his obesity, and I was heading down the same path quickly. Even my dad told me I was getting fat and needed to lose weight. I was so shocked that he said that.

When you look at my photos from when I joined the City Council to when I finished being the mayor, you can see my face change from being thin to getting very chubby with fat cheeks.

Once I finished my term as mayor, I began the gruelling challenge of carrying out due diligence for the sale of our family company. An American company made us an offer that was too good to be true. As they were a large publicly listed international company, they had teams of accountants, lawyers etc., throwing questions at me. I was working all hours of the night to get them the information they needed. Another reason to make poor food choices and the weight continued to come on.

On the completed sale of our business, I was able to concentrate on myself. It was Liz's time to shine. I stopped drinking, started playing tennis a few times a week and took up Pilates. The result was most of the weight come off, and my favourite jeans fitted me without the need for lying on the bed first.

I am fortunate to be tall enough to carry the extra weight, but I needed to be nine feet tall to carry my mayoral weight. But, of course, having a large bust doesn't help either; it gives an impression that you are more heavier than you are.

Mike, on the other hand, is well over 6 feet tall and very lean. He has always been very good with what he eats and has incredible discipline with his exercise. His whole family are fit and look fantastic. He has that gorgeous olive Italian skin and thick grey hair. It was black when I met him. Mike reckons being married to me for so long has turned it grey!

Our three daughters all take after Mike. I swear that I was just an incubator! All three girls are tall with lovely olive skin and long dark hair. Two have Mike's brown eyes, and one has my blue eyes. Not one of my daughters got my blonde hair.

Mike and I started our family business the same year we got married. We started with one truck and hired it out, then purchased the next one and so on. So you can find our trucks all over the country. We ended up with over 550 trucks that we hire out.

Because of the size, our family business had become desirable to the American company that purchased it and sent us into retirement. So Mike was very quick to buy that big luxury boat he had always dreamed of.

Now we have more time to play tennis, golf, bike riding and spending time on our new boat.

Life is good!

CHAPTER EIGHT

FRIENDS COME AND GO, BUT YOUR FAMILY WILL ALWAYS BE THERE. So just keep an eye out for the friends who try too hard to be your best friend.

It was a gorgeous summer afternoon, and I enjoyed a ladies lunch at my friend Zina Parkin's house. Zina would often hold these events to raise money for different charities. She had the most fantastic home set on massive acreage: fifteen bedrooms, twelve bathrooms, and even a four-hole golf course.

After enjoying a delicious lunch, we were all sitting in and around the pool, drinking French champagne. At this lunch, I met Tracy Kardan. She lived in a small house behind Zina's Estate. She struck up a conversation with me, and I found out that her daughter was the same age by a few days as my daughter. In addition, Tracy and her husband owned a business which is something else that we had in common.

Tracy was hilarious, bordering on crazy, that day. The more she drank, the louder she became. Tracy was really in your face when speaking to you and had quite clearly attached herself to me for the rest of the afternoon. We exchanged numbers when I left, and she messaged me within five minutes of leaving Zina's.

I joined the local tennis club and booked in for lessons with the resident tennis pro. The tennis pro took groups of six, and the classes started in a week. I was excited to start a new hobby, tennis is a game that I have always wanted to play, and apart from playing at school so many moons ago, I hadn't had the chance to play. I was talking to Zina about the lessons, and she decided to join me. There were only a couple of spots left in the classes I joined, and I loved the idea of Zina joining me.

Then Tracy called me. "Liz, it's Tracy; I hope you don't mind, but Zina told me about the tennis lessons you are both going to, and I have joined up too. Isn't that exciting!"

I was surprised by this phone call as I felt like Tracy was starting to suffocate me. I don't know her, and she is inviting herself to something that I was looking forward to sharing with Zina.

So, I replied, "Hi Tracy, yes, that is exciting news; we can all get to hang out together." Not sure what else I could have said. You never want to be rude to someone, especially when you don't know them. She is a friend of Zina's, so she can't be all that bad.

Tracy continued, "So, after the lesson, I thought we could all go out to lunch. I have booked us into that cheeky little tavern near the coast." "Thanks, Tracy," I replied. "Have you checked with Zina to see if she is free to join us?" "Not yet," replied Tracy. "I am sure she will come, but if not, it will just be the two of us. Wouldn't that be fun!"

Tracy was putting me in a difficult situation. How would it look to Zina if Tracy and I took off to lunch without her? I was feeling the pressure now, so I thought I should check in with Zina. "Hi Zina, how are you going?" "Great, thanks Liz, what's up?" I continued, "you probably know that Tracy is joining us for our Tennis lessons." Zina replied, "Yes, I hope you don't mind Liz, I was talking to her about it, and she jumped right onto it." I was quick to reply, "No, I don't mind at all; I know she is a good friend of yours."

"I wouldn't put her in my 'good friend' category, Liz, she is my neighbour and a friend, but she is not someone I hung out with a lot." "She can go off the rails when she drinks, so I have learnt to be very careful to invite her only to events that are suitable."

The advice I should have taken on board for future events, Zina quite clearly warned me in this conversation, but it flew right over my head.

"Tracy has booked us in for lunch after our lesson next week. Are you able to join us, Zina?"

"Sure, Liz, any excuse for food, bubbles, and a chat sounds good to me."

Saturday morning came around fast, and I headed off to my first tennis lesson, with my new racquet that still had the plastic on it! The old ladies at the club were busy preparing morning tea for the new players joining the lessons.

I politely poured a cup of tea and took a fresh scone with jam and crème. These lessons were not going to see me lose any weight! Zina and Tracy then walked in; they shared a car, making sense seeing they live next door to each other.

The lesson went well; then, we headed off to lunch. It was a cute little restaurant attached to a tavern: beautiful ocean views and a great menu. Tracy ordered the champagne before we were even seated at our table. Zina was driving, so I gathered Tracy wasn't going to hold back on downing the drinks.

Tracy didn't disappoint; she became drunk within half an hour of being at the restaurant. She needed to get food in her belly before going hard on the booze. I found out that Tracy likes to gossip after a few. Wow, she knew so much about so many people. Some of her stories were quite shocking, and I became aware that people at nearby tables were starting to glance in our direction.

"Tracy", I begged, "Please keep your voice down; people are starting to look at us". Tracy didn't care, "They can get fucked! I can say what I like."

Wow, no class with this woman. Now I understand what Zina meant when she said she chooses her invites carefully with Tracy.

I was feeling somewhat embarrassed by Tracy's company. I made an excuse to leave and left cash with them on the table for my share of lunch. Then, driving away, I thought, shit! How can Zina be friends with someone like that? Zina will always look immaculate, speaks eloquently, even with her Spanish accent, and her makeup and hair look professionally done every time we go out. My effort is usually tinted sunscreen with my hair tied back in a ponytail.

The next day my phone rang, "Liz, it's Tracy. Have you got time for a quick chat?" "Sure", I replied. "Fantastic," enthused Tracy, "I'll be there in five minutes".

What! I thought she meant a quick chat on the phone. I didn't want her coming over to my house. I didn't even know she knew where I lived.

Sure enough, in five minutes, there was a knock at the door. I was surprised by what greeted me at the door. Tracy was standing there with a large ice cream container filled with Chicken and vegetable soup.

"Hi Tracy, what's up," I asked while looking at the container Tracy cradled in her arms. "Can I come in?" Tracy asked. "Sure, come on in. What do you have in the container?"

Tracy replied, "Chicken and vegetable soup; I was making a large batch and thought you might like some. I make the best soup in the whole world!" "You didn't look happy when you left us at lunch yesterday, and I wanted to check that you are ok!"

"I am fine, thanks, Tracy; I was just starting to feel very uncomfortable with the way the conversation headed."

"Sorry Liz, I get carried away sometimes, and the lips get loose once I have had a few drinks; I hope you don't judge me on one lunch. I like you and thought we could be best friends. And, you do know that I only ever tell the truth!"

"Thanks for the soup Tracy, you didn't need to bring me food, but I am sure my family will enjoy it." "I am wary of people who like to gossip, Tracy, I have had people talk poorly about me, and I can't understand the mentality of those who repeat such garbage." "All I ask of you is to never talk about people around me; I detest gossip."

"Liz." Tracy quickly replied. "Let's go outside for a smoke; I just got these beautiful pink ones from Zina; she brought them back from Spain."

I didn't smoke, and my husband hated the smell of smoke. Mike had gone out to play golf with his brothers, so I had the house to myself. We walked out to the pool area, which has wind protection.

Tracy can be a bad influence! After her second cigarette, I caved and decided to try one. Unfortunately, it wasn't as pleasant as I thought it would be, and I could feel the head rush from the nicotine. Tracy laughed at me, struggling through the cigarette.

"Here," Tracy encouraged, "I'll leave you with this packet. Zina gave me a whole carton; she sneaked them through customs in her luggage. She has that personality that she never gets checked by customs!"

"No, that's ok Tracy, I don't smoke. Please take the packet home." "Nonsense", Tracy exclaimed, "You must keep them here, hide them in the cupboard in your outside pool toilet. So no one will find them there!"

Tracy jumped up and confidently walked over to the toilet and then returned without the pink cigarettes. She left shortly after that.

I am feeling that Tracy is forcing her friendship on me. She is very confident and quite overpowering and not one that takes no for an answer. I called Zina to get a feel for her relationship with Tracy.

"Hi Zina, It's Liz." Zina is always so bubbly when she answers the phone, "Hello beautiful Liz, what is going on?" I continued, "I just had Tracy turn up at my house with a container of chicken and vegetable soup!" "Is this something she normally does, Zina? She is freaking me out a bit!"

"I am sorry, Liz, she asked me for your address after you left us at lunch. She was aware of her behaviour and wanted to make it up to you." "I think since she found out you are the mayor of the city, she wants to be your friend." "I am not condoning her actions but realise she can be a bit clingy." "Tracy is not a bad person, just a bit needy, so be gentle with her."

"Thanks, Zina", I replied, "Let's not do lunch after our tennis lesson next week; I think I need to move slowly with Tracy; I get the feeling she is a bit desperate to be my friend."

I decided to host a party for my Birthday, only a small event as it wasn't a special birthday. I invited Tracy and Zina along because I started to spend more time with Tracy and thought it was easier to ask here than explain why I didn't. Zina has been my friend for a long time, so she was always on the list. My other friends commented on Tracy during the night. Everywhere I went, she attached herself to me like glue. If I approached someone to speak to, she would fly over to me and find out what we were talking about and butt in. Her obsession with me was becoming very evident to my other friends.

Two days have passed since my birthday, and I haven't heard from Tracy. I finished at an official function and pulled into my driveway when I noticed Tracy's car parked on the verge out the front. Great, I can't believe she is here again! I parked my car in the garage and closed the garage door after entering the house through the carport entrance door.

Tracy was sitting on the front porch, holding another casserole dish. I opened the door and reluctantly greeted her. "Hi Tracy, what are you doing here?"

"I'm so sorry for not calling first; I was so excited to bring you this cottage pie I made; I left my phone behind in the kitchen and didn't realise until I got here and you didn't answer your door."

"I have a hectic schedule, Tracy," I replied. "Just today, I have three functions and two meetings to attend, so I can't stop to chat now."

"Well, it's a good thing your best friend has made you dinner!" Tracy exclaimed. "I make the best cottage pie ever; you will love it."

"Thanks, Tracy, but you don't need to make me dinner, I am very prepared with my meals, and Mike loves to cook too." "Thank you, though, for your thoughtful gift."

Tracy was very quick to intercept, "Do you have time for a quick smoke? Or have you smoked them all?"

"No", I replied, "The packet is where you left it."

"Great", Tracy said as she pushed past me to put the pie on the kitchen bench. She then proceeded outside to the pool area and grabbed the packet of smokes from the toilet cupboard.

I kicked my heels off, then took my jacket off and laid it over the dining chair. By the time I walked outside, Tracy had already lit two cigarettes, one for us both!

The last thing I needed was to attend my next meeting stinking with smoke.

"No thanks Tracy, I have to head off to another meeting soon, and I don't want to smell like an ashtray."

"Bullshit", Tracy exclaimed, "I have gum and perfume so that no one will notice the smell!!" "Here, take your ciggy; I have already lit it for you!"

I was not too fond of the way Tracy forced me. But still not trying to offend Tracy, I reluctantly took the lit cigarette and drew the poison into my lungs.

"You're not going to believe what I got up to last night?" Tracy spoke with such excitement; I thought she was going to explode.

I replied, "I have no idea what you did last night, but you look like you are going to pop if you don't tell me soon!"

"I caught up with Paul Aldman, you know, the CEO of the city! I joined this online bondage group and got talking to this guy who lives in Wanjup. He booked this dodgy motel on Ellen Street, near the old train station. You should have seen his face when I knocked on his door. He went as red as a beetroot and looked as awkward as fuck!" Tracy said.

This information I can't un-hear! I felt repulsed that Tracy had chosen me to confide. I don't know her that well, and to tell me this! I was shocked and really couldn't hide my expression.

"Please tell me, Tracy, you turned away and went home to your husband?"

"Haha, you are so funny, Liz! After Paul got over his embarrassment of knowing me, we got our funk on! He has some fucked up gear in his kit bag. I'm talking ankle sling loops, leather floggers and wrist cuffs, even a ball gag. He would have spent thousands on this stuff."

I wanted the earth to open up and swallow me. Tracy needed to stop talking because I have to work with Paul. How was I going to look at him in the face after this conversation?

"Paul is keen to catch up every month!" Tracy continued, "Paul is a bad boy; he likes to play rough and enjoys a good beating. I think I left a few scratches on his back; he will have fun explaining that to his wife!"

"Oh my God, Tracy!" "Is this the only reason you came over today? To tell me about your sex romp with my CEO?"

"No", Tracy replied, "I've got even more interesting news to tell you!"

"Please don't Tracy, I have heard enough today."

"Liz, my news involves your sister Lisa! I think you want to hear this."

"I will not believe my sister is involved in this bondage crap Tracy!"

"Correct, Liz, Lisa isn't involved, but her husband Scott is."

"What! How on earth do you know that?" This news was alarming to hear. Scott and my sister had been married for twenty-five years and went to church every Sunday. Scott was even a Catholic Acolyte to the Parish Priest.

Tracy was so excited to spread this malicious gossip with me; you could tell she enjoyed sharing this information. "I recognised him, Liz, from your birthday party. If I had my phone on me, I would show you his photo. He is one sick puppy! The photos he has posted show him in the full-body leather gear, you know, where he has a zip for a mouth, and only his eyes are visible under all that black leather. There are even photos of him with animals! He has his regular partners on this site; one of them even calls herself, Vagina breath!!"

I felt sick to the stomach! I know you shouldn't shoot the messenger, but my gun was loaded. "How dare you come to my house and tell me such horrible things, firstly about Paul and now you have thrown Scott into the mix." "Surely you have made this up; people don't go around doing this stuff."

Tracy gave off this shrieking sound that made my skin crawl. It was somewhere between a high-pitched laugh and a snarl. "The truth hurts, don't it, Liz!"

Excellent English, Tracy! She was smiling like the Cheshire cat. Very pleased with herself.

"I am sorry, Tracy, this has been a lot for me to take in, and I have to decide if and how I will tell my sister. I need to prepare for my next meeting and clear my thoughts. If you don't mind, I have to ask you to leave."

"You ok, Liz?" Tracy asked, "Sorry for dumping so much on you, but I thought you needed to know about Scott and also what type of freak Paul and Scott both are."

"Thanks, Tracy." "I know you had the right intentions by telling me this information, but I do need to get ready and head off."

"No worries, Liz, I hope you enjoy the pie for dinner tonight! Think of me when you are eating it. It will be the best pie you have ever eaten!"

I watched Tracy drive off the verge and around the corner. I didn't feel very well. That was a lot of stuff to hear about people you thought you knew.

Funny how Tracy can accuse Paul and Scott of being 'freaks' when she was playing a big part in all this!

I knew I had to tell my sister, poor girl. She will be devastated when she finds out. So I walked into the kitchen, opened the bin, then slid the pie into it. Who knows what Tracy put in that pie!

CHAPTER NINE

My sister Lisa is a beautiful person, inside and out. I indeed wouldn't have said that growing up in the same house as her. Our parents made us share a room, and we fought about everything. We were horrible to each other, and we drove our parents mad. Finally, one day, Dad gave up his home office and made it a bedroom for me. He made an office in the back workshop so he could have peace in the home.

Thinking back to those days, I can't even remember any significant reason why we did fight. Lisa was always the smart one who did her homework and received good grades at school. I struggled at school because there was always too much fun elsewhere. My dad would compare our school grades, which made me feel dumb and resentful of my sister.

Her clothing style was also very different to mine. Lisa loved frills and lace, while I loved Denim and tee shirts. She would listen to classical music, and I loved whatever was the latest on Countdown, the music program of the '80s. Lisa loved to read massive books, and I enjoyed the Mad comics, you know, the ones where you fold the back page to reveal another picture.

Lisa took off to travel around the world for a year, just after I married Mike. When she returned, I greeted her at the airport with my newborn daughter Carla. Lisa looked terrific; all that backpacking through Europe toned up her body. I probably noticed this more because I had just given birth, and I think I was pregnant in every part of my body. I swelled up to an additional 20 kilos. Considering Carla was only three and a half kilos, it was all me!

Lisa was dating a sleazy encyclopedia salesman before she went off travelling. Mike and I would see Scott out in the city, and he was always with many women. I wouldn't trust this guy as far as I could throw his short fat body!

On Saturday, while Lisa was still overseas, I received a phone call from Scott.

"Liz, are you free tonight?"

"Yes, Scott, I am; why?" I replied with curiosity.

"Well, as Mike is away on business for the week and Lisa is still overseas, I thought it would be nice for the two of us to catch up for a meal. We will be related one day, you know!" Scott said.

"I guess that would be ok! Where did you want to go?" I replied.

"There is this great new restaurant just opened up in town, you will love it! I will pick you up around 7 pm, ok?"

"Sure, Scott, I'll see you at 7 pm."

Scott was on time, and we enjoyed a lovely meal together. For a dickhead, he had some funny stories to tell. I could see how he charmed my sister. Then on the way home, Scott showed his true colours! He pulled into my driveway and turned off the ignition. Then without warning, he leant over to kiss me.

At first, it appeared he leant over to give me a goodnight peck on the cheek, but no, Scott went straight for my lips. Then, as I tried to pull away from him, he grabbed the back of my head and moved me towards his face and thrust his revolting tongue down my throat. This foolish move by Scott made me gag so bad; I threw up my dinner in his car.

Being mortified, covered in vomit, I struggled to undo my seat belt and slid out of his car. I didn't realise how much I had to eat and drink! I slammed his car door shut and walked away without looking back. I heard his car start up; then he was gone. He was driving back to his hole with the stench of my vomit in the air. He deserved every bit of it.

I later told Mike and my parents about what Scott had done to me. Mike never trusted him before and didn't like him now. My mum asked me not to say anything to Lisa. which I thought was strange. Knowing what type of man Scott is, why would you want him to marry your daughter? My mother knew how awkward our relationship was and thought she would only blame me if I told Lisa the truth.

When Lisa returned from Europe, she got back together with Scott, and they moved into a home they jointly owned. My mum warned me again about telling Lisa the truth about Scott, especially after they announced their engagement. She said that if I make Lisa break off her engagement to Scott and never marry again, it would be all my fault.

So, my lips sealed. Lisa married Scott. It was a beautiful wedding; she asked me to do a reading at the church wedding. But she was never going to ask, her only sister, to be her bridesmaid. Her excuse was, "you are already married, and married women can't be bridesmaids or a matron of honour!" Gutted that my beautiful big sister had shafted me. I had nothing to do with the wedding planning; I received no invitation to any hen's night or any real part in the whole wedding. I am sure she only asked me to read at the church because no one else wanted to do it.

Time passed, and Scott decided to leave the encyclopedia sales business and go to university. Lisa paid for Scott to attend university to gain his business degree. It took him longer than most to finish because he would fail units and re-enrol to study it again. After six years, he completed a four-year degree and gained employment in the government organisation called Centrelink, which looks after the welfare payments in Australia.

Thankfully now they had two incomes coming into the house, and Lisa had her first son. He was the cutest little fellow, with big chubby cheeks and thighs to match. Three weeks later, I gave birth to my third daughter. When Lisa and I stood back-to-back, we looked like bookends with our large pregnant bellies. Lisa's son Sean was born at the end of January, and my daughter Stella was born in mid-February.

Lisa and Scott lived in Adelaide, so we didn't catch up much. Maybe at Christmas and Easter only. We never really called each other or just caught up for a coffee. I found out years later that Lisa was expecting identical twin boys but had to abort after she found out that they had Anencephaly. One of the poor boys had already died. It was on the doctor's advice at 24 weeks to let the surviving baby go. They assured Lisa that her surviving son would only last a few days.

What a horrible decision to make; by the time Lisa had spoken to her parish priest and sought counsel from other doctors, she finally decided to say goodbye to her remaining son. None of this I knew. Lisa went through this without the comfort of family around her. Lisa's babies had Birth and Death certificates drawn up, and their ashes were blessed and spread in the memorial gardens at the hospital.

Lisa finally confided in me, years after the event that she had lost twin sons. I was so shocked. She also told me she had suicidal thoughts that some days she just wanted to drive straight into a tree because her grief was so overwhelming. Why I never knew this information before? It was at this point; I knew I had to work on my relationship with my sister.

Four years after losing her twins, Lisa gave birth to a gorgeous little girl called Rose. Now with her two beautiful children, their life seemed perfect.

Scott's parents were starting to become unwell; it happens to us when we get significantly older. So he started driving to their house a couple of nights each week to help them out. He would cook them meals and do the odd job around the house for them.

Or so Lisa thought! She watched a documentary on the ABC channel one night, when Scott was over at his parent's house, about how much information is stored about us, without us even knowing! Fascinated by this story, Lisa logged onto Scott's Google account and checked out his timeline. Not expecting to find out any juicy information, really just checking to see if it worked. This is when she found out that Scott would leave his parents' house at 9.30 pm, probably after he tucked them in bed! He would then drive to a place around 30 minutes away and stay the night. He would return to his parent's house at 6.30 am and join them for breakfast. Then off to the office for an honest day's work.

She was genuinely shocked, so to further investigate, she went onto his emails. This is something Lisa had never done before and probably why Scott hadn't locked his computer. She discovered a booking made for a hotel in Melbourne, a trip he told her was for a work conference! But the idiot had the booking in both his and his mistress's names.

Further checking of his emails uncovered numerous hotel bookings all over Australia. One booking he made was to spend time with an old friend dying of cancer, and Scott wanted to spend as much time with him as he could. Again, Scott made the hotel booking in both his and his mistress's names. What an idiot.

She then uncovered love letters and an online bondage group the two of them had met. Lisa was so upset, she googled the mistress's name, and it came up like a rash all over the internet. She was always selling stuff and had her kinky online website for selling bondage gear. The fucked up things you only see in horror movies.

Lisa located her house through Scott's Google timeline and armed with her name and phone number, which was easy to get because she posted it on social media to sell crap. She then went through Scott's phone records and discovered that they had been calling, texting etc., for more than three years. That is how far back she could get the phone records. So, who knows how long he had been cheating on her?

Lisa kept this information to herself for a while, for fear of our dying father finding out. She didn't want to disappoint our dad. After our dad died, Lisa finally confronted Scott with what she knew; he denied it.

"There is no way I would ever cheat on you, my love!" Scott asserted. "I have too much respect for you and our family even to consider doing such a thing."

"Well, Scott," Lisa replied. "Have a look at this love poem you wrote to someone called Veronica Banks, or VB as you have nicknamed her". "I have printed out your timeline on Google to see that you have been going to her house after leaving your parents' home. There is also booking confirmations on your emails. So here, have a look at my solid proof, you dick head!"

"Well done, Lisa, you think you are so clever, don't you!" "I finished my relationship with Veronica months ago, we are just good friends now, and I have only been going to her house to do some maintenance for her."

"What a load of crap Scott, I can see that you are still seeing her." "I want you out of the house now. Collect your belongings and get out of my sight."

"I think you are a bit hasty, babe, nothing is going on, and you are overreacting." "Why don't you have a glass of wine and calm down. Then we can talk about this properly without the false accusations."

"No, Scott, you are not going to smooth talk your way out of this. I also discovered your online bondage site where you and Veronica are members. That is some messed up crap that you guys are into." "Curiosity got the better of me, and I logged into the site using your login details; you need to start using a different password!" "I also noticed that Paul, the CEO from the city of Wanjup, is a member of this club. It makes sense because from what Liz has told me, he is a sick bastard too."

"Don't be so judgmental Lisa, remember how you liked me tying you up, years ago when we used to have sex!"

"Bullshit Scott, I hated it. You forced me to do that, and I never liked it."

"Come on, honey; I know you liked it! You used to call me 'Big Daddy'."

"Get out now, Scott! You are a liar and a cheat. Just the sight of you is making me feel sick in the stomach."

"Fine, Lisa, if this is really what you want, I will move in with my parents for a while until you sort yourself out."

"Thank you, Scott. I'm going to the shops and would appreciate it if you were gone by the time I get back."

Lisa's hands were shaking; she was so upset by Scott's blatant lies and the smug look on his face when he realised that she had caught him out. But, on the other hand, it was as if he was relieved that she now knew the truth.

Lisa rang me that afternoon to tell me what had happened. I was very proud of her. It takes many guts to say to the man you have been married to for 25 years just to get out.

I let her know what Tracy had told me and that Scott was still cheating on her with other sickos in the bondage group. It was a relief that Lisa had already dealt with Scott, and I wasn't the one to tell her. People always shoot the messenger when there is bad news to be said.

CHAPTER TEN

THE MONDAY MORNING, AFTER THE SATURDAY NIGHT ELECTION, I entered my new office and was greeted by the former mayor's personal assistant Yanel Winley. She was very friendly and was keen to help me learn my new role. However, sometimes being a nice person isn't enough to successfully do your role. I had my first meeting with her, and that is where the fun begins!!

Imagine a significantly overweight woman, past retirement age, and the secretary of the former mayor, who was in office for eight years. When Yanel sat down at my office meeting table, I was sure her buttons would take my eye out under the straining pressure. You could see her white pasty skin bulging through the gaps in her shirt, where the fabric could no longer hold itself together. Yet, she was not prepared to budge on anything new and insisted that everything was as it was for the previous mayor. The previous mayor was a good but hard man who could not have been more different from me if he tried; I am putting this down because he was in the army.

Back to my secretary Yanel, this woman couldn't organise anything! My husband Mike had a saying for Yanel, "That woman couldn't organise a root in a brothel". Her desk was always in disarray, and she had virtually no idea of current software. She commented to me, "Microsoft Word can do anything Excel can," really!! Because she couldn't navigate herself around the Excel program, she would use Word and tab across to put figures in a line.

One day she sent me off to a meeting at the Port Pirie Harness Racing track. It took me 30min to drive there, and the car park was empty. When I called her to find out if I was at the right place, she confirmed that I was, but she got the time wrong; I was half an hour early. So, I sat in my car and waited. As people starting trickling into the building, I joined them and took my seat in the middle of the rows. One lady recognised me from a neighbouring shire and asked me why I was at this meeting. I told her I had no idea and that my secretary had it on my calendar to attend. It was a meeting for people in the racing industry to update the latest rules and regulations from Racing SA. I didn't need to be there and felt quite stupid. I stayed till the end and joined them in a cup of tea. I was furious that I had my day taken up with a pointless meeting.

Yanel never allowed for travel time in my calendar. On many occasions, I would have to excuse myself from meetings to race off to another across town. She never checked to see how long my attendance time was. On one occasion, I even accepted an invitation to attend the local Catholic school's opening of their new gymnasium. I arrived at the school and was escorted around the gym by a group of very excited and enthusiastic students. Then the other dignitaries and I were seated in the front row to listen to speeches, and the students were going to perform a few songs for us. So far, so good.

My niece passed away in a car accident the year before; her daughter was in the choir that sang for us. I love this little girl; she had been rehearsing for this day for weeks, and she knew I was coming to listen. As the first speech finished, my phone started vibrating. It was Yanel! I never took the call, and she continued to ring me. Finally, she sent a text message asking me where I was. Seriously! I am sitting in the front row with dignitaries speaking, and my excited niece is looking at me with the biggest smile. I rudely took my phone out and had to reply to her. She then texts me back saying a state minister was waiting in my office, and I had to return now. It broke my heart to have to stand up during someone's speech and leave. It wasn't like I could sneak out either. I will never forget the look on my niece's face. She was visibly upset, and I never got to hear her sing.

On returning to my office, the minister had left. They couldn't wait any longer. Yanel forgot to put the minister's meeting into my calendar, and she never checked to see how long the school event was going to take. How the previous mayor put up with her is beyond me. I can only assume they are great friends and looked out for each other.

The mayoral office was very basic and didn't work well as a mayor's office. The main desk faced away from the door and up against the wall. Covered in old coffee cup stains, you know where you place a hot cup on varnished wood, and general wear and tear of a desk that was around twenty years old. Then there was the meeting desk. A round laminated table with four chairs, something you would find in a cheap motel room.

The first day in office was a massive day. After spending the first hour with Yanel, I was to meet with the CEO, Paul Aldman. As I had been on council for a few years, I knew Paul quite well.

The CEO has worked in the city offices for over 25 years, starting as a bookkeeper, then worked his way through the ranks to finally being promoted to CEO. I believe that any organisation should not have a powerful position for more than 20 years. A change is needed to encourage fresh ideas and limit manipulation and bullying, especially when that person is a misogynist! Yes, that is not only my opinion. I would be told regularly by other CEOs of local governments, the way that this CEO spoke about me in public was disgusting and quite frankly hurtful. He would politicise the council by promoting arguments based on political decisions made. As a member of the local political branch, I would never be the flavour of the month with this man. He would staunchly bellow he was not political, as local government shouldn't be political. Actions speak louder than words.

The CEO has his first meeting with me, and we went through the mayor's role expectations, etc. Paul arrived on time and came into my office with his arms full of files we needed to go through. Most of it was documents I needed to sign off. Paul said to me with a smile during the meeting, "I thought Lincoln would have beaten you by at least two thousand votes; we are all shocked that you won". Wow, just slap me in the face with a wet fish. I never saw that comment coming. How rude and arrogant to say that to an incoming mayor. He never said congratulations Mayor Valenti; I am looking forward to working with you over the next four years of your term. No congratulations came from his pursed lips. He made me feel like I had stolen the position, and I knew then that moving forward with this man wouldn't be easy.

Then to make the conversation head south, he added, you are what we call an accidental mayor! So now I am genuinely pissed off and had to sit there and be polite because I could not handle this situation. Looking back on this conversation, I wish I could have said so much more, but I said nothing.

I am aware that the former mayor took Lincoln under his wing and was preparing him to be the next mayor, and the CEO was right in there pushing for him to step up to the role. I found out from friends around town that Paul and Lincoln would meet up every week to discuss what was happening in Wanjup. Some conversations I had with Lincoln at different events were surprising to me, as he seemed to always have the heads up on what was going on around town before I did. Yes, Lincoln would receive invites to nearly every event that I was hosting or even just attending. Lincoln never ran for his council position because he was sure he would become the mayor; he lost his seat on the council for the next four years. It was either Yanel or Paul who were sending him the invites. As he held no position on council, he had no right to be attending these events but somehow kept showing up.

I questioned Paul about his meetings with Lincoln at one of our weekly meetings and voiced my concern that he was sharing confidential information with someone who was not privy. He became very flustered and agitated that I should question him on whom he shared information. Then I argued that it wasn't correct that he tells someone not on the council details of sensitive matters before he had the decency to say to me, the mayor. My request fell on deaf ears as he continued to have his little catch-ups with Lincoln; Paul tried to hide the meetings at neighbouring towns.

Paul wasn't the only one keeping Lincoln in the loop. Sharon and Derwent would have lunches with him and feed him anything he needed to know. Lincoln quite clearly had a cult following within the council.

Being the mayor of any City is a colossal role and one that I honestly didn't realise until I was in the position myself. Chairing the monthly council and other meetings was not difficult as I was previously a sitting elected councillor, so I knew the workings of the meetings very well. However, I wasn't familiar with public speaking, including speaking on the radio and being interviewed by television reporters.

The first time, shortly after I was in office, I had three TV crews setting up outside my office to interview me on something that had happened in Wanjup. I was like a deer in the headlights. I looked like I was going to vomit. Every question asked had me spinning my head to work out which camera to look at or which reporter asked a question. I spoke too fast and umd and arrd too much. Watching my efforts on the news that night had me cringing and disappointed at how I came across. Unfortunately, I wasn't the only one that noticed, and the city's media team got straight onto it. You can't have the city leader not being able to conduct herself with a simple TV interview.

I felt blessed that this gorgeous media personality had the time to spend with me and teach me everything about speaking in public. Even providing me with some great tips like "don't look at all the reporters and cameras when being interviewed by more than one, just pick one reporter and one camera, keep your head still". So now I know when I watch politicians etc., being interviewed by a crowd, they keep their head on one reporter while listening and responding to questions.

Every fortnight I had a radio interview with the local radio station. The city's media team would put a script together of what was happening in the city and anything newsworthy that the public would like to know. My first, and I am sure a few after that, radio interviews had the public ringing into the station saying they couldn't understand what I said because I was talking too fast. I was so nervous that I would put my head down and just read straight from the script prepared for me. It took a few months for me to settle into this new challenge. I hated listening to myself on the podcast. But, the radio announcer called Golfie was so supportive, kind and understanding. He helped me to slow down, breathe and enjoy the time on-air. Finally, I owned this program, we joked on air, and my personality shone through.

The media team in the city were so accommodating to the fact that there are certain words I couldn't say without stuttering. I would see the word written down, and one of two things would happen, I would freeze, or I would quickly find a replacement word. Every script

I had, I would read out loud several times to become familiar with it, to memorise most of it, or remember keywords to speak off the cuff too. When you are nervous and speaking in front of large crowds, you don't want to get stuck on delivering one word. It could unravel your entire speech. You also don't want to stand there with your head down just reading from paper. Giving an address is more than reading and speaking. It's about how you deliver and interact with your audience.

It's incredible the journey I went through with my public speaking. Within five months of being elected mayor, I had many speeches to deliver at the city's Festival event. This event showed how far I had come, and it felt good to rise to my commitment to represent the city. The festival is a two-day event attracting more than 100,000 people and has many activities; fantastic music acts, TV celebrities, cooking shows, bars, hundreds of food outlets, with lots of seafood of course!

I would open the event with an address to tens of thousands of people, then race over to the next marquee, where I would put on an apron and wireless headset microphone, to prepare a meal with a celebrity chef. Here's something I never let the public know, I don't eat seafood!! Not allergic, but even the smell makes me nauseous. So, there I was, on-stage cooking seafood-inspired dishes, all the while pretending to love eating them. How can the mayor of a city, well known for its seafood, at a seafood festival, not eat seafood! I felt it best not to let on to the truth about this one.

The chef knew I didn't eat seafood, so I was conscious not to try the Lobster meat while preparing the dishes. However, this chef was a bit cheeky and would ask me to comment on how good the dish was at the show's end. I would carefully pick out pieces not touched by the Lobster, so to the audience, it looked like I was genuinely enjoying the dish. My husband Mike was sitting in the front row at one of the shows, a beautiful, supportive husband. We made a chilli Lobster gourmet burger, so I ate a bit off the side of the bun then graciously gave it to Mike to enjoy. No one was the wiser; they just thought I was looking after my man. After my first cooking show, I was excited, knowing that I nailed my performance; I quickly went backstage to tell my team how well I did. What I forgot was that my microphone was still on, and the audience could hear every word I said. I took one step down the stairs into the back room, and I've yelled out, "Oh my God! That was amazing!" Then my head ripped backwards with the audio technician grabbing the microphone off my head before saying something I could never take back. He was onto that very fast; I think it's not the first time people have forgotten they are wearing the mic. It tucks under your chin, so after a while, you do forget you are wearing it.

CHAPTER ELEVEN

AUSTRALIA DAY HAS ALWAYS BEEN ONE OF THE HIGHLIGHTS OF BEING the mayor, and our city does it very well.

The most significant event for the day is not the fireworks display but the Australian Citizenship ceremony. We have monthly citizenship ceremonies in the city; however, the big-ticket event is being naturalised on Australia Day because it carries much more significance.

In my opinion, Australia Day is all about every nationality coming together to respect each other's culture. To show respect to our great land's original custodians and welcome the new people, to join us in being all one great nation.

It is also a day that we recognise our fellow citizens awarded for outstanding achievements within the community, sporting achievements, and even academic achievements.

No matter what the colour of your skin or religion you worship. We are all human beings who deserve to be loved and welcomed. We need to cohabit this planet, so it makes sense that we all make an effort to get along. No one nationality is superior to another.

The city would generally nationalise around 100 people on Australia Day. They would come in groups of ten people, on stage in front of thousands of people making their pledge to country, and they all did so, with so much pride.

After the big celebration on stage, we would welcome the new Australians to enjoy a big Aussie breakfast of bacon and eggs, with lashings of tomato sauce, all wrapped up in a bun. There was then the cutting of the traditional chocolate cake made in the shape of Australia and the lamingtons and meat pies.

The day has many events happening during the day and always finished with the most beautiful fireworks display in the evening. Everyone is generally well behaved and proves that we can all get along together, even if just for one day a year!

I always have loved conducting the citizenship ceremony because of the smiles on the faces of the newly naturalised Australians; it gives me the pride to be an Australian. Everyone would turn up in their finest clothes and be beaming with happiness at their achievement, with their family and friends present to cheer them on and bear witness to them taking the citizenship pledge.

The city would hold citizenship ceremonies every month, with around 20 people taking the pledge. They stand on stage in front of their families and friends and pledge their allegiance to Australia and the Commonwealth.

Every new citizen would hold the Bible in their left hand and raise their right hand for the duration of the pledge and would have to repeat after me. "From this time forward, under God, I pledge my loyalty to Australia and its people, whose democratic beliefs I share, whose rights and liberties I respect, and whose laws I will uphold and obey."

There is a second pledge for those who have no religious beliefs or hold God as their higher power. Again, there is no Bible to be held, but they still must hold up their right hand to pledge and repeat after me. "From this time forward, I pledge my loyalty to Australia and its people, whose democratic beliefs I share, whose rights and liberties I respect, and whose laws I will uphold and obey."

The monthly ceremonies followed up with a photo opportunity with the mayor then a small meal of good Aussie tucker. My jaw constantly ached after these ceremonies because I had to smile so much and for so long. But I did not mind one bit. They loved having their photo taken with the mayor and the Mayoral chain sparking in the pictures.

One lady from Uruguay was so happy to meet me, she cried. "Mayor Valenti, I am so pleased to see and speak with you. In my country, you never see or ever get close to someone in your position. I feel so fortunate tonight. Thank you for giving me your time to speak with me. Again, thank you!" It truly is amazing how we go about our lives and don't stop to respect where we are in our own lives and how much we have achieved. That lovely lady made me feel special, even though she told me that I made her feel special. You never really know how people perceive you until they speak up.

Every citizenship ceremony started with a welcome to the country by our local Aboriginal Elder, a lovely old and very kind man. He spoke of his troubles growing up in our city, trying to fit in with the white people, and the problem he had with alcohol and how it destroyed much of his old body. However, he would always conclude his speech by connecting with all the different people from other lands that came to Australia to make it their home.

My secretary Yanel is responsible for organising the Australian Citizenship awards for our city; it's a part of her job. Unfortunately, in the last ceremony Yanel did, she spelt names wrong on the certificates, which, as you can imagine, caused a lot of people to be distraught. This paper is such an important document, and most people are hanging out to use it to obtain their passports or enter university. The months' time delay in having it changed to their correct name is unacceptable.

Yanel's time as my secretary was up. She needed to go and join her husband at the retirement village. She had passed her use-by date. I couldn't sack her because the city employs her, so Paul eventually had to get rid of her. Unfortunately, Paul is a weak man, and it took him over a year to sack Yanel. It's a pity that she didn't leave six months after I became the mayor as she had promised. She just hung on to the job until Paul finally let her go. Paul waited until I was ready to explode before he sacked Yanel. I am sure he did it on purpose.

CHAPTER TWELVE

Councillor Belinda Stump was elected onto the council to fill Lincoln's councillor position. However, as Lincoln was so sure he would be the mayor, he never backed up his position on the council by electing to also run as councillor, leaving his councillor position vacant.

Belinda was a peculiar person. She didn't say much or mingled with the other councillors. Keeping to herself and just turning up to the council meetings, and that was about it. She never turned up to citizenship ceremonies or other official events when required that councillors attend and represent their wards.

During the council meetings, Belinda wouldn't ask questions about the reports or have any input with any conversations that were taking place. She never moved or seconded a motion nor spoke to any reports or presentations put forward by the city officers.

She would just sit there, eat her lollies and put her hand up to vote once she could see which way the favourable vote was going. She only voted because she had no choice. If you are sitting at the council chamber elected member desk, you must vote.

About a year after Belinda joined the council, I had councillor Barney Jones come to my office to complain about Belinda. "Mayor Valenti, you need to do something about Belinda. She and her husband are thieves."

Wow! What a big statement; how was Barney going to back this up? "Are you sure, Barney?" I asked, "You need to be very careful with what you are accusing Belinda and her husband Harry of."

"Let me tell you, mayor." Barney continued, "I gave them my car to sell on consignment, and they sold it but never gave me the cash for it. I have repeatedly asked them and have been chasing them up on this for months now. You need to step up and sort this out, or I'm going to the police to file criminal charges."

"I had no idea that Belinda and Harry sold cars! I just thought he restored antique cars." I added.

"They sell cars as a side business; they have a factory unit in the industrial estate, where they store cars for sale on consignment," Barney explained. "They offered me a great commission price and promised to get me a higher price than what the car yards had anticipated receiving." "I'm a bloody fool for trusting them!" "I even signed the paperwork, giving them control of my car to sell, before an offer had even come in."

"How do you know Belinda sold the car?" I asked.

"I saw it being driven around by a young man," Barney replied. "I followed him into the supermarket car park and asked him where he got the car from." "He confirmed that he brought it online through Belinda and Harry's dealership." "I then enquired about how much the car cost him, and I nearly fell over when I found out what this sucker had paid."

"Oh no, Barney, this is so disappointing. I gather this guy paid more than Belinda and Harry told you it would sell for?"

"Too right he did." Barney was furious, "Now I know they have sold my car and have refused to hand over my money." "You need to sort this out because it will look terrible on council if I have to go public with it."

"You are right, Barney; I will get Belinda into my office tonight, before the council briefing, to have a chat with her."

"I hope you do a hell of a lot more than just chat to her mayor!" "I am at boiling point now and will struggle to hold back in council if not resolved."

"I understand Barney, leave it with me, and I will let you know how I get on."

My assistant came into my office. "Mayor Valenti, councillor Stump has confirmed that she will come in half an hour before the briefing to meet with you. She inquired about why you wanted to see her? I told her that I had no idea; I hope that is ok?"

"Thanks for organising the meeting," I replied. "It's best that no one knows about the meeting because it is very private and confidential."

My assistant just nodded and left my office.

Councillor Stump arrived at my office a few minutes late. Not uncommon for her to be late. And she looked a little concerned as to why I asked for this meeting.

"Thanks for coming in early, Belinda." I began, "I have a sensitive matter I need to discuss with you."

"Really!" Belinda replied. "What on earth have I done now?"

So, I continued, "Councillor Jones has come to me with a complaint about yourself and Harry, apparently selling a car for him and then refusing to pay him his money!"

"What a load of crap!" Belinda shouted. "As far as I know, the car is still sitting in our factory." "Barney is just trying to cause trouble; we haven't even charged him for space that car is taking up in our factory." "This has nothing to do with you, and I am through talking about it. Mind your own business in future!"

Belinda stormed out of my office without even the courtesy of a goodbye! She never turned up to the briefing and arrived right at the start of the council meeting. She did well to avoid Barney. Although, if looks could kill, these two were eyeballing each other all night, throwing daggers with their eyes. She never came to the dining room after the meeting to have dinner with everyone. Quite obviously avoiding Barney, the act of a guilty person, for sure.

Barney came up to me at dinner. "Did you speak with Belinda?" Barney asked.

"Yes, I did," I replied. "The meeting didn't go as well as I thought it would. I knew it was going to be a tough one, but Belinda's response surprised me."

"Am I going to get my money?" Barney asked.

"Sorry, Barney." I continued. "Belinda refused even to admit that she sold the car." "The conversation with her became very heated, very fast!" "She told me it wasn't my business and to butt out." "Have you tried speaking with Belinda?"

"She won't answer my calls," Barney replied. "She and Harry are both ignoring me, and I'm getting fed up."

"Well, Barney." Trying to remove me from this matter carefully. "Being convinced that your car is sold and that a young man was driving your car. All I can suggest is that you do take it to the police."

"I was trying to avoid that, Liz, but it seems that is my only option now." "I just hope it doesn't come back on the council."

I shrugged my shoulders at Barney. It isn't a council problem but a personal one; however, I am concerned about Belinda's reaction. I couldn't imagine owing someone money. Belinda didn't care. Council meetings will become very awkward because I am sure Barney will tell the other councillors.

The next day I received a phone call from Barney. "Hi Liz, it's Barney. I just wanted to give you the heads up; I have gone to the police to report the car theft. The cops are not considering it theft because I signed the car over to Harry to sell on my behalf. Can you believe that! I now have to get a lawyer to sue the bastards to get my money out of them."

"I am so sorry to hear this, Barney. I will give Belinda a call to see if I can convince her to pay you and to avoid the whole lawyer process."

"Thanks, Liz; I would appreciate anything you can do to help get this matter sorted."

I am so disappointed in Belinda's reaction to this mess. Hopefully, it was just her being shocked that I questioned her, and now that she has had a couple of days to calm down, she may be more receptive to my request. I gave her a call.

"Hi Belinda, It's Liz. Have you got a quick minute to chat?"

"Are you calling about a council matter or Barney's car?" Belinda snipped.

"Unfortunately, the car Belinda, I was hoping that you had it sorted by now."

"Well, it's not Liz, and I told you to mind your own business."

"This matter involves two of my councillors, and I have made it my business, Belinda. I hope you can see reason and pay Barney what you owe him."

"Heads up, Liz, I don't owe Barney anything. The business is in Harry's name only; Barney signed a contract for the car to Harry, not me. This whole process has absolutely nothing to do with me, so Barney can take a running jump, as far as I am concerned."

"Thanks for clearing that up, Belinda. I will let Barney know the situation and that you are not involved in it.

"Maybe you should have asked me first before you started accusing me of being a thief!" Belinda responded with such odium towards me; I was shocked.

I informed Barney of this conversation between Belinda and myself.

"What a bloody cop-out, Liz!" Barney fumed, "Are you seriously telling me that she has wiped her hands clean and dumped Harry in this?"

"Yes, Barney, it certainly seems that way."

"Well, Liz, I've got more bad news about Belinda!" "Councillor Day has just given her car to Harry because I told her about the great price he had offered me for my car."

"Sharon went in to see Harry the day before I discovered that they sold my car. He is refusing to give Sharon back her car. Sharon drove over to the factory unit yesterday and saw her car still sitting in there."

"No, this is terrible news, Barney. I am sorry that I can't help you guys, but this is not a council matter, but a personal one. Unfortunately, it sounds like you will have to see a lawyer now."

"Sure, Liz, that is a weak and pathetic answer I would have expected from you. Thanks for nothing."

"Are you serious, Barney! You are the one who signed over your car without a contract, and somehow, it's my fault! You talked Sharon into using Harry's business, too, so that is totally on you. Don't you dare blame me for your foolishness!"

With that, Barney hung up on me halfway through my last word; I gather he heard as much as "fool" before ending the call.

Great! Now I am suddenly the bad guy in this messed up situation. My hands are tied, I am not the law, and I have no idea what Barney wanted me to do. Belinda has shown her true colours and has lost what little respect she had. Somehow, I also have lost respect from all three of them by trying to help them out.

Councillors' whispers spread throughout the corridors, and everyone knew what had happened with Barney and Sharon's car. I think Belinda and Harry are incredibly dishonest and unscrupulous individuals.

It is unbelievable how bold Belinda and Harry are; the next council meeting called for three councillors to attend a conference in Melbourne.

Sharon and Barney were quick to raise their hands, and then Belinda raised hers! The look on Sharon and Barney's faces said buckets! What a stupid woman, I thought. These two will eat her for breakfast.

The day following the council meeting, my assistant informed me that Belinda had requested a family apartment in Melbourne, as her husband Harry and their two daughters would be joining her on this council conference trip. I have to admit, Belinda has massive balls to be so audacious in taking this trip and especially knowing that Barney and Sharon have such hatred for her and Harry. Or is she just plain stupid!

CHAPTER THIRTEEN

"Ok, everyone is here now, so let's get started," Paul announced as he gestured for me to start the council briefing.

"If everyone doesn't mind, I would like to start with agenda item five," I asked to ensure we had time to discuss it. "Is everyone familiar with the new railway station proposed for Coonamia?" The councillors all nodded in agreement, so I went on. "The federal government has agreed to spend five million on this new station which will alleviate many of the parking problems we are having at the main city station. The government has asked for our approval, which is why I am putting this motion forward tonight".

Councillor Day tersely replied, "You are aware that this will add seven minutes to the train trip!"

I replied, "I don't believe it will add that much time; I have an assurance of only a four-minute extension to the trip."

Under her breath, Sharon muttered, "If you did your homework, you would know it's seven minutes!"

I continued, "Does anyone have any questions regarding the new station? The government is not seeking funding from us; the land developer in that area gifted the land the report states."

Apart from the general murmuring in the room, no one had anything else to add, which I found surprising. The agenda briefing continued without any issues, so I finished it early to allow the smokers ten minutes to suck down the poison into their lungs before sitting in the Council Chambers.

It's always interesting to see who turns up to listen to a council meeting. The press has a permanent table raised at the rear of the room. The press reporters can record the meeting, but photos are prohibited.

Then there are the regulars who regard these meetings as the highlight of the month. The public can ask questions and make deputations, but only from advance notice and the questions must be relevant to the items on the agenda.

As mayor, I sit in the middle of the long arched table with the CEO, Paul Aldman, on my right and the council lawyer Tony Bancroft, on my left. Every councillor has a name plaque in front of them, so they know where they are sitting when they enter the room, and the public can see their name. I like to change the seating arrangements monthly to stop collusion between the councillors.

Every councillor has a microphone with two buttons. The green button indicates that you want to speak, and the red button is depressed when you have permission to speak.

Because some council meetings can go on for as long as five hours, we are all given a water bottle and a bowl of nuts and lollies to nibble on during the meeting to sustain us and, I am pretty sure, to keep us awake.

Councillor Belinda Stump ate her bowl of sweets within ten minutes of arriving at her seat; her hand is in one continuous motion of bowl to mouth and back until it's finished. My God! You can't watch her eat as it's disgusting to witness her chewing with her mouth open as she forces the next lolly in on top of the half mauled preceding lolly.

I commenced the meeting with a welcome to country to recognise the traditional landowners then jumped straight into the agenda. This night it was all proceeding well, and I came to agenda item five. As I put this item on the agenda, it was up to me to move the motion. "Before I can speak to the motion, I need to have a seconder," I asked. "Can someone please second the motion?"

The whole council sat there in silence; not one councillor was prepared to second it. I was shocked; not one councillor had a problem with the new station, apart from Sharon's earlier spat regarding the time delay. There was no expense to the city, and I could only see that the new station will only benefit the city, especially with the parking problem.

This move not to second my motion was purely a political one. Certain councillors didn't want the opposing side of government to receive any acknowledgment from the city; what ridiculous and stupid people.

With no seconder, I had to announce, "As there is not a seconder for this motion, the motion is lost; moving on to item six, can I have a mover and seconder."

I felt like shit; the councillors did this on purpose to make a point. I was annoyed, and the rest of the meeting continued with an air of contempt. A few councillors are too weak to stand up to the strong bullies like Sharon and Barney.

As a part of being the mayor and generally being a councillor, you attend conferences held either in your state or interstate. Most of my travel was to Canberra to speak with ministers on matters that concerned Wanjup.

During this council meeting, agenda item 23 required three councillors to attend a sustainability and renewable energy conference in Launceston, Tasmania. Councillor Sharon Day and deputy mayor Derwent Peabody were quick to nominate themselves, and I also nominated. Having never been to Tasmania, I was keen to check it out and see what new developments there are in environmentally sustainable ideas and products.

Paul Aldman and his wife Sonja attended, Sharon and Derwent and Derwent's wife, Patricia. Unfortunately, Sharon and I didn't bring our husbands because they couldn't get away from work. It's a pity because Tasmania was such a beautiful city full of incredible history. I know they both would have enjoyed exploring the city while we were all at the conference.

This motion was adopted and passed without any fuss. I felt everyone was getting tired and were ready to hit the dining room for a well-earned dinner. During dinner, I overheard Paul talking to Sharon about the Launceston trip we just voted on.

"This will be an excellent conference, Sharon," Paul said. "I have checked out the program, and there are quite a few good seminars I'm interested in also attending. I am thinking about joining you and the other Councillors and will bring Brian Molloy as well; it makes sense to bring Brian, seeing he is the director of sustainability."

Sharon replied, "That would be fantastic Paul, we can share notes and check out how Tasmania is leading the way in sustainability." Paul and Sharon then sat together and chatted the whole way through dinner. They were looking very cosy.

My alarm woke me at four am to get ready for my six am flight to Tasmania. I couldn't believe how fast the date came around. Mike is so beautiful; even at that early hour, he got up and made me a coffee while I got ready. "Have you called the cab?" Mike yelled out. "Yes, just did it. Should be here in around ten minutes." I replied.

I wished Mike was coming away with me as I always miss him when we are apart. Finally, the taxi turned up, and Mike carried my luggage out to the taxi for me and put it in the back. "Have a wonderful time, honey, and I'll see you in five days," Mike crooned as he placed a gentle kiss on my lips.

I gave Mike one last instruction. "Please don't forget to walk Nessy every morning; you know her morning walks are the highlight of her day." Our little dog Nessy is getting on in years now, and apart from her daily walk, all she does now is sleep and eat. Mike assured me she would be well looked after.

When I arrived at the airport, I could see Sharon, Paul, and Sonja were already there enjoying a coffee together. As I approached them, I could hear them whispering about something very private. I put on my biggest morning smile as I gave them my cheeriest greeting. "Good morning guys, you all look very awake for this time in the morning." Sharon smiled and replied, "Morning Liz, would you like a coffee?" "No thanks." I replied, "I've already had my morning coffee quota, but thanks for your kind offer."

Shortly after my arrival, Brian Molloy turned up. He was very excited to be going to this conference. As the director of sustainability at the city, he was keen to see what Launceston was doing in this field. Brian is a nice guy, and we talked while waiting for the flight.

We checked our bags in and made our way to the departure gate. Sharon and Paul continued their private conversation, and I spoke general chit chat with Sonja and Brian. Just before boarding, a very red-faced, sweaty Derwent and Patricia came running around the corner. Not a pretty sight watching an extremely obese woman manoeuvring her body in a hurry with a very unfit Derwent by her side. Her belly and bosoms bounced, rising to hit her chin, then falling just north of her knee caps with every stride. Their alarm clock didn't go off.

We arrived safely in cold Launceston, and the coach took us to our hotel. Sharon and I had rooms next to each other on the seventh floor, and Paul and Sonja, Derwent and Patricia and Brian, were all on the third floor. "Once we have settled into our rooms, does everyone want to meet at reception then head off for lunch?" I asked. Everyone agreed, and we all went up to our rooms. So let the Tasmania experience begin!!

Before we went towards lifts, Sharon gestured towards Paul to come over to her for, obviously, a private conversation. "Hi Paul, I'm not happy with my room being right next door to Liz," Sharon complained. "I'm going to reception now to see if they can move me." "Agreed." Said, Paul. "The last thing we need is having Liz getting suspicious about us." Sharon went over to talk to the receptionist about changing her room but was unable to move.

"I am very sorry, Mrs Day, but the hotel was fully booked months ago because of the conference." The receptionist apologetically said to Sharon. "Shit!" snapped Sharon, "surely everyone hasn't checked in yet?" "Unfortunately, Mrs Day, the management has allocated the rooms, and I can't override the system to make any changes. Is there a problem with the room?" the receptionist asked. "No." replied Sharon, "I am sure the room is fine; I was just hoping to be on another level, that's all." Disappointed, Sharon went in the lift up to the seventh floor, then later joined the rest of us downstairs to head out to lunch.

While we were in Tasmania, I noticed Sharon and Paul were spending a lot of time together. They sat together during the conference and breaks, and I saw they both didn't turn up to some meetings, gone for a few hours during the day.

Sonja was a nail technician who worked out of Wanjup and didn't spend much time here. They had another home in Wolftown which was the major city north of Wanjup. For a lady in her sixty's, she held herself together quite well, quite a tidy package. I couldn't get my head around why Paul would be interested in Sharon, a dowdy woman who tested human crap for a living. Sharon had the personality of a gnat, while Sonja was quite the socialite and very beautiful.

As we left the hotel and went down the road to find a restaurant, it was very noticeable that something was happening with Sharon and Paul. They were mumbling about something that they were right royally pissed off about and were walking a few steps behind the rest of us.

Derwent and Patricia didn't turn up. "Hey Paul, have you heard from Derwent?" I asked.

"Yeah, he sent me a text saying that they would be checking out Tasmania's sights today and won't be joining us," Paul said.

Thanks for sharing that information, Paul, I thought to myself. What a wanker; he never tells me anything.

Lunch was a beautiful Japanese Teppanyaki meal which was as entertaining as it was delicious. We all agreed to an early dinner because we had an early start in the morning as it was the first day of the conference.

We all joined up for dinner, and sure enough, the seating arrangements were Paul with Sonja on one side and Sharon on the other. You don't have to be Einstein to work out what was going on here. I felt sorry for Sonja as she had no idea. Derwent and Patricia were missing again.

We all headed back to the hotel for a good night's sleep. Sharon's phone rang, "Sharon, it's Paul, is the coast clear for me to come to your room now?""

Sure," Sharon replied. "I haven't heard any noise coming from Liz's room, so I am guessing she is either still out or asleep."

Paul quickly got in the lift and made his way up to Sharon's room on the seventh floor. He gently knocked on the door, and she let him in. "Did anyone see you?" Sharon asked. "Not that I'm aware of," replied Paul. "I was conscientious about checking the hallway before entering."

Sharon greeted Paul wearing a black silk negligée that was short enough to see that she wasn't wearing any knickers. "Wow, Sharon! You look fuckin hot," exclaimed Paul. "I'm getting a bloody roger just looking at you!" Sharon blushed a little. "This is all so new to me Paul, I was very nervous about what to wear, I had to be careful packing my case, so Shane didn't see it and ask me why I need to bring sexy underwear away for work conference." "Well, I'm glad you did because I love it!" purred Paul.

Sharon had already ordered a bottle of champagne which was chilling on the bench in a silver wine bucket. "Champagne Paul?" Sharon asked. Paul replied, "Is the Pope Catholic? Absolutely Sharon, let me pour it for you."

They sat on the bed, sipping nervously at their drinks, like a couple of teenagers on a first date. Paul put his glass down and slid his hand onto Sharon's thigh, and slowly stroked it, inching up towards her juicy pussy with every stroke. He then moved closer and gently placed his other hand behind her head and pulled her closer so her lips could meet his.

They kissed passionately as Paul pressed his body against Sharon's and softly forced her to lay back on the bed. He then removed his clothes, faster than Superman, and joined her on the bed. He was rock hard, and she was ready to receive him. Paul carefully entered Sharon, and they made love. Unfortunately, Paul was a little too eager, and the whole process only lasted a couple of minutes.

He felt like he had let Sharon down as she wasn't even close to enjoying an orgasm. Paul had a shower and got dressed. He looked devastated that their first encounter was over and done with so fast. "I am so sorry, Sharon; I was just too bloody turned on and excited to see your naked body," Paul said with the saddest tinge in his voice. "I promise to make sure it's all about you next time." "That's ok Paul, it was exciting, and now that we have the first root out the way, we can concentrate on enjoying it more the next time we do it!" Sharon replied.

Sharon had her shower and returned to the room wearing the hotel dressing gown. They finished the champagne then Paul went back down to his room. Not much conversation followed while they drank the last of the bubbles. It's a bit hard to liven up the party after a massively disappointing sex romp.

At breakfast the following day, Sharon and Paul were very quiet. Sonja, on the other hand, couldn't shut up. She had been exploring Launceston all night, been shopping and tasted champagne at every bar. We had to hear about all of it. Sharon and Paul haven't stopped talking since they arrived in Launceston, but now not a word; I knew something was up with these two. Call it female intuition. Still, the two of them were inseparable. I attended a couple of seminars with them but sat as far away from them as possible.

On the second day of the conference, I noticed the two of them leave the function centre, and they didn't return until the last session of the day. I seriously doubt they are off on council duty. These guys are doing the horizontal tango! I am sure of it. So gross, I couldn't imagine these two in the sack. It's just wrong on so many levels.

Later that night, we had organised to do a ghost walking tour. It started at a pub not far from where we were staying. Launceston has so much history and beautiful old buildings. The young tour guide was enchanting as she talked about the ghosts that haunted the facilities we visited. We started at the Royal Oak, a pub with a few spirits, then moved down the laneway to the Coffin Room. There was a pine coffin sitting on wooden stilts, empty with the lid raised. I moved over toward the coffin to check it was open! While I was standing there listening to the stories of ghost sightings in that very same room, the coffin next to me suddenly had its lid slammed shut. It was so loud; it forced the air out of its cavity onto my arm. I screamed so loud, my heart was racing, and I thought I was going to faint! Everybody thought it was very amusing. I failed to see the funny side of it. The weird thing is, no one was standing next to me, so how did it slam shut like that? The rest of the tour was a little scary to me. You felt the presence of souls stuck on Earth.

We learnt about what the Grave Yard shift meant. They would bury people alive, by accident, of course. People got so drunk they would pass out. Have you ever heard of the term 'dead drunk'? As there was no refrigeration back then, they would bury people straight away before their bodies started to decompose.

When they buried the dead, they tied a string on their toe, which was attached to a bell on the surface. People accidentally buried alive would wake up and move their legs, which in turn rang the bell. The person on the graveyard shift had the job of digging them up to live another day. They were 'saved by the bell'.

I learnt lots of fun facts about the history and the ghosts that haunt Launceston. I was glad we ate dinner before taking this tour, as my stomach was not doing so well after the tour. However, everybody enjoyed a good laugh during the tour, and it finished off a long day in a good way.

The third day in, the same routine, breakfast, then a quick walk to the function centre. And what do you know, Paul and Sharon exit the conference again, straight after they checked in and sat through the opening address. Curiosity got the better of me, and after the next seminar, I walked out and headed back to the hotel. I could hear noises next door when I entered my room. So, I grabbed a glass from the minibar and placed it against the wall. I've seen people in movies do this to somehow listen more clearly through the wall. It works! Oh my, what I heard nearly made my ears bleed. Why did I listen? I can't un-hear this. I need to wash my ears out.

Later that evening, we headed out as a group to dinner. I couldn't look at Sharon or Paul. I was seriously grossed out by what I heard. Big Daddy and Who's your Mumma are two catch cries I never want to hear again! These two are becoming too comfortable, and I believe Sonja was finally waking up to something going on with Sharon and her husband. It took her a while to click on to this.

"Has anyone seen Derwent and Patricia? I swear they disappeared as soon as we arrived at the hotel. I have not seen Derwent at one seminar during this conference. Paul, have you heard or seen Derwent?" I asked.

"He mentioned something about a stomach bug and was going to stay in bed for the day," Paul said as he screwed up his face.

I figured that Derwent and Patricia were just using this conference as a holiday or a honeymoon. All paid for by the good ratepayers of Wanjup. It's incredible how much money the city pays for these trips, and no one ever questions them. What little respect I had for them both, as well and truly gone.

Sonja sat next to me at dinner. During the meal, she quietly asked me about the night meetings we were having. I knew what she was asking, and it put me in an awkward position. I don't want to lie to her, and I don't want a shit fight here at the restaurant either. "Not sure Sonja, I haven't been invited to any night meetings. You will have to ask Paul about that."

Paul's ears pricked up when he heard me mention his name. "What about me, Liz? Did you have a question?"

"Not me Paul, Sonja just asked me about the night meetings you have been attending in Launceston. I don't know anything about them."

I replied. How did he think he would get away with this? Bringing your wife along to a conference and then proceeding to bang your mistress under the same roof!

Paul's face went red as he stumbled through a pathetic answer, something to do with a CEO only meeting. "I thought you knew Liz; being away with other CEO's is a great opportunity for us to catch up and share information about what we are all doing in our cities."

"Nope, Paul, this is something that must have slipped your mind, but it's not unlike you to forget to tell me something!" I said with a smile.

Paul just glared at me. Sonja caught this glare, "Sorry Liz, I don't think you have a fan with Paul. I didn't mean to get you in trouble. I was just curious about him coming back to the hotel after dinner then heading out again. You know Paul wanted Lincoln to become mayor. He is such a flamboyant and fun man, always great to take clothes shopping too. He has the best taste in women's clothing."

Sonja is a sweet woman, but she is so dumb! I just wanted the conference to finish so we could all go home. I was missing Mike now and knew I had to endure one more day at the conference before heading back to South Australia.

Friday finally came, and we caught the flight back home. Mike and Nessy went to the airport to pick me up. I was excited to see them. Nessy jumped onto my lap so I could stroke her all the way home. I loved it as much as she did. I filled Mike in on what happened at the conference, including all the saucy stuff about Sharon and Paul. Mike couldn't believe it. Sharon is such a stuck-up righteous bitch and is ten years younger than Paul, and God, Paul is no oil painting either. Mike just couldn't understand what the attraction was between them. He was glad I was home, as was I. He had prepared a beautiful dinner of steak and three vegetables, Mike's speciality.

On arriving back home to Wanjup, I would see Sharon's car parked out the front of Paul's office a few times a week and see them in his office discussing the next agenda. It was starting to become embarrassing that they weren't even trying to hide their affair. Just Sharon and Paul attended the next conference that was in Queensland. Who knows if they even turned up to the conference?

CHAPTER FOURTEEN

MY HUSBAND MIKE NEVER WANTED ME TO RUN FOR THE MAYORAL position, but he always supported my decision. He was getting tired of being called the mayor's handbag, Mrs Mayor and the First Man. He didn't mind one name being hailed as the Italian Stallion because he was servicing the mayor! The first year in office, Mike attended nearly every event with me. Still, as his own company was getting busier and busier, he started to pull back from accompanying me, as he put it, to the opening of an envelope and only attending a few selected essential functions.

My friend Tracy was very keen to be in the limelight and jumped at the opportunity to attend as my plus one. The first event she came to, she picked up Mike's name badge off the table and placed it on her blouse. She then proceeded to tell everyone she was 'fill-in-Mike' for the night. It was funny the first time, and then after a few events, it wore very thin, very quickly. Tracy liked to drink and wasn't a pleasant drunk. She would become very flirty with anyone that didn't run away fast enough. At one event, I saw her at the corner of my eye flirting with Paul. I thought, poor Paul, you have no idea if you are even considering hooking up with Tracy.

Although you would never know this by the way she carries on, Tracy is married and has a young daughter. She is a heavy smoker and drinker and loves to brag about her money. Tracy is a lot of fun to go out with because you never know what crazy thing she will do. But, as it worked out, not the appropriate girlfriend to bring along to council events. Sometimes we learn the hard way.

About two months after the last event I took Tracy to, we caught up for a girl's night out. After a few too many Gin and Tonics during the dinner, she confided in me that she had caught up with Paul in Melbourne. She went away on a girls' weekend to Melbourne with some tennis friends. She hadn't planned on seeing Paul, but he magically just happened to be in the same place as her. A tremendous amount of detail followed as she slurred her way through what transpired in Paul's hotel room. Not much left to the imagination.

Tracy is in love with Paul! Great, I seriously hate this man, and he is now bonking my girlfriend. I didn't care that I figured he was fucking Sharon, but Tracy!

Tracy's problem is, she likes to brag about what and who she has been with sexually. I feel for her poor husband. Tracy said that after the Melbourne trip, she had been catching up with Paul regularly. Paul is madly in love with her and will leave his wife to start a new life with her.

She hasn't told her husband about the affair yet; she waited for Paul to make their love public and announce he is leaving his wife. Some women can be so stupid. At this point in our friendship, I had started to pull away. She is psycho and dangerous. I'm a little annoyed with myself for not picking up on it earlier. I began to make excuses for not going out to dinner or lunch with her and our friends. I became very involved in my work and had no time to spend with them anymore.

At the next Council meeting, we had the usual catch up to go over the agenda with the CEO and officers. During this meeting, Paul announced he was taking the next month off to take his wife to Italy for their 20th wedding anniversary. The look on Sharon's face was priceless. She couldn't hide her shock and disappointment. It was self-evident that she had no idea this news was coming. After that, however, she and Paul continued to see each other regularly.

After the council meeting, I asked Sharon to stay back for a quick discussion. As she came into my office, I closed the door behind her. Sharon looked very uncomfortable and snapped at me, "What do you want"? I replied, "You looked troubled when Paul announced he was taking a month off". "It would have been nice to have had a bit more warning; a lot is going on right now" growled Sharon.

I knew there was more to it, so I pushed just a little more. "Sorry Sharon, but I need to know if you are having an affair with Paul?" My question didn't go down well at all. Her face gave it away in an instant. "I don't know what you are talking about," Sharon said, "you have no proof". Well, this is true, but a woman's intuition can be spot on. I just shrugged my shoulders and watched her walk out of my office. At least she knows that I am on to her now, and I am sure she will run to Paul and confide in him too.

Lucy came into the council chambers to print off some documents the next day, and I asked her to go into my office when she finished. I know how close Lucy and Sharon are and thought she would know if Sharon was having an affair. Lucy knew something was up when I asked her to close the door behind her on entering my office. I started with my concern for Sharon and the way she has been acting lately. Lucy agreed that Sharon's attitude had changed. When I asked, "is Sharon having an affair with Paul?" her response was sheepish, and I knew she wasn't going to spill the beans on her best friend. "I have no idea what you are talking about, Sharon and Paul have a good working relationship, and that is where it ends; they are both married and respect each other very much." Yeah, right, I don't believe a word Lucy said; things aren't always as they seem.

I let it go for the weekend, and after my Monday morning meeting with Paul, I asked my secretary Yanel to leave my office and close the door. Yanel attended every meeting held in my office to take notes unless I ask her not to follow. Paul straight away looked worried, his face became flushed, and he started twitching, scratching his nose and looking around the room to avoid my glance. I knew straight away that Sharon had spoken to him about our quick meeting.

I congratulated Paul on his wedding anniversary and commented on what special gift you give someone for the twentieth anniversary; I think that 20 years is a silver gift. Have you bought Sonja something nice? It was like he was waiting for me to stop the small talk and get to the point of asking him about the affair. So, I jumped right in. "The reason I wanted to speak with you is to ask if you are having an affair with Sharon?" Paul's face went purple, far from the earlier redness; he twitched, looked up at the ceiling and giving off every piece of body language that screams 'guilty'.

This man hates confrontation, and unfortunately, this question was right in his face. He denied it until I told him what I had seen, what other people had seen and the fact that the two were AWOL during the Launceston conference. I strongly recommended that he break off the relationship with Sharon as it is not going anywhere. Especially seeing he is taking his wife to Italy for a romantic Italian holiday to celebrate their 20th wedding anniversary. My threat was that I would tell his wife if he didn't end the relationship with Sharon today. I never mentioned the affair I knew about with Tracy; I figured it had finished its normal course. Tracy can be full-on, and this would have pushed Paul away.

Paul slammed his fist on my small table, red-faced and starting to sweat; he began to yell at me. He wasn't going to back down on this one. He was rightfully pissed off that I had found out about his affair. I carried on calmly, "Sharon was in my office last week, and we spoke of your relationship. I feel the announcement of your Anniversary trip to Italy has come as a shock to her"! "Mind your own fucking business", Paul shrieked "you have no bloody right to interfere in something that has nothing to do with you." I interrupted his rant, "No, Paul, this has everything to do with me; you are screwing around with a married elected member of the council. How do you think this will look on the front page of the newspaper?"

"It's not how it looks," he said. "We never planned on this happening, and I do love Sharon." "I owe Sonja this holiday; it's the least I can do considering how I have treated her."

"Now I am confused Paul, are you going to leave Sonja for Sharon?"

"Sharon was going to leave Roger and has changed her mind, so now I have to decide to either rebuild my marriage or leave Sonja," Paul answered.

Paul promised that he would end his relationship with Sharon on his return from Italy but not before. For what reason he wanted to wait till he returned, I don't know, but he begged me not to tell Sonja. I gave him the benefit of the doubt and graced him for the period of leave to get his head around what he had to do. This was never going to end well. Who knows who else he has been having an affair with? Paul is not an attractive man, overweight, but not obese, thick glasses with greying hair. Beady little eyes that never make eye contact with you. I would never trust and know full well how he speaks about me to other people. I think Paul is a horrible man and a total waste of good oxygen. He should have been sacked years ago for his misconduct in how is runs his position.

Just as a side note, have you ever found out someone is having an affair and thought, No Way! I never saw that coming. Incredibly, you think you know someone, only to find out that what you perceive outside is not always what is going on behind closed doors. I have always thought that only attractive, beautiful people would have affairs; the fat and unattractive were safe! I was wrong; it takes all types to jump in the sack as the moral compass flies out the window.

CHAPTER FIFTEEN

As mayor, you try to attend as many things as you can to show the public that you care about your city and the people in it.

There was a walk happening in the local park to raise awareness of missing children. My heart truly goes out to any parent who has lost a child but even more so to the parents who have no idea if their child is alive or dead. You can't mourn for the loss of your child because somewhere deep inside, you don't want to believe they are finished.

I decided to register and join in the walk. There were so many young parents there with lots of children happily running around. I attended on my own and started walking in the silent march. There was one man in his mid-thirties walking on his own just in front of me. I thought I would be friendly and walked a little faster to catch up to him. About four children were playing just in front of him. To be polite and to make conversation, I asked him if the children in front were his. I didn't expect nor deserve his response!

It was like a switch had gone off in his head. He glared at me like daggers were flying from his eyes directly into mine. "How dare you ask me that!" he yelled. "None of those are my children; I am just walking to support the families that have lost children." "Who the fuck do you think you are asking me a question like that, you insensitive bitch." "I could have lost a child, and you ask me if they are my children." "You had better watch yourself, or it will be you that disappears, you stupid mole!"

I have never been spoken to like that before. Shocked is an understatement. Councillor John Driver joined the march and walked up behind me as this man started his crazy rant. I stopped dead in my tracks and just listened. I couldn't respond to this guy because anything I said would only fuel his irrational psychotic behaviour. Then, when he finished, he just walked away. I couldn't move, paralysed with what had just unfolded.

"Are you ok, Liz?" John asked. "I just heard the last part of what he was saying and couldn't believe it. Does he not know who you are?" "What on earth did you say to set him off like a firecracker?"

I replied, "You wouldn't believe it, John, but all I said was are the children playing in front of him, his?" My hands were shaking, and I was upset from what this man had said. John kindly put his arm around me and said, in the most comforting way. "You haven't done anything wrong, Liz, especially didn't deserve to be spoken to like that." "The man is quite clearly off his meds; stay away from him. I think you should call it a day and go home and have a cup of tea instead of continuing with this march."

John has always been a kind and mild man, and today, I needed his support more than ever. So I took his excellent advice and went straight home.

Unfortunately, this man's rant at me didn't end at the park. Later that night, I went onto my mayoral Facebook page and was surprised to see so many comments on a post I made about attending the walk for missing children. I did the post the day before to encourage people to support the walk and wasn't expecting anyone to comment on it, or if they did, it would have been only positive words of encouragement.

The comments were disgusting personal threats to me! Who are these people that hide behind a keyboard and say the most horrible things? The threats were so appalling and rude. I wonder if they even know what I had said to deserve this backlash.

Any public office is demanding, and now with social media, it makes it even more challenging. All I can say is, thank God Facebook wasn't around when I was young!!

People have become keyboard warriors and hide behind what they say, using phony names and slander you publicly because our laws give no protection other than suing them for money. So broke, no worries, say what you like, and there is no come back apparently!!

One horrible, nasty woman went on Facebook and said awful lies about me, my husband and generally my family. Well! I got lawyered up and sent out a notice of intention to sue if she didn't remove her post, only to have her publicly abuse me again on Facebook, telling people that I am trying to silence her truths!! Great, how do you combat stupid people who think that saying crap on social media is ok? It is not ok, and someone needs to come up with a law to stop this. I genuinely feel sorry for politicians and anyone in the public eye these days to live an everyday life and ignore these uninformed idiots, which believe their hollow words matter.

Then there is Messenger. Another tool these low life's use as a weapon to attack people. The first few I read were direct death threats. How frightening and bloody ridiculous over what I thought was, a friendly gesture to strike up a conversation with a lonely person. Then my Messenger page was full of posts removed by Messenger with a comment left behind; Removing the content because it contained offensive language. Bloody hell, if they didn't remove the direct death threats, what had they written that I never saw.

I reported the posts to the local police, which recommended increasing the security at my house, which we did the very next day. More CCTV security cameras around the house and added extra security gates. So I now live in Fort Knox!

It dawned on me about a week later that the charity walk debacle was probably a set-up. It was four months out from my term finishing, and the election was coming up in October; this was only a taste of what was to come.

CHAPTER SIXTEEN

EVERY YEAR THE COUNCILLORS HAVE A RETREAT TO BRAINSTORM IDEAS about making Wanjup a better place to live. The CEO and the executive staff also attend. This particular year, we went to the big city of Adelaide and stayed at a beautiful resort. My husband Mike came along too. I already had my room, so there was no extra cost to the city. He brought his pushbike along to ride during the day when I was in meetings.

Sonja also attended with Paul. I hadn't seen her since Tasmania, and my heart just felt so sorry for this poor woman, being married to such a misogynistic bastard.

A few councillors brought their partners to the retreat, so we decided to invite them to our final night event. It was only a BBQ on the hotel's rooftop, but it was a beautiful night, the sky so clear you could count every star, the food was glorious, and there was plenty to drink.

As we were mingling, doing the pleasantry chit chat with people, Sonja made a beeline for me and pulled me aside. "Sorry to dump this on you right now, but I have a feeling that Paul is sleeping with someone, and I think it's Sharon!"

Wow! I nearly fell off the rooftop. I can't believe that she just said that. My first reaction was, 'You think! Yes, obviously!' but then I remembered that Paul had also been hopping into Tracy.

"Oh, that's awful Sonja, why would you say that?" I was trying to act as if I knew nothing.

"Come on, Liz, you saw the way those two were carrying on in Tasmania. I could smell another woman on him when he came to bed. I was trying to pretend I didn't notice, but it is getting a bit pathetic now. Please tell me if you have noticed anything going on between them."

"I haven't noticed anything, Sonja; I would be surprised if Paul were interested in Sharon. Look at the way you dress and the way Sharon presents herself! There is no comparison; you are so much classier than her!"

"I know, right! I spend a lot of money and time looking this good. Sharon looks like she has bought out the bargain bin at Kmart! You're right; I am just paranoid at the amount of time he has been spending with her. I guess it is all work-related."

Sonja and I enjoyed a drink together, laughing about me screaming at the coffin slamming shut in Tasmania and other general chit chat, then we returned to our husbands.

When Sonja returned to Wanjup the next day, she received a phone call from Tracy.

"Hi, is this Sonja Aldman?"

"Yes! Who is this?" Sonja replied.

"My name is Tracy; I was hoping to catch up with you for a coffee to talk about Paul."

"Why would you want to catch up for a coffee to discuss my husband with me?"

"I know things that I think you would be interested to hear about, things that Paul does behind your back!"

Sonja nearly hung up the phone; who is this woman, and how dare she accuse her husband of 'doing things' behind her back. But she knew better; her female intuition was in overload and had been for a while.

"I have no idea what you are talking about, but my curiosity has the better of me. Ok, let's meet in town at the Cheeky Monkey café. I can be there by 2 pm if that suits you?"

"Perfect, you will love what I have to tell you. I have been to places and done things that would blow your mind, and with the most prestigious people in town. Your husband is no exception. But I won't say any more; I will see you at two." Tracy said with a very obvious grin in her voice.

Who is this, Tracy! Sonja thought, and why does she want to tell me things about Paul. What has she got to gain from this?

Sonja was rightfully concerned but went ahead with the meeting. But, as she said, her curiosity had the better of her.

Two o'clock came, and Sonja was patiently waiting for Tracy. Sonja had chosen a seat in the corner of the café where hopefully no one would notice her, and she waited for Tracy to arrive. But, instead, Tracy bounded into the café as she had just skulled two Red Bulls and yelled, "Hi Sonja, great to see you! Do you mind if I join you?"

Sonja thought, how bloody obvious Tracy. "Hi Tracy, sure, come and join me."

Tracy came and sat next to Sonja and said, "LOL, how funny is this? It's like we are secret agents or something! God, I have got some juicy info for you bitch! You are going to love it!"

Sonja was shocked by Tracy's brashness with her. Tracy doesn't know Sonja and should be going a bit slower with the best friend's bullshit.

"Ok, Tracy, you called this meeting; what do you have to tell me about Paul?"

"Are you shitting me, Sonja? You don't know anything, do ya! Lucky you have a best friend like me to keep you in the fucken loop!" Tracy laughed.

"I have no idea what you are talking about, and I would appreciate it if you would keep your voice down."

"My apologies, Mrs stuck up! I am just here to help you. Your husband Paul is a lying, cheating prick, and he owes me money."

"Owes you money for what?" Sonja queried, still trying to get her head around this meeting.

"I have done some pretty fucked up things for your husband, and he owes me. I am only telling you because he didn't pay up, and I threatened to tell you if he didn't. Simple!"

"Are you trying to extort money out of my husband?" Sonja asked.

"No, we are too far past that point now. Paul owes me. We are a part of an online bondage group, and we meet every month at this crappy motel in Port Pirie. He asked me to 'go the extra mile with him, and it freaked the shit out of me. You know! Where you strangle someone until they nearly pass out. He got the biggest hard-on from this, but he has heart problems, and he nearly had a heart attack on me. He promised me he would pay me for the stress this caused."

"Please stop talking! Seriously, are you just blurting out, in a public place, that my husband had sex with you? Sorry, but I don't believe a word that you are saying. Paul hates being in a confined place; you should see him in an elevator, he starts to sweat. So what is it that you are after because I am about to get up and leave?"

"You don't know your husband, Sonja, let's face it. I know that he has been banging that scrag councillor Sharon for a few years. You didn't even know that he is in a bondage group, right here in town, either. You know, nuthin' bitch! I want fifty thousand dollars in my bank account by noon on Monday, or the press will know about everything. I've got pics and shit on Paul that you wouldn't imagine."

"I need time to process what you have told me, Tracy. I am sorry that Paul owes you money; maybe we can work that out. I have a little money on the side that could tide you over while we sort this mess out!"

"Cool! Let me know when it's a good time to come over to collect the cash. I will bring you the most amazing spaghetti Bolognese that you have ever tasted; I am a great cook."

Sonja was thinking, how the hell do I get rid of this woman! She is annoying, and I can't believe what she is saying about Paul; there is no way he would stoop this low.

Tracy got up and left the café, waving goodbye to Sonja, "see ya soon, love, have a great day." She yelled as she sauntered out.

Sonja was numb; how can this woman know so much about a man she loves and lives with. How did she not notice anything, and for years he has been having an affair with Sharon? This can't be true. Sonja decided to get to the bottom of it.

"Hi love, what's up?" Paul answered Sonja's call.

"I just had an interesting meeting with a woman called Tracy; you owe her money for sex acts? And she told me you are having an affair with Sharon. Please tell me it's not true?" Sonja blurted out. She was sick and tired of the games and wanted to know the truth.

"Honey, can we not talk about this now? I'm about to go to a meeting. I will come home after I finish this meeting, and we can talk then." Sonja's accusations dumbfounded Paul. He couldn't believe that Tracy had told Sonja about them. Tracy is a backstabbing little bitch.

While Sonja was angrily waiting for Paul to come home and fess up about his sex affairs, she decided to do a bit of snooping herself. Sonja went into Paul's Google account and located his movements on Google maps. For example, she could see that he was at a motel in town every Wednesday night, arriving at 6 pm and leaving at 9 pm.

Further investigation into the motel to see what type of a place it was, shocked Sonja. This place looks like the main tenants would be rats. It's over 100 years old, terribly run down, handrails missing in areas on the old wooden staircase leading up from the car park. You could see some ripped and torn curtains and the paint was peeling off the walls, probably asbestos. What a dump; why would Paul be going to this place?

Sonja then went onto his web page browsing history to find that he had been visiting a Tie up your Teddy Bear! What an odd name, thought Sonja. She then went onto the website to see what Paul had been doing. Sonja felt like someone punched her in the gut! The images that came up on the screen were of people in black leather, with certain parts of their bodies exposed and the usual parts covered up! It took the wind right out of her. What the hell has Paul been up to? Is he really a part of this group? Where does he keep this gear if he does wear it? Sonja had a lot of questions for Paul to answer. She was very anxious to talk to him. It can't be real!

CHAPTER SEVENTEEN

SOME PEOPLE IN LIFE ARE JUST BORN BAD! AS CHILDREN, YOU WOULD SAY they have spirit; as teenagers, they become uncontrollable, and as adults, you are cautious around them.

Paul Aldman is one such man. A genuinely heinous individual who preys on the weak. He has destroyed women through multiple marriages and risen through the ranks at the city to become the CEO, a position he will kill to protect. He virtually controls the city where he lives. The mayor is not the boss of this city, but the CEO and all his underhanded ways to ensure total control.

Paul will manipulate everyone from staff, tenders, contracts, even to the elected members on the council.

I knew nothing of this man before being elected onto the council. As a councillor, he came across as a weak man, almost shy at the council briefings, one who didn't like any form of conflict. However, I never took him for being the piece of crap I got to know once elected as mayor.

You can only imagine my surprise when I became the mayor and got to know this individual better. He would rarely look at me when speaking. At first, I thought he was shy, but then I realised he detested me and refused to respect me. Any man who looks over your shoulder when speaking or refuses to look up, in my opinion, is a pathetic person.

He would big note in public and say unkind things about me. Other CEOs of neighbouring cities would tell me that he spoke of what I wore being inappropriate, that I was an accidental mayor, wasn't mayor material because I couldn't handle public speaking etc.

A close friend of mine came to my office one day to discuss a tender he had submitted. Cornelius Smith, or Neils as his friends call him, was disappointed not to win this tender.

His company is local, employing local people, and his price came in well under the winning contract. Nevertheless, he came to my office to ask why he missed out on the tender. I could see no apparent reason why, so I called Paul into my office to discuss the tender process.

"Why are you asking me about a tender process, mayor?" Paul demanded. "It is not your job to concern yourself with the day-to-day operations of the city. That is my job."

I replied, "A close friend of mine owns a company called Wanjup Lighting. It is a local business employing locals, and his tender price came in a lot lower than the winning tender. My question is, how did you decide on the weighting of the tender? How did you decide to honour points towards what? I would have thought a local company would have had a higher weighting than a big Adelaide company!"

It pissed Paul off that I questioned the tender process. He proceeded to explain how the weighting worked. I instantly picked holes in it, and the meeting went south very quickly.

I discussed my CEO meeting with Neils, who lost the contract. Neils had done a bit of digging himself mainly because he was upset with losing such a large contract.

"I contacted a few of the other companies that put their tenders in for this contract," Neils said. "Nearly all of them weren't even given the courtesy of a reply to say they were unsuccessful with the tender."

Neils has been in this industry for a long time and caught up with a guy, Joe Sharps, who was sacked recently, from the business who won the large lighting contract from the city. There is nothing like a scorned employee to spill the beans on their boss.

"Let me know what you need to find out?" Joe asked. Joe had recently been laid off due to his asthma problems. "I still have computer access to the server; those dickheads have forgotten to remove my password."

"Brilliant" replied Neils, "I need to find out how much the tender for the last city contract was. It was tender 20190255, and Beautiful Lighting won the tender."

"I remember that tender; I worked on it. It came in quite low because we had a massive shipment of decorative lighting come in from Guangzhou, and we needed to move them. I am fairly sure the tender price was around $300,000."

"Are you sure, Joe?" Neils asked, "The tender approved by the city was for $500,000, that is a mark-up of $200,000." "My price was for $385,000 using local products and staff. So I was going in at cost price to win the work."

"Leave it with me, Neils; I will go onto the server and retrieve the original tender that I submitted to the city." "I reckon they are all bloody corrupt at the city. I hope you can do something about it."

Neils and Joe finished their coffees and went about their business. Neils was seething after hearing what Joe had told him. He knew damn well that his price was the best, and he needed the job to keep his staff employed. Times were tough, and hearing that he lost the contract to a big Adelaide firm left him very angry.

It took a couple of days, but Joe came through with a copy of the contract stamped with a received stamp from the front reception desk at the city. So, somewhere between the reception desk and the CEO's office, the report to the council for approval of the contract had significantly changed.

Neils pondered about how to best deal with this information. The CEO was quite clearly skimming the top for his benefit, which wasn't a small amount. The CEO's salary was around $400,000, including a car, travel, study, phone, expense credit card and a whopping 25% superannuation guarantee. Not a bad wicket considering he lived five minutes from the office and managed to play golf most Fridays.

Paul would not let anyone, especially the mayor challenge his position as the CEO. It would be a brave man to take him on. He had eyes and ears everywhere throughout the city.

Neils asked me for confidential copies of previous tenders to check on their pricing. I didn't feel comfortable doing this, but Neils assured me that only he would see them, and he just wanted to confirm the winning contracts with the company's tenders.

I trusted Neils, especially Mike's best friend, and I am a close friend of his wife, Julie.

He didn't disappoint me; Neils kept everything confidential and went about his work, proving that Paul is as bent like a banana!

Neils uncovered at least five companies that had won contracts for a lot more than their original tender. He just needed to prove now that Paul was skimming off the top.

Did Paul have an offshore bank account where he hid his money? Was the account in his wife Sonja's name? There are so many questions that are difficult to prove.

Typical of small city gossip, word got around quickly that Neils was hunting to bring Paul down. Unfortunately, Paul didn't have a lot of fans in the city. If you are an arsehole for long enough, it will eventually come back to bite you. I call it Karma!

Armed with his evidence, Neils made an appointment with the South Australian Local Government authority. There, he presented his facts and voiced his concern about the corruption going on in Wanjup under Paul's control.

They assured him they would look into it, as it was most concerning that someone of Paul's calibre would stoop to do doing something so despicable. It was stealing from the local companies and the ratepayers at large.

My office phone rang, "Mayor Valenti, do you have a minute to chat?" Paul asked.

"Yes, I am in my office for another hour until my next appointment," I replied.

"I'm coming down now; see you in five minutes". Paul sounded agitated.

I wonder what he wants to chat so urgently?

Paul knocks at my door and walks right in. "Thanks for seeing me at such short notice, mayor."

"No worries, Paul, what so urgent?"

"I have just received an email from the South Australian Local Government minister who wants to chat to me about our tender process!" "Do you know anything about this?"

Paul was looking very agitated, and I knew what he was talking about, and he knew, damn well, that I knew too.

"Why do you think the Minister is concerned?" I asked. "I always thought the process was reasonably straightforward."

"Cut the bullshit, mayor!" "I know your mate Neils is behind this crap. How did he get the confidential tender reports that the Minister suddenly has?"

Oh shit, Neils gave the confidential papers to the Minister. The bugger has thrown me under the bus this time.

"I have no idea what you are referring to; I am sure the tender process is above board, or do you have something to hide, Paul?" I responded.

"You will get what is coming to you, Liz! Mark my words. You don't cross me and get away with it!"

"Are you threatening me, Paul? Be very careful with what words come out of your mouth next because I am reporting you to the local government Minister myself."

With that, Paul stormed out of my office and slammed the door. I have to admit; I was pretty shaken after his outburst and rang my husband straight away, who then called Neils. But, unfortunately, I only got two words out when I heard Mike's comforting voice and burst into tears.

Paul had gone too far this time, and he was going to get what was coming to him very soon.

CHAPTER EIGHTEEN

Sonja heard Paul's car coming down the road, his Audi had a very distinctive tone, and she knew his car. So Paul sped into his driveway and slammed on the breaks, so hard his car left a black skid mark on the driveway.

Sonja knew he was angry; she must have pissed him off with her earlier phone call. Then, finally, Paul came into the house. "Sonja, where are you?"

"I'm in the kitchen, Paul." Sonja pretended to make herself busy, wiping down the benchtops.

"You wanted to talk, so let's talk; I haven't got much time. Shit is going down back at the office; I've just had a crap meeting with a guy called Neils" said Paul as he moved toward the kitchen stools and sat down.

"Ok, I will start with Tracy" continued Sonja. "How do you know this person? She is a common slut and came to tell me you are having an affair with her!"

"For starters, I don't know anyone called Tracy, and I am not having an affair with her!"

"Tracy is trying to extort money out of me for compromising photos she has of the two of you. She is threatening to go to the papers with them. I offered to pay her, to protect you."

"What, why the hell would you do that? What bullshit. That Tracy bitch is just trying to cause trouble." Paul's face was starting to turn red like he usually does when he gets angry.

"Tracy also told me that you have been having an affair with Sharon from the council. I noticed how close you both were in Tasmania. I guess you are going to deny that too!" Sonja was past upset with Paul. Now she was angry. How dare he lie to her face? As much as she disliked Tracy, she now sadly believed what Tracy had told her.

"What a load of crap, councillor Day and I are work colleagues. Nothing is going on. She is sleeping with Angelo from the office. Not me." Paul's face was almost turning blue; he was mad.

"I'm sorry, Paul, but I don't believe you!" Sonja then pulled out a manila folder she held her printouts. "Here is a copy of Google maps, showing where you have been driving. I checked out the motel you were driving to; look, here is a photo of it. God, I hope your Tetanus injection is up to date! What a dive! Oh, but wait! There is more!" Sonja is feeling very pleased with herself for being able to find this information. "I went looking for bondage clothing, seeing Tracy told me you were a part of some group, and look what I found!" Sonja holds up a Gimp mask. "I found it, stuffed down the back of your underwear drawer, you sick prick; when were you going to tell me about this?"

"Are you seriously going to believe a woman, who you don't know and who is trying to extort money from you, over your husband of twenty years?" Paul pleaded.

"I don't think I know you anymore, Paul. What is the story with this mask?" Sonja asked.

"Someone gave it to me as a joke; that's why I stashed it at the back of my undie drawer. I have never worn it. It's bloody disgusting!"

"How does Tracy know so much about you then? You have never mentioned her. How is she a part of your life!"

"Tracy is a best friend of Liz Valenti. You know how much I hate Liz; I reckon this bitch is trying to set me up."

"Interesting Paul, five minutes ago you said you didn't know anyone called Tracy! How is your memory now?"

"You got me on the hop Sonja; I panicked when you accused me of having an affair! I haven't done anything wrong, and these bitches are trying to destroy me and my marriage. Don't pay Tracy one cent, and don't believe anything they are saying. Liz and Tracy are nasty, vindictive cows." Paul's whole body had gone the shade of red now; he was ready to boil over with rage. "I've got to get back to work, a lot is going on right now, and I haven't got time to listen to this bullshit. Are we good?" Paul asked Sonja as he got up to leave the house.

"I don't know if we are!" Sonja was pondering over the papers she had on her kitchen bench. This evidence still hasn't been explained, and Paul was in a hurry to leave.

"I have to go, honey. We can talk later tonight. I'll grab something for dinner on my way home so you can have the night off. You seem upset, and I am sorry that you met Tracy." They were Paul's last words as he flew out of the house and back into his car.

CHAPTER NINETEEN

DEATH WILL HAPPEN TO ALL OF US, AND THERE IS NEVER A GOOD TIME to die. During my term as mayor, my mother-in-law passed away, my mother the following year and then my father the year after my mother.

I was chairing a meeting at Wallaroo, an hour away from Wanjup, when the meeting was interrupted.

"Sorry to interrupt mayor Valenti." The council receptionist quickly said as she walked into the board room. "I have an urgent message for you. Can you please step outside for a minute?"

"Sure!" I replied as I got up to leave. "Excuse me, everyone; I don't belong. Let's all take a five-minute break while I get this message."

I walked out into the foyer, where the receptionist was waiting for me.

"Ok, what's this urgent message all about?" I asked.

"Your secretary just rang me with a message from your husband, Mike." "Your mother-in-law passed away this morning, and Mike wants you to be with him."

"Oh, how awful! Thanks for letting me know; I'll give Mike a call now."

I went back into the board room to grab my phone out of my handbag. There were four missed calls from Mike. My phone was silent as I was in a meeting. I called Mike back straight away.

"Hi Mike, I just got the news about your mum. How are you?"

"Please get here as soon as you can, Liz; I want you here with me."

"I carpooled to this meeting Mike, I'm in Wallaroo, so it will take me at least an hour to get back to Wanjup." "I'll see if I can get someone to drive me back."

"Thanks, Liz, please hurry."

"I love you, Mike; hang in there! I'll be with you soon."

Poor Mike sounded shattered. I got Paul to drive me back to Wanjup after I gave everyone my apologies in the meeting. It felt like the longest drive ever. When I got to the retirement home, I ran down the long corridors to Mike's mum's room. When I walked into the room, I could see Mike sitting next to his mum's bed, holding her cold hand. His head was down, and tears were dropping onto his lap.

"Mike, I am so sorry it took me so long to get here".

"What took you so long? It feels like I called you hours ago." Mike was upset and annoyed that my mayoral position had taken me away from being by his side at this horrible time.

I walked over to him and wrapped my arms around his shoulders, and gently kissed his wet cheek. Mike let go of his mum's hand, stood up to give me a big cuddle, and then buried his head into my neck and sobbed. His mum looked so peaceful laying in her bed. She was 87 years old and had lived a good life. Mike's father had passed away from leukaemia seven years earlier, and his mum missed him so much that she kept asking why God was keeping them apart.

My mother-in-law was one of the most beautiful souls that I have ever met. She worked hard and loved her family. She was incredibly generous, even to total strangers. If someone asked her for something, she wouldn't hesitate to give it to them even if it was the last or only one she had. I believe that both Mike's parents are together again and at peace.

The family worked together to give Mike's mum a beautiful funeral. We held the wake at the local football club. Everyone in the family attended and celebrated the beautiful person that she was.

Five months after Mike's mother had passed away, my father rang me from the Adelaide hospital. It was just after lunch on Christmas Eve. I thought he was calling me to confirm the times for our Christmas catch up.

"Liz, it's dad. Are you busy?" Fair question because every day, I had commitments to fulfil.

"I am free dad; what's up?"

"I'm at the Adelaide Hospital, and the doctor wants to talk to you."

I thought this was a bit strange, so I replied. "I don't understand, dad! Why would your doctor want to talk to me? Where is mum?"

"Your mother is at home. So just shut up and listen to what he has to say!"

"Ok, dad, put the doc on." I was apprehensive about whatever the doctor was going to tell me. My dad wasn't sick, neither was mum. He sounded distraught like I had never heard that fear in his voice before.

"Hello, are you Mr Van Ottom's daughter?" The doctor asked.

"Yes," I replied. "What's wrong?"

"Your father has a stomach tumour, and we estimate that he has around two weeks to live. We have organised palliative care for him, and he wants you to contact your mother." The doctor delivered this news without compassion and professionalism. It was like he was telling me my car had been serviced and was ready for collection.

"Put my dad back on, please!" I was so shocked, not only about the news but also the way it was so coldly delivered.

"Dad, are you ok?"

"What do you bloody think! I have two weeks to live. Can you pick up your mother and come to the hospital."

"I am so sorry, dad. Yes, I will grab mum and will be there in around two hours."

At that moment, I hated the fact that we lived so far away from Adelaide. We had no large hospitals around us, and this was the only option for anything significant.

Mike and I jumped in the car and drove to my parent's house. Mum had spoken to dad and had a few vinos to settle her nerves. Maybe a little too many.

Mum was ready, by the front door, with dad's hospital overnight bag set to go.

"Hi mum, how are you going?"

"I'm fine, love; it's your dad that I am worried about right now."

"Jump in the car, mum, and we can chat on the way down to Adelaide."

As we drove along the freeway, mum started telling us about how dad had indigestion for about a year, and the doctor kept giving him Nexium or other indigestion tablets. He was popping Quick Eze tablets like Tic Tacs. Nothing seemed to help.

Funny how I had noticed him burping a lot but took no notice of it. I just thought, how rude, older people must think it's ok to burp whenever they like!

Dad's belly had started to swell; like most men in their early seventies, they begin to get a bit of a potbelly. Dad was always fit and was never carrying extra weight, but now was maybe his time to relax and put a bit of extra pudd on! He ate well and was very active. His only devil was his cigars. He enjoyed a cheeky cigar with a neat scotch at night. Nothing too bad. It was his little bit of indulgence.

Mike dropped mum and me off at the entrance and then searched for the elusive car bay. We sat in reception and waited for Mike to join us. When Mike came through the hospital entrance doors, I had already ascertained what ward and the room where my father was.

We all headed up to his ward and was shocked to see him sitting on the bed in a shared room, wearing only his hospital gown. He looked devastated and lost.

"Hi dad, sorry it took so long to get here. How are you feeling?" I asked.

"I just want to go home," Dad replied.

"Have you seen the doctor? Has he said you could go home?" I just want to make everything better for dad. There is nothing worse than seeing the man who has protected you all his life suddenly need your help!

"Since the doctor spoke to you hours ago, I have sitting here waiting; no one has come to see or speak to me about anything." Dad was so upset; I could tell he was trying to be strong for all of us.

I was so furious that I stormed out of the room, straight up to the reception desk, and demanded speaking to someone regarding my father.

The nurse said. "I am sorry, but no one is available to speak to you about your father right now. When there is, I will send them into your father's room."

"The doctor has just delivered the news to my dad, that he has two weeks to live! It's Christmas Eve, and this is the best that you can do. Seriously!!"

Yes, I was wildly pissed off. I stomped back to my dad's room and picked up his bag.

"Dad, you are coming home with us now!" I demanded.

Dad replied. "I think I need to get the doctors approval to leave the hospital?"

"What did the doctor say to you, Dad?"

"He said I have a stomach tumour that was too large to operate on, and judging by its mass; I would only have a couple of weeks to live. So he was going to organise palliative care for me back in Wanjup."

Dad continued. "This is shit news to hear, but to say it to me with no family around, no warning of this horrible news, and to have it said in a public place! The guy in the bed next to me had a whole hoard of people visiting him, and they all stopped to listen and gasped when they heard my diagnosis. I was feeling miserable anyway and this just added embarrassment, humiliation, and he had just given me a death sentence!"

I was livid at the cruel treatment of my dad. My protective and warrior side kicked into overdrive.

"Dad, you are coming home with us now," I commanded.

I marched up to the nurse's desk and told them my father was coming home with me now.

"I am sorry, but the doctor has to sign you out before you can leave." The nurse instructed.

"Sorry, but I don't play by your rules. Your doctor has just delivered a death sentence to my fragile father, and I am bringing him home for a second opinion. You cannot legally hold someone here without their consent!" I was glad my legal skills kicked in at the right moment. I suddenly had balls as big as King Kong!

I marched back to my dad's room and announced he was coming home now.

"Dad, get your bag ready. We will wait outside while you get back into your clothes."

My dad got dressed, faster than Superman in a telephone box, and met us out in the corridor. It felt like we were breaking him out of prison. He certainly felt like that.

As we approached the elevator to leave, a young doctor came up and nervously asked us to wait a while, as they needed to do the discharging paperwork.

"No, I am sorry, but we are leaving." I snapped at the doctor. "My father has received the most horrendous care at this hospital, and he will not be staying a moment longer."

I turned my back on the doctor and ushered my family into the lift. Then, just before the doors closed, I yelled back. "You can send the discharge papers to his GP. I am sure you have his details."

Mike bolted to the car and drove it to the entrance; we all got back in the car, I put Mum in the front, and I sat back with dad. Mum hadn't said a word since we arrived at the hospital or on the way home. The poor love was in so much shock. Dad was everything to her.

On the long drive home, the car was silent. After about an hour, dad squeezed my hand so tight; I thought it was going to break. He leaned in towards my ear and whispered, "Thank you".

I called my girlfriend Steph, a doctor, to ask for her opinion on how best to deal with this situation.

"I can't believe a doctor delivered terminal news to a patient without the courtesy of having their family present! That is terrible." Steph empathised, "I know of a brilliant oncologist who will look after your dad. I know it's Christmas Eve, but I am sure I can get your dad in to see him in the next few weeks."

Steph was my Angel and my families, that night. Finally, dad met with the oncologist on the 27th of December, who gave him hope.

Christmas Day was a sad day that year. It was like a dark cloud was hovering over our heads.

We were fortunate enough that the oncologist was able to squeeze Dad in on the 27th. He was so busy. I knew he only fitted my father in as a favour to my friend Steph.

"There is a new drug we can start you on right away. If it works, we can operate within three months to remove the tumour." The oncologist said.

My dad now had so much hope. It was like having a hangman's noose around your neck, only to have it removed just before the trap door opens.

"Thank you," my father said. "You have no idea what this means to my family and me."

Dad walked out of that office with so much hope and a new love for life. You don't realise how precious your life is until someone tells you that you will die!

As the weeks passed, dad regained confidence in his future life on this earth. Finally, the medication was working, and he was starting to plan overseas holidays.

Three months later, my husband Mike and I were at the same football club, where we had his mother's wake the last year when my mobile rang.

"Liz, it's dad." He sounded upset. It takes a lot to rattle my father, so I was instantly surprised and concerned.

"Hi, Dad, what's up?"

"It's your mother, Liz; the ambulance has taken her to hospital. She was having trouble breathing."

"Poor mum! Where are you, Dad?"

"I'm still at home packing a bag for mum. Can you meet me at the hospital?" "I am worried about her."

"Sure, Dad, I'm just down the road at the football club. I'll grab Mike and meet you in there. I'm sure mum will be ok. See you shortly."

I grabbed Mike and took off to the hospital. We were there in minutes. Mike can drive fast when he wants to. Unfortunately, he has a lead foot and has the speeding tickets to prove it!

We went into Emergency and waited to speak with the Triage nurse. My mother had been brought into Emergency and was waiting for a bed to be ready. The nurse allowed us to go through to be with mum. Mum smiled when we walked into the ward. An oxygen tank was assisting her laboured breathing.

"Hi, Mum," I said as we approached her bed.

"What's going on with your breathing? "You have certainly got dad rattled."

Mum obviously couldn't respond, but she shrugged her shoulders and smiled.

The doctor came over and introduced himself to us.

"Hi, I'm doctor Nalder. Are you Mrs Van Ottom's family?

"Yes," I replied. "I am Mrs Van Ottom's daughter, and this is my husband, Mike." "My father is on his way in now. He will probably be another 10 minutes."

Dr Nalder shook our hands and pondered over his clipboard for a minute before responding.

"Unfortunately, we can't keep your mother here as we don't have the correct breathing equipment. I have just ordered an ambulance to take her to Jamestown."

"Thanks," I said, "I'll give my dad a quick call now so he can head straight over there. Hopefully, he will get there at the same time as mum arrives."

I rang dad, just as he pulled into the car park at the Wanjup hospital and told him to keep driving to Jamestown. It was a good 40-minute drive from Wanjup.

"I'll stay here with mum until she leaves in the ambulance," I told my dad. "I'll send you a text message when she leaves here."

Poor dad sounded so worried. I should have driven with him, for company, to Jamestown.

I chatted away to mum while we were waiting for the ambulance. She looked happy enough, just a little concerned about her breathing.

Once I saw the ambulance pull out of the hospital, I text dad and let him know that mum was on her way. After that, Mike and I jumped in our car and headed up there too.

It took us nearly as long to find a car park as it did to drive to Jamestown! By the time we got in to see mum, she was already attached to some severe breathing equipment. There was a massively thick tube going down her throat.

"Hi, mum," I said as we entered her room. Mum just smiled back at me.

"Have you let Lisa know that mum is in here?" Dad asked.

"No, I'll do it now; I'll give Patrick a call too." I felt terrible because I didn't even think about calling Lisa. She only lives about half an hour away from Jamestown, and Patrick lives in another State.

I went outside and called my sister and brother. Lisa said she would drive straight into the hospital now. So I grabbed three coffees and went back into mum's room.

"I just spoke to Lisa and Patrick, dad," I said as I handed out the hot coffees. "Lisa is about half an hour away."

"Thanks, Liz; your mother would want to have both her girls here".

We sat there with mum, chatting amongst ourselves and sipping away at our coffees.

Lisa turned up and looked as white as a ghost when she walked in and saw mum.

"Hi, mum," Lisa said as she leant in and gave mum a soft kiss on her cheek, trying to avoid the tubes. "What have you done to yourself?" Mum just smiled and shrugged her shoulders again.

Dad explained how mum went to lay down for an afternoon nap because she was feeling exhausted. "I went in to check on your mother, and I knew, straight away, that something was wrong." "She was taking these short breaths, like a panting dog. Her face was full of sweat like she had done a huge workout."

"I asked if she was ok and she shook her head. That's when I called the ambulance." Dad explained. "By the time the ambulance arrived, mum looked like a fish out of water, grasping for what little breath she could get in her lungs."

"How frightening for mum!" I said as I took hold of mum's hand. "You are in good hands now; the doctors will look after you and get you back home soon."

We sat with mum for another hour. Then, Mike and I decided to head off back to Wanjup because mum would be in for the night, and we both had work the next day. But, Lisa said she would stay for a few more hours with mum and dad, making me happy. Dad looked like he could do with the support.

I headed into my Mayoral office the following day. Mondays are always busy for me. My secretary seems to fill up my calendar effortlessly. I was sitting with my secretary going through the day's meetings, speeches, etc., when my phone rang. I saw my dad's name come up on the screen and knew something was wrong. So I excused myself and took his call.

"Hi, dad."

"Liz, can you come to the hospital now. I need you to be with me. Something has happened to your mother during the night, and I don't know what is going on."

"Sure, dad, I'll be up there inside of an hour. I just have to cancel a few meetings."

My secretary had to cancel my day's meetings, including the poor people, who had just walked in. Some people wait months to get an appointment with me. I had two speeches to deliver, so the deputy mayor had to step up and take over for the day.

When I got in my car, I called Mike and let him know that I was driving up to the hospital to be with my parents.

Being a Monday morning, the car park was a bit emptier than it was the night before, saving me about ten minutes of driving around. I walked into mum's room, and she wasn't there. So I rang dad, and he told me the hospital moved her.

Mum was placed into a coma sometime during the night. There were machines and tubes everywhere.

"What has happened to mum?" I asked Dad.

"All I know is that, during the night, one of the Doctors thought mum still wasn't getting enough oxygen, so they increased the oxygen flow. Unfortunately, the increased pressure blew a hole through mum's lung. They have put her on this machine to take over her breathing."

Poor dad looked sick with worry. No doctor had been in to see mum since he got this news when he arrived at 6 am. So, again, I called on my good friend, Steph, who, at that time, was the doctor in charge of Emergency at the Adelaide Hospital. I gave her a call to see if she could get any more information about my mum.

Steph was amazing. It was one of her rare days off, and she drove to Jamestown to be with me and help us out. Steph was like a saint, coming into the hospital and helping us out at such a critical time. I will never forget what she did for us that day.

"Thanks, so much Steph, for coming in," I said as I wrapped my arms around her. "Any information you can give us will help." "We feel like a couple of mushrooms sitting here." "Doctors keep coming and looking at the chart, then walking off without even the courtesy of an acknowledgement. It's as if they don't see us or don't want to see us and have to deal with our questions."

"I'm so sorry, Liz," comforted Steph. "Now that I am here, we will get to the bottom of this."

Steph took mum's chart and studied it for a bit. She was trying to conceal her worried look, but I knew her well enough to spot it.

"Give me a minute, Liz," Steph said. "I'm just going to talk to the doctor in charge, and I will be right back".

"No worries, Steph, thanks." I watched her leave the room, armed with mum's medical chart.

I rang my sister Lisa and asked her to come into the hospital.

"Hi Lisa, how are you?" I asked.

"Good Liz, how is mum?"

"Not good. I have asked Steph to come in to tell us what is going on. No one is saying anything, and mum is in a coma."

"What!" replied Lisa. "Why would mum be in a coma? Ok, I'm coming in right now. I'll be there in half an hour."

Steph was gone for nearly an hour. When she returned with the doctor, they asked us to come into a room down the hallway. Lisa had turned up about 10 minutes before and looked like she was going to puke. We were all concerned, but Lisa can't handle things like this very well.

You know the news you are about to receive is not good when you walk into a room with water glasses and boxes of tissues. The doctor looked pleased to let Steph be the one to give us the news about mum.

"I have looked at your mum's medical file and spoken to the doctors who have been in charge of your mum's care. Your mum has a lung disease called Idiopathic Pulmonary Fibrosis." Steph was speaking very slowly and with compassion to ensure we were absorbing what she was saying.

"Steph." I interrupted. "Mum has never smoked or showed any signs of lung disease. Are you sure this is the correct diagnosis?"

"It is Liz; I have read your mum's reports." Steph continued. "When your mum came here, she was struggling to get any oxygen into her lungs, so they put her on a mechanical ventilator. Unfortunately, this machine wasn't delivering the proper level of oxygen required, so they put her onto a larger machine and increased the airflow." "The unfortunate result of the increased airflow, as it blew a hole in her right lung." "To avoid any stress to your mum, she has been put into an induced coma."

"So, what now?" I asked. "Are we waiting on a lung transplant?"

Steph shook her head and looked so sad. "I am so sorry, but your mum is 72 years old, and she is past the age that they would perform a lung transplant.

"That is crazy!" I snapped. "Does mum have to be on an oxygen machine for the rest of her life?"

Steph said "This is the news I wished I didn't have to give you". "Your mum is on a life support machine now. When we turn it off, your mum will die." "The hospital is prepared to give you a few days to sit with her and say goodbye, but there is nothing else that can be done."

My poor dad was so shaken. I just put my arm around him, and my sister sat on his other side and cuddled him too.

"Can you take her out of the coma so we can say goodbye to her?" My dad asked.

"No, unfortunately, as soon as we bring her out of the coma, she will be unable to get a breath and will be in great pain. It would be extremely cruel to do that to her," Steph said.

We sat there for a while, trying to understand how mum was alive one minute and now told to say our goodbyes. Then, finally, dad asked me to get the priest in to give mum her last rites.

He was dealing with his own health problems and relied on mum to be there for him, how your life can change in a day!

Dad continued to drive up to the hospital every day and just sit and read to mum. The doctor said she could hear what we were saying to her, but we wouldn't see her reaction.

After three days, the doctor came to dad and said it was time to let her go. He refused to give his consent. Every day dad would do this same thing, pack his sandwich and coffee, drive to the hospital and read to mum for the day. Every day the doctors approached dad and asked for permission to turn the machine off on the sixth day. I went in to sit with dad and mum, and the doctor comes in the see us. Dad instantly got his back up.

"No! You are not killing my wife today!" he shouted at the doctor. I texted Lisa and asked her to come straight into the hospital. Dad was losing the plot.

The hospital needed the life support machine, and mum's time was up. However, dad couldn't permit them to turn it off. It was just, so final, and his love for her was so great; he couldn't bear the thought of her dying.

I took dad outside for a walk around the hospital gardens. "It is time, dad; you have to let mum go. You know she never wanted to be kept alive on a machine."

"It's the 13th today!" Dad begged. "Your mother is not dying on an unlucky day like the 13th!"

"Dad, remember you got married on the 13th fifty years ago." "It isn't such an unlucky number then, is it?"

Dad had a horrible decision to make, and he knew there was no point keeping mum alive on the machine. So we went back into the hospital, and dad told the doctor to terminate mum's life. The doctor gave us one hour to say our goodbyes.

I spoke to Lisa. "You go in first. I am still getting my words together. I think I will tell her about what is about to happen so that she can make peace with God."

"No! You can't." scolded Lisa. "That is a cruel thing to do to mum. I am just going to tell her how much I love her. Please don't tell her she is going to die."

Lisa went in to see mum. Dad just finished a phone call to the local priest and burst into tears. "Have I done the right thing, Liz? I can't believe your mother will be gone forever shortly, and there is nothing that can prevent it. I just want her to get better and to come home with me."

"Dad, you have been left with no choice. Mum can't survive without that machine and has already lost any quality of life. Being in a coma is not living. You are making the right decision. Mum will be getting things ready for you to arrive in Heaven."

Poor Lisa came out of mum's room sobbing so hard; she could hardly catch her breath. Dad grabbed her with both arms, and they stood there hugging each other for comfort. I then went to see mum.

She looked so peaceful. I watched her blood pressure and heart monitor to see if there was any change when I walked in to be with her. "Hi mum, I am not sure if you have heard what is going on with your body? Your lungs have become hard, like an old basketball, and they can't expand anymore. This is because the doctor accidentally blew a hole in your lung, which is unrepairable. So they have decided to turn the machine off, and this will kill you. After that, you won't feel anything but will peacefully slip off to be with God."

I quickly looked at the monitor to see if her pulse increased, but nothing, no changes in any of the monitors. I hope I had done the right thing by telling her this information. I just know that if it were me lying on the bed, about to be killed, I would want the opportunity to pray in my mind. But, I felt like I had done the right thing. I told her how much I loved her and thanked her for being such a wonderful mother. I also assured her that I would care for dad, which he will need with his imminent death.

The priest arrived as Mike arrived, and we all went into mum's room to join dad. We all joined in praying for mum. It was one of the saddest days of my life. After the last prayer, we all went out to that horrid small room with the tissues and water and waited for the doctor to join us.

About ten minutes later, the doctor walked in and told us our mother and wife had passed away. It's strange how we knew what was about to happen, but the reality was still shocking. We were all shattered and walked out of that hospital for the last time.

CHAPTER TWENTY

I WENT INTO WORK ON MONDAY MORNING IN SHOCK. MY NEW secretary, Wendy, brought me in my morning coffee and weekly file. Wendy was so super-efficient at her job. I finally felt like I was in control of my daily routine. Wendy came highly recommended and has already proven herself to be a great asset. I love the way her desk is always so organised. She drank green smoothies every morning, looked after herself, and kept an eye on the meals prepared for me.

Wendy stopped when she came into my office and looked at my face; before she opened the file, she asked, "Are you ok, Mayor Valenti? You don't look well!"

The look on my face gave it away. Before I could even say, "My mum!" I burst into tears which is unlike me. I am a strong woman. I don't cry, I don't take crap, and I certainly don't ever let people see my emotions.

"I can cancel your meetings for today, mayor! What has happened?" Wendy asked.

"My mother passed away on Friday. She appeared well when I last saw her. I am so worried about my dad!"

"I am so sorry, mayor, don't worry about your meetings or anything else you have on this week. Take the time to be with your dad. I will make arrangements for the deputy mayor to take over."

Just as Wendy was working out what meetings, events etc., she could move to other councillors, there was a knock at my office door.

Paul did knock! But then he just abruptly stormed into my office and threw his files on my meeting table. "You are not going to believe the mess that councillor Donald Geary has put the city in!"

Wendy started to put Paul in his place. "Excuse me, Paul, but the mayor is not ready for your meeting. We have not finished going through our stuff!"

"Stuff!" Paul said in a highly demeaning way. "I am here to talk about real things, not stuff. You can have the mayor back in ten minutes."

I was upset already, and the way Paul spoke to Wendy was so awful. He is the most misogynist man I have ever met. "Excuse me, Paul, do you mind the way you speak to my staff! You were quite rude then."

Paul was annoyed that I spoke against him in front of my secretary.

"Need I remind you, mayor, that I, the city employ Wendy, and not you. The people elect you, and I employ the staff. So remember your place here."

Paul just actually said that to me! Wow, he has no idea about his place on this earth.

Lucky for him, I was devastated by my mother's passing and still dealing with my father's terminal illness. So I chose to be the bigger person and let it go.

"I am sorry, Wendy; we can pick up our meeting after Paul leaves."

"Ok, Paul, what is so important that you have to be rude to Wendy and disrespectful to me?"

"I have no idea what you are yapping on about! This is our regular time slot." Do you have a problem with our meeting this morning? Is it that time of the month, and you can't handle the big boy's job?"

"Fuck you, Paul, my mother died on Friday, and I was going through my appointments with Wendy when you interrupted us!"

Paul looked stunned like someone just shone a flashlight in his face. "Shit, I am sorry. No one told me."

"I have only just told Wendy and was going to tell you before you rudely forced your way into our meeting!"

"Don't worry about Councillor Geary; we all know he's an idiot. What can I do to help you out?"

This man is like a real-life Jekyll and Hyde; one moment, he hates you, and he cares and wants to help you!

"Right now, nothing, thanks, Paul. I appreciate that you care. The funeral arrangements are complete. My mum had pre-organised her funeral, right down to the Sunflowers and readings."

"Did she know that she was going to die?" Paul asked.

"No." I replied, "She has just seen a few of her friends pass away and thought it would make our life easier if she had her wishes written down, and it did." "Wendy is aware of what is going on and will make arrangements for the deputy mayor to step up and take over my weeks appointments."

"Fantastic," Paul said. "She is a good egg, much better than that Yanel! I have no idea how you put up with her."

The fact that he kept Yanel looking after me for so long reflects on him, not me. Remember, you idiot, you employ the staff, not me.

"Yes, she is pretty good, thanks, Paul. You picked a good one!" "Now tell me about Donald. What has this guy done now?"

"Are you sure you want to hear about this now?" Paul asked.

"Yes, it will distract me from what I am going through."

"Donald was at the local Irish pub on Saturday night, grabbed the microphone and started taking over the evening. They were having a quiz night, and Donald thought he could suddenly be a better quiz master. He commented on women's breasts and even their arses! Slurred his way through questions and made an idiot of himself." "You know this reflects badly on the council!" "You need to do something about this fool!"

"I am sorry, Paul, you just made it quite clear that I do not employ people; the people of Wanjup elect them. Therefore, I have no authority to sack him or reprimand him."

"Well!" retorted Paul, "You need to at least speak to him about his public behaviour. He can't keep getting pissed every weekend and expecting people to continue to respect him or his behaviour! Last week, that idiot Donald walked over to the minister for health's chair at our citizenship ceremony and bent down to sniff it after she stood up. He had quite obviously been drinking. He then asked the minister if she had fish for dinner! She had to hold herself back from slapping him. Then to top it off, he puts his arm around her for a photo and snaps her bra strap, which undid her bra. It was embarrassing for her and everybody else, she has a double G cup, and when her strap came undone, her large breasts flopped out and hit her belly."

"I don't think that Donald is my biggest problem right now. It's not like I can sack him; I agree something needs to be done, but my head is not currently in this place."

"He fell off a table, drunk while gyrating to an Elvis song! Everyone at the pub saw him and were disgusted that he was a councillor and, not to mention, his poor performance of Elvis." Paul said. "He can't continue to carry one like this. He and councillor Pauline Ashley are an embarrassment to this council. They are both always drunk, and they suck down at least two packets of Wini blue's a day! Councillor Pauline Ashley was at the same pub, encouraging Donald with his antics. She was no better; the silly old cow was sitting on guys laps and trying to fondle them, can you believe it, a woman of her age doing that. People thought it was funny at first, then it just became embarrassing."

Knowing what I am going through, I am surprised that Paul is pushing so hard on my fellow councillors.

"Paul, right now, I have a lot of personal issues going on, and the actions of councillors Donald and Pauline can be put aside. You know they are both good people, with bad habits, but good people, nonetheless. Can you please speak with them?"

"My mother's funeral is on Friday, and I have planned a health retreat to Bali on the following Monday. I will be gone for a month. I just feel that I need to have some time to myself. I haven't had a break since I became the mayor two years ago."

"I am sorry for harping on about these matters, Liz. However, I agree you should go away to spend time recovering from your mother's sudden death." Paul said.

"Thanks, Paul, you have no idea how much I appreciate you saying that. I felt guilty about leaving my post for so long, but I cried like a baby on Saturday night, at the anniversary of the senior citizens centre. During my speech, they brought up photos of the local people who regularly attended different events. Then my mother popped up on the big screen, wearing her purple shirt, with all the other ladies doing a jazz dance. Then, there she was in her best Christmas gear, smiling as she would live for 100 years." I continued.

"I was ok, delivering my speech, until I spoke about the purple haze girls, and thought of my mother in the photos. I inhaled a deep breath and kept on, then I talked about the crazy times the seniors had with their organised outings and social get-togethers, and the photo of mum in the Santa costume came to my mind. I just stopped and couldn't continue. I cried and couldn't stop. It was more of an uncontrollable sobbing than a cry! Councillor Malcolm Dunbar stepped up and took over for me. I truly respected that man for helping me out."

What was I thinking, going straight back to work! I didn't want the public to see the weak emotional side of me. But, of course, being a female, you always think that people will judge you on your weakness.

Paul agreed that I needed time to grieve and set about helping my secretary Wendy make arrangements for other councillors to take over my commitments.

CHAPTER TWENTY-ONE

I ORGANISED MY HEALTH RETREAT IN UBUD, BALI. IT WOULD HAVE TO be one of the most beautiful places in the world.

I arrived in Bali, went through the customs and collected my luggage. The guy holding my sign was on a call and had his clipboard facing down when I walked by. There must have been 100 guys holding signs, and none of them had my name on them.

I went to the help desk and asked about company drivers. The lady was just so gorgeous, she called the number on my travel voucher, and the driver came to the desk to collect me.

It was the longest drive from the airport to Ubud, but it was worth it. This place is Heaven on Earth. The scenery on the drive up, up, up to Ubud is spectacular! However, when I arrived at my accommodation, I wasn't impressed. There was no TV, no pool, no radio and no transport. It indeed was a health retreat.

The owner came to greet me with a bag of quinoa and mango. That was going to be my breakfast! He assured me; he would be here in the morning to cook for me.

I sat there in the darkness that night, listening to monkeys jumping all over my roof and other animals; I still have no idea what they were, screaming during the night.

I rang Mike to chat and tried to sound confident! Even though I was shitting myself. What was I thinking coming to this country to recuperate?

The owner of the 'Recovery & Rejuvenate Centre' was from America. He had no idea what he was doing and paid everything in cash! So ample warning, guys, if someone from Bali insists on cash, don't go there.

Ron was originally from America and a recovering alcoholic. He thought he could put a recovery centre together for people going through grief, drug abuse, alcoholism and people who needed to reconnect with life. Thank God he didn't put us all in the same house!!

The following day, the business owner, Ron, came to collect me for our morning Yoga session. I walked outside to see his moped!

"Are you kidding! Is this the transport you offered in your brochure!" I exclaimed.

"Yes," Ron replied, surprised by my concern.

"There is no way that I am getting on the back of that!"

"There is no other transport Mrs Valenti. We don't have Uber in Ubud!!"

I had no choice; I had to get on the back of a moped and drive down the mountain to the Yoga centre in Ubud.

Then we went to a delicious juice bar. After that, Ron took me to another restaurant, and we had the most amazing Vegan meal ever.

We rode around Ubud for the rest of the afternoon; then, he dropped me back at my apartment in the hills.

The next day started the same, early pick up, after a breakfast of home-cooked quinoa, then meditation and yoga.

Ron then decided I needed to speak to a healer from America, who brought out my fears, and I cried tears for days.

By now, I was ready to go home. Only a few days into the retreat and I was homesick.

Then on the third day, I met another victim of Ron's retreat. She was in her late twenties and a recovering alcoholic. She told me that Ron had taken ten thousand dollars off her, two thousand transferred and eight thousand in English pounds when she arrived. Yet, she was so trusting and believed this guy could help her.

I bumped into her at one of our meditation sessions. When Ron arrived to pick me up, she was shocked that I knew him.

"How do you know Ron?" Maria asked.

"He is the guy who is looking after me while I am going through my grief," "How do you know him?"

"This is the Ass that took my money and has given me nothing!"

"I am so sorry, Maria." Maria was such a beautiful person; her husband had sent her from England to recover, only to have Ron take her money and give her nothing in return.

My very Ballsy attitude kicked in. I went to one of the ladies I had met at a yoga class and knew she had contacts! I explained this poor lady's situation, and she jumped right in to make it right.

"Tell Ron that you will contact the tourist police in Bali, and he will shit himself. Then, tell him that you want all your money back!"

Brilliant advice, Ron gave this poor girl back her money. I have never heard from her since, but I know that she was thrilled; she could go home with her head held high, with her money in her pocket.

Ron wasn't exactly happy with me the next day and never came to collect me for my morning meditation.

You have to understand, I was in a mountainous cabin, with no communication and no transport. So it wasn't like I could walk outside and grab a burger or something to eat, or even water for that matter.

My survival mode kicked in. I walked down the road to a place that had a sign, Motorbikes for rent.

It could have said free ice-creams for all I cared at that point. But, unfortunately, I needed transport, and there was nothing available.

I have never driven a moped or a motorbike. So as you can imagine, I was a little bit scared about the whole process. But when you know that the only way you can leave the confines of your apartment is by moped. It suddenly becomes the most critical part of your day.

I walked across the road and offered the moped renter $25 for the month. Remember, we are not in the tourist centre of Bali here. He was happy with our arrangement and gave me the bike.

He accepted, and I walked the bike across the road to my apartment. I looked on the internet, how to ride a moped. It didn't help.

I got on and started down the road, then a dog ran across the street, and I ended up in a rice field. So I was not confident at riding one of these things.

The next day I went to yoga on the back of Ron's moped. I didn't have the confidence to tell him I had hired one of these death traps!

I caught up with a local who cared for abandoned dogs at one of my yoga sessions. She was also an artist and a beautiful lady. I told her about my bike purchase, and she offered to give me some riding lessons.

The following day, before Ron arrived, Lucy came and showed me how to ride a bike. She was amazing. I had my confidence up in no time. I took off down the mountain to Ubud and swayed my way around cars like they weren't even there.

Ron took a back step then; I didn't need him anymore. I could transport myself and found accommodation with a television and the internet! I never asked him for a refund, which he owed. But sometimes, we have to look at where we are in our lives, and what matters.

I stayed at my new apartment for a few weeks then headed home.

After sitting in my business class seat, after a month of no alcohol and no meat, the air hostess asked me if I would like a drink and something to eat!

I am sorry to disappoint, but after a month, I said YES to everything.

The wine tasted even sweeter and the meat even juicier!

I fell asleep soon after my meal. Then, as I arrived at the airport and walked through the opening doors, there was Mike, waiting for me with the biggest smile and most comforting cuddle any woman could want!

CHAPTER TWENTY-TWO

My trip away to Ubud gave me time to consider my decision to contest my seat for mayor. I needed to clear my head, and the health retreat was the perfect time to reflect.

I was only home one day when Tracy knocked on my door. Arm filled with Spaghetti Bolognese sauce in an old ice cream container. It was too late to try and hide; she had her face pressed against the glass panel on the front door and had spotted me.

I opened the door, "Morning Tracy, how are you?"

"Morning Liz, I am so glad you're home." Tracy sounded almost too excited to see me at home.

"I have got too much to tell you! Put the kettle on and let's grab a ciggy outside!" Tracy smirked.

She can be so selfish; what if I was busy and had lots to do! Which I did. "Sure, Tracy, I'll go turn the coffee machine on; it takes five minutes to heat up."

"Perfect!" said Tracy as she bounced outside to my pool toilet to collect her stash of coloured cigarettes. She prances around my house as if she owns it!

"Oh, and by the way, Liz, that ice cream container I just put in the kitchen has the best Spaghetti sauce you would have ever tried. So just cook some pasta tonight, and you will be in for a treat."

"Thanks, Tracy, we will enjoy that. It's very kind of you to cook us dinner."

"No worries, Liz, I am a good cook, and I love cooking."

I popped the Spaghetti Bolognese sauce into the fridge, made our coffees and brought them outside. Tracy was sitting, perched upon my outdoor lounge, with her feet tucked under her bum.

She held the packet of cigarettes to my face and gestured for me to take one. "No thanks, Tracy, I'll pass. I haven't had one since I left for Bali. Didn't even feel like one the whole time I was away, and I don't want to start that habit up again!"

"Are you serious!" Tracy exclaimed, "These are good for you; it's a bit like how red wine is good for you."

"I don't think so," I replied, shaking my head at her. "They will kill you."

"Oh my God, Liz! You are such a party pooper! One cigarette won't hurt you. Go on, keep me company."

I picked up my coffee and pointed to the cup, "This is the only drug I am interested in right now!"

"Mike has gotten to you!" Tracy groaned, "You were much more fun before you went away."

"Maybe this is a good thing Tracy, I am starting to look after myself better."

Tracy was starting to fidget and move around in her seat.

"Ok, Tracy, What's up? What is it that you are dying to tell me?"

"Well," Tracy starts, "while you were away, Zina and I started spending a lot more time together. We had a ball hanging out; the problem is, though, Zina can be very naughty!"

I laughed, "I think you girls are both equally as naughty; what has Zina done?"

Now Tracy was more settled in her seat as she settled down to start her story.

"Let's see, it all started the week after you left. There was a ladies night at the fishing club; it was great. They had a male review show with lots of alcohol. I am sure there was plenty of food too, but you know! Eating is cheating!" "It got to about 11 pm, and Sam wanted to pick me up. He kept ringing my phone, but I didn't want to go home, so I didn't answer. I knew why he was calling, so I got Zina to answer."

Tracy continued. "Zina answered and told Sam that she would bring me home. Sam was angry because he had been sitting in the car park for half an hour waiting for me."

"Why on earth would you do that Tracy, you put Zina in an awful spot. Sam is your husband; you should have talked to him."

"Nah" she said, "it was funnier watching Zina do it! Sam has been furious at me lately for coming home drunk, way too often, and he hates the fact I'm smoking so much more now."

"I get that, Tracy; Mike hates me smoking and worries if I drink too much."

"It's different with Sam," Tracy continued. "He is controlling now!" "He has turned into the fun police; if I'm having too much fun, he has to stop me. It's like being arrested for having a good time. He is driving me crazy."

"Is that the only time you have pulled Zina into your marriage turbulence?" I asked Tracy

"God no! I have used Zina as my scapegoat many times. Every time I came home late, I would tell Sam, it was Zina who gave me one more drink!" "It was hilarious."

"I don't understand Tracy, why has Zina been brought into your messy web of deceit? So now she is in trouble with Sam?"

"She started it by buying us those coloured cigarettes. Sam asked where they came from, and I told him, Zina!" "You know how forceful Zina can be!"

"Unless if Zina has changed in the last few months, I don't remember her being like that; she likes to have fun and is extremely generous, with sharing whatever she is indulging in, but not forcefully!" I said.

"As I said, Mr Fun Police came along and had been restricting my social life; with you away, I only had Zina to play with." "Because she is who I was out with the most, I just blamed her for not coming home till late." Sam is so annoyed with her; it's pretty funny, Zina hasn't done anything, and she has taken the fall for it!"

"That's terrible Tracy, Zina is your friend who you should be protecting. Instead, you have made Sam mistakenly hate her."

"I know, right!" Tracy laughed. "It's hilarious, I look innocent, and Sam loves me and hates Zina, which is better for me. I don't want my husband hating me! But, sometimes you have to understand; it's all about survival, girlfriend."

I was starting to dislike Tracy, who does that to a friend. But, unfortunately, it will only be a matter of time before she does the same to me.

"Here's the kicker, Liz! Remember that auction item I brought at the political function I went to with you and Zina?"

"Nope!" I said, "Remind me."

"Come on, you know, the dinner with the politicians at Parliament House," Tracy replied.

"Oh yes, I had forgotten about that," I replied.

"Sam was asking me about it the other day, and he doesn't want Zina anywhere near me, or him, for that matter. I think he is ready to punch her. What can I do?" Asked Tracy.

"You did this, Tracy. You made Sam hate Zina, and she has done nothing wrong. I have no idea what you can do other than come clean with Sam and tell him the truth. Zina will be devastated to find out that Sam hates her."

By now, Tracy had told me about four different events, that she had directly blamed Zina for her misconduct. I felt terrible for Zina and didn't like the situation Tracy had put me in. How sad is it when you lie to your husband and blame an innocent person in the process?

"Come on, Liz, you must have some idea on how we can have this Parliament dinner without asking Zina?"

Zina is my friend, and knowing Tracy will hold this dinner without asking Zina will only upset her.

"I know that Zina is going to Spain to spend time with family for a couple of months; why not hold it then, so she doesn't know or gets upset." My intentions were pure; I was only trying to protect Zina.

Shortly after Zina went overseas, Tracy held the Parliament house dinner. Then life went back to normal.

A few months had passed, and Zina returned home. We caught up and had a lovely lunch. During lunch, Zina asked about the Parliament House dinner; she was the local socialite and loved being in the middle of attention, especially at prestigious places.

"So," said Zina, "We need to organise the Parliament house dinner with Tracy!"

I fell silent and looked down at my plate. Zina instantly knew something was up.

"What, Liz, why do you look sad? What's happened? Is Tracy ok?"

"Yes, Tracy is fine, Zina; it's just that the dinner went ahead while you were away."

"What!" shouted Zina, not caring about how loud she was. "How did this happen? Why didn't Tracy wait for me? I was only gone two months."

"I don't know, Zina!" Again, I lied to protect both Zina and Tracy. It wasn't my place to bring up Tracy's problems with Sam and to tell Zina of Tracy's lies about her to Sam.

"You must know Liz; I don't believe you!"

"Zina, it was Tracy's dinner to organise; she can ask whoever she likes; you will have to ask her?"

I didn't want to be involved in this and was upset that Tracy had pulled me into her web.

The rest of our enjoyable lunch wasn't so pleasant.

A few days later, Tracy came up to me at our local football club. "What did you tell Zina about the dinner? She seems angry with me!

"I didn't tell her anything, Zina brought it up, she asked about organising the Parliament house dinner, and I got put in a very awkward position. I told her we had already had the dinner while she was away, and she was quite livid."

Tracy was so mad with me. "Really! Why did you tell her we had already held the dinner?"

"Like I told Tracy, I was put on the spot and didn't want to lie."

Tracey sneered "You could have made up something, anything, other than the truth!"

"No, Tracy, it had nothing to do with me; you were the one who didn't want Zina near Sam because of your lies!" "I only told you that Zina was going away. So the dinner was ultimately up to you to organise."

I arrive at the tennis club early on Wednesday morning, get my bag out of the car and head into the clubrooms. There Zina and Tracy are standing, watching me walk in. You could have cut the air with a knife!

"Morning, ladies!" I said.

Zina yells out across the club room, "You are a liar!"

She was so loud, every woman stopped and gawked at me. I'm sure a few ladies out on the court stopped too.

"What are you talking about, Zina?" I asked.

"Tracy, she tells me the truth about what happened. It was your idea to make the dinner when I was away seeing my family."

"Really!" I was shocked that Tracy had gone to tennis early to ensure that she could get in Zina's ear first. She had dumped me in the shit with Zina.

"I can assure you, Zina, that it was Tracy who had the problem, not me."

"I don't care what you say. All lies. You will pay for this!" Zina was so upset; she was yelling very loudly at me; I just couldn't believe her anger over a bloody dinner. What the hell did Tracy say to her?

I left tennis after Zina's outburst. I was very embarrassed by the way Zina spoke to me. I have never heard someone be so crass, so low that they would need to bring a room full of judgemental women into our conversation, even though it turned into a one-sided yelling match. Zina considers herself a socialite, but I only saw gutter vomit that day.

In the afternoon, I tried to call Zina and Tracy to talk to them about what happened. Zina was my friend, and her comments significantly hurt me. But neither of them answered my call.

Later in the week, Tracy rang me. "Hi Liz, how are you?"

Just like nothing had happened, how could Tracy forget how she lied about me to Zina!

"I've been better; why have you rung Tracy?"

"You are not going to believe this. Liz, Zina's husband Russell, has decided to run against you for mayor. Isn't that great!" Tracy said this with a horrible cackle in her voice. Yet, she somehow thought this was funny.

"Zina just rang me and said, "Do you have any dirt on Liz? I want to bring her down! Isn't that hilarious?"

"Are you serious, Tracy? No, this is not funny at all. But, lucky for me, you don't have any 'dirt' on me."

"Maybe not!" Tracy replied, "But you know, I love the saying, never let the truth get in the way of a good story."

"Don't be stupid Tracy, this is not a game; this is my life you are messing with." I was so annoyed with Tracy right now.

"Put the kettle on, Liz; I'm coming over to chat!" Tracy said as she hung up on me before I could answer.

Within minutes she was out the front of my house. I was so upset with her; I refused to answer the front door. I felt betrayed by this witch. How dare she brazenly waltz up to my front door and expect me to welcome her in. No, she had entered my house for the last time and would never be welcome again.

My phone rang, "Liz, I know you are home." Tracy laughed. "Big mistake for not letting me in. Now I'm pissed off, and you have no idea what stories I will make up about you. This town is going to eat this shit up. Everyone loves to gossip. Good luck running for mayor!"

About a month after this, Sam left Tracy. Sam told Mike that he had organised a dinner at home for their wedding anniversary and Tracy had promised to be home by 6 pm. Sam and their daughter sat at the dinner table and waited till 8 pm. Then they ate dinner, and their daughter went to bed. Tracy turned up pissed and stinking of cigarette smoke around 9.30 pm. No apologies about the anniversary dinner. She had brought a new girlfriend home and continued to smoke and drink until they passed out around midnight. Sam found them asleep on the couch the next day.

Sam packed his bag and left her. He married a beautiful Asian lady who doesn't drink or smoke a few years later. He has never been happier.

Everywhere I went, every club I was a member of and every function I attended, Zina would be there ranting crazy bullshit about me. I heard from people that Zina told them that Mike and I were swingers, drug dealers, Tracy's husband had an affair with me and broke up their marriage. Zina believes it is all true because, you guessed it, Tracy told her it was the truth.

These words were absolutely the worst things you could say about anyone. But, unfortunately, people do love gossip, and mud does stick. If people hear the same bullshit from enough people, it must be true. I was heartbroken that two people that I welcomed into my life would turn on me like this. And for what!!! A stupid dinner with bloody politicians! Looking back, I wished I had asked Tracy to leave and to sort out her lies.

I believe that Karma will bite Tracy in the arse. You don't treat people like this, and you don't make up crap, just to be mean. I know for sure that she will never be my friend or welcome around my family ever again. After her husband left, I haven't seen her around town at all. I guess people found out what she was like!

Funny thing about Zina. She said so much, so loudly and so often, that people grew tired of it. She was toxic to be around, and people could see through her bullshit. So I just carried on with my life and beat her husband in the mayoral race. Sweet Justice!

Zina continued her rants for more than two years. No wonder she started losing her shine in social groups. No one wants to hear what foulness was spurting from her plastic lips. But, on the other hand, I continued to become a well-respected and loved member of society, and my husband and daughters have lived an enjoyable and fortunate life.

Zina's husband made some poor business decisions and lost their wealth. They are now living in the suburbs, driving a twenty-year-old BMW, pretending they still have money.

CHAPTER TWENTY-THREE

TYPICAL CRAZY MONDAY MORNING. I WAS LOOKING FORWARD TO MY meeting with Brian Molloy this morning. Paul is away at a conference, and he appointed Brian as acting CEO in his absence, as my first Monday morning meeting is always with the CEO.

I walked into the council chambers and instantly noticed my secretary looked upset at her desk. So I put my files down on my office desk and went out to find out what is wrong.

"Morning Wendy, what's wrong? You look terrible, has something upset you?" I asked.

Wendy closed her eyes and shook her head; tears started running down her face. I put my arm around her, and I could feel her shaking. "Please tell me what has happened. I want to help."

Brian Molloy then interrupts us as he bounds into the room full of cheerfulness. "Morning mayor, morning Wendy, isn't this a gorgeous day! Ready for our meeting, mayor?"

"Yes, Brian, please go right in; I'll be just one minute."

Brian walked into my office and got settled.

"Wendy, go wash your face, and we will chat after I meet with Brian." Wendy nodded, wiped her eyes and left her desk.

I went into my office, where Brian was waiting. He looked like he was so excited to be alive; it was bordering on being annoying!

"Sorry about that Brian, Wendy is upset about something."

"That's no good. What's wrong?" Brian asked.

"No idea! I didn't get a chance to find out. So what's on the agenda today, Brian?" I asked, trying to change the subject quickly.

Brian went through the paperwork I needed to sign, and then we started going through the council meeting agenda. There wasn't much happening this month. "Looks like this will be a quick meeting, Brian. Nothing contentious, no deputations. I guess we will have to see if any questions come up on the night.

"Well, mayor, I have always said, a good meeting is a quick meeting!"

"You have picked a good month to be acting CEO Brian. Thanks for coming to go through the agenda with me!"

"My absolute pleasure, mayor!" Brian then gathered his papers and left my office.

I went back out to Wendy's desk to see what has happened to upset her. "Wendy, did you want to pop into my office for a minute to chat?"

"Ok, mayor." Wendy switched her phone over to the main switchboard so they could take her calls. She came into my office and closed the door, then sat at my small meeting table. She looked miserable. Wendy is a beautiful young lady in her early thirties. A brunette with a very fit body. She teaches aerobics at the local gym most nights and runs every morning. Wendy insisted on an ergonomic standing desk, so she has the option of sitting or standing at her desk, and her chair is a large Fit Ball. It is perfect for strengthening your core, spine and stability.

Wendy came into my office, and she closed the door.

"Please tell me what has upset you, Wendy?"

"It's embarrassing, mayor. I can't believe I let it happen to me!" She then burst into tears as soon as she said it.

"What happened? It's ok to tell me, Wendy, I want to help you, and I hate seeing you so sad."

"It's Donald Geary, mayor. He touched me up!"

I was surprised! "How did this happen?" I asked.

Through Wendy's sobbing, I could make out that Donald Geary came in drunk on Friday afternoon and started harassing her.

"He just came over and started massaging my neck! I didn't know what to do, I should have told him to fuck off, but I was so scared."

Poor Wendy was a mess; she was crying so hard, she could hardly get a breath in.

"The next thing I know, his bloody hands are down my top, and he's got my boobs in his hands, and he squeezed them hard; it hurt so much!"

"How dare he touch you like that! That is disgusting; what an arsehole!" I said, trying to soothe her.

"All I could do was run away to the toilet and wait till he had gone," continued Wendy, now bawling.

"You have done nothing wrong, Wendy; Donald has done buckets wrong, and I will sort this out. Can you please write out what has happened in a statement for me? I want to contact the police and will let them know what has happened?" I handed Wendy some tissues.

"I am so angry with myself. Why didn't I stand up for myself? I said nothing; now he probably thinks he can do it again. I should have called security; I should have told him to fuck off, sorry, mayor." Wendy burst into tears again.

"That sleazy bastard! He will pay for this. You must press an assault charge against him."

"I don't know that I can go through repeating what happened again. It's so embarrassing, mayor; I am so disappointed with myself. I would hate for him to do this to another woman."

"I understand, Wendy; I am so sorry you have been through this. It's just horrible. Can I ask that you type up a formal complaint, and I will witness it? This statement may prevent you from having to repeat your story, over and over again."

"Yes, I can do that. Can I leave please, I will type it up at home? I just don't want to be here right now."

"Please go home, Wendy; I can't imagine how you must be feeling. Leave Donald to me. "Thanks, mayor, thanks for listening and understanding; you have no idea how much I appreciate it." Wendy left my office, gathered her things and went home.

I rang Brian and asked him to come back to my office for an urgent matter. Within five minutes, Brian walked into my office.

"Where's Wendy, mayor?"

"I let her go home. She is the reason we need this meeting."

"I saw she was upset this morning when I came in; I'm guessing everything is not ok!" Brian said.

"That easy month I mentioned earlier is about to change. Councillor Donald Geary sexually assaulted Wendy on Friday night in the office. In a nutshell, Wendy was alone working at her desk, and Donald came in drunk to collect his council papers. He started massaging Wendy's neck, then put his hands down her blouse and grabbed her breasts!"

"Stupid bitch! Why would you let a drunk man massage your neck? She was asking for it, and now what! It's a sexual assault!" Brian exploded, quite clearly defending Donald.

I was shocked at this response; how the hell is this Wendy's fault, and why is she a stupid bitch? "Are you kidding me, Brian? I can't believe you just said that"

"Come on, mayor, I have seen the tight clothing she wears; she wanted that kind of attention!"

Now I was mad, what a misogynist! I always liked Brian; now I wanted to slap him. "No person has the right to touch another without their consent sexually. What action are you going to take to sort this mess out, Brian?"

"Sorry, mayor, I deal with the staff; you deal with the councillors. I'll get human resources to give Wendy a call to see if she needs anything, you know, to make all the right noises! Donald is your problem!"

"Wendy is writing up her statement today. I have told her to press charges against Donald. The media will have a field day with this news." I said,

"You know it will be her word against his, mayor. Good luck." Brian retorted as he got up and just walked out of my office.

Wow! I thought Paul was a prick, but this place is a breeding ground for them! My brain hurts trying to figure out how that meeting went south so fast. The assault of a young lady is not her fault. This situation is so very wrong. I called the police for advice on how best to deal with this situation.

"Hello, this is constable Jones; how can I assist you?"

"Hi, it's mayor Valenti from the city of Wanjup. My secretary has just informed me of a sexual assault by a city councillor last Friday night in the council building. Can you please tell me the correct procedure to press assault charges against the councillor involved?" I asked.

"This is a terrible thing to happen to your secretary, mayor. Can you bring her into the station so I can take a statement from her?"

"She is struggling with having to repeat her story. I have asked her to write it down. Can I bring her written statement into the station on her behalf? I will have her sign it, and I can witness it."

"Yes, we can get started that way. Ask for me, constable Jones, when you come into the station, and I will take you to an interview room."

"Thanks, constable Jones. Hopefully, I will get the statement to you this afternoon. Goodbye."

Wendy emailed me the statement of events from Friday night, just after lunch.

I printed it out and drove to the police station in town. I asked for constable Jones, and she arrived at the reception desk to take me through to the interview room. Constable Jones is a beautiful young woman; I would guess the late twenties. She tied her blonde hair back in a tight bun, and you could see she was physically fit. "Thanks for seeing me, constable Jones; I am fuming that this has happened to my secretary. She is such a beautiful person. Here is her statement."

The constable took the statement and read it out loud to me.

"I was working back on my own on Friday afternoon, finishing off some paperwork ready for tomorrow's council meeting. I had two hours to kill before taking a class at the gym. It wasn't worth me driving all the way home just to turn around and come back, so I thought I would use my time wisely.

Councillor Donald Geary came in to collect his council papers around 5.30 pm. He told me he had just come from lunch, like he deserved a medal or something, for having such a long lunch! I could smell the alcohol on him as soon as he walked in and was intoxicated.

He went out the back and picked up his papers, then came around my desk and sat on it. He just wanted to chat. So I kept working, hoping he would get annoyed with my lack of input into the conversation and bugger off. But he stayed and dribbled shit.

My neck was sore; I rubbed it without thinking. Just a normal reaction to a stiff neck, I guess. Then, Donald jumped up off my desk and came over to me. He put his hands on my neck and started to massage it. I was horrified; I froze and didn't say a thing to him. How did I let him get so close to me? My mind was racing; I know this person, a trusted councillor, can be sleazy, but he won't harm me; he is always very friendly to me. I wanted to scream at him, but logically, I was telling myself not to be silly. After all, he was just trying to help me, wasn't he?

Then he started to massage my shoulders. My fight or flight sensors had gone on holiday. Now I was screaming inside, but I just sat silent! I knew what he was doing was wrong; he needed to stop and leave me alone.

Before I knew it, the wanker slid his hands down my top and under my bra cup and squeezed my naked breast. Donald's movements were so effortless that I knew he had done this before to other women. I could feel his hard cock pressed against my back. I jumped up and just ran to the bathroom. I locked the door and sat in there for over half an hour, hoping he had left.

When I came out, my fit ball was on the other side of the room, he must have kicked it, but Donald was gone. I turned off my computer, tucked my Fit ball under my desk and went home to a very long hot bath where I scrubbed myself multiple times; I felt so dirty. I had to call in sick to gym; I couldn't conduct the class after what had happened. I was shaking all over and felt physically ill.

I apologise for my language. This statement is from my heart.

Yours sincerely

Wendy Hunt."

"This poor girl needs to know that this is not her fault. However, this councillor is definitely at fault. Do you have CCTV at your office?" The constable asked.

"Yes, we do, and outside the building, and there is a camera on the car park too," I replied.

"Interesting, if the councillor drove his car to the council building, we may be able to get him on a drunk driving charge as well as sexual assault in the first degree. It would help if Miss Hunt could provide photo evidence of her breast where the bruising is, as she mentioned in her statement that the councillor hurt her. I will also head down to the city's security office to retrieve the footage from Friday night. Thank you for coming down on your secretary's behalf and also for her contact information. I will give her a call shortly to confirm her statement." The constable then stood up and offered me her hand to shake. I was so impressed by her compassion and how this young constable conducted our meeting; she was very professional.

I left the Police station and went back to my office. How am I going to deal with councillor Donald Geary? I want to bring my boxing skills into play right now and beat the crap out of him. But, unfortunately, that will only lead to an assault charge against me!

The next night was our regular monthly Council meeting. Wendy didn't come into work that day, so I had a temp called Tanya Riser fill in for her. All the councillors, myself and the city executives were all in the briefing room, talking our way through the night's agenda when two police officers were escorted in by Tanya. "Sorry to interrupt mayor Valenti, but these policemen would like to speak with councillor Geary," Tanya explained as she stepped aside to let the police enter the room.

Donald stood up with a stupid smile on his face and held out his arms in front, with his wrists together. "Ok, cops, arrest me! What have I bloody done now?"

Without a blink of an eye, one of the policemen stepped forward and announced. "Mr Donald Geary, you are under arrest for sexual assault in the first degree."

"Bullshit, where is the candid camera? What a bloody joke! I haven't assaulted anyone." Councillor Donald Geary shouted.

The policeman said, "Mr Geary, understand that any statements you make become evidence in a court of law."

"You guys are not real cops; you don't even know how to arrest someone with the correct Miranda; how about, you have the right to remain silent etc." Councillor Donald was trying to make a joke about an actual situation.

"That is only applicable in the United States, Mr Geary; there are no Miranda rights in Australia. Please come with us now." The policemen led councillor Geary out to their waiting police van and took him to the holding cell.

Deputy mayor Derwent Peabody said, "What the fuck just happened. Did councillor Geary just get arrested in front of us?"

"Yes," I replied. "There is nothing more I can say on the matter; it is in the hands of the police now.

"Did he try to mess with you, Liz?" Asked councillor Sharon Day.

"No, he did not. Now let's get back to the council agenda." I tried to change the subject to stop the questioning. But I could hear everyone whispering under their breaths. Thank God this was going to be a quick meeting. I noticed that Brian Molloy sat silent during the whole debacle.

CHAPTER TWENTY-FOUR

Paul had taken Lincoln under his arm. So when I won the election against Lincoln for the mayoral position, Paul was equally devastated as Lincoln.

Paul had done his absolute best to get Lincoln elected as mayor, as had the former mayor Ron. They invited him to every well-published event, keeping him in the loop on what was happening in the city. They both held regular weekly meetings with him for this very reason.

These meetings also doubled as a chance to ensure that his 'charitable organisation' had enough city funding and enough public exposure to ensure his success at a run for the mayoral position at the election.

After I became the mayor of Wanjup, Paul made sure he continued his weekly updates on the city's events etc, and former mayor Ron Yag stepped back a notch. He was still there supporting Lincoln in every way possible but had taken up other public positions, as he couldn't show his support for Lincoln publicly. Ron had purchased a caravan, and he travelled around Australia with the love of his life.

One night, at an invite-only event organised by the city of Wanjup, I ran into Lincoln! He had no formal invitation, even admitting to me he had no right being there, but Paul had insisted that he attend.

Lincoln arrived directly, strutting towards me, with his white crocodile boots and matching tight white pants. "Hi, mayor Valenti, how do you feel about the new nightclub proposed for the centre of town?"

"Lincoln! Why are you even here?" I asked

"Paul gave me a personal invite!" boasted Lincoln.

"And you want to talk to me about what?" I asked

"The new nightclub is approved to open in the centre of town. A maximum of 900 Persons!" "It will be amazing, Liz. It will bring so much money into the local economy; you will be so proud this happened on your watch!"

"Hang on!" I asked, "How has it been approved? Why is this the first that I hear about something so massive for Wanjup? Was council consulted about this nightclub?"

"Paul told me about it last week!" Lincoln said. "The Press is going to have a field day with this. Imagine 900 drunk people leaving one location when it closes! There will be fights, business windows smashed and broken glass everywhere."

"I don't understand how city officers could have the right to approve something like this? Surely a project of this significant scale and importance to the community should have come to council for approval first?" I asked.

"I know, right!" Lincoln said. "Shit is going to hit the big fat mayoral fan when this gets out!"

Lincoln stood there with this stupid smirk on his face. I was so angry! Angry at so many things. Why would Lincoln tell me this information now, at a city function? How dare he know before me, how dare Paul tell someone, not even involved in the council this information before me! Now I had to make a speech, and my blood was at boiling point. I sucked in more air than the room had to share, smiled and delivered a faultless speech.

After Lincoln walked away from our earlier conversation, knowing he had pissed me off, I walked up to Paul and told him that I wanted him in my office first thing in the morning. He agreed but looked concerned. I was as mad as hell and wasn't doing an excellent job of concealing it.

Lincoln avoided me for the rest of the evening. Still, I could tell he was bragging to other councillors about his superior knowledge of things happening around Wanjup that I am oblivious to!

At the end of the evening, I left, still feeling very annoyed and once I got home and into bed, I couldn't sleep. I tossed and turned all night, being so cross about Lincoln. I felt the whole injustice of it. What had I done to deserve this treatment?

The following day, Paul was waiting outside my office. "Morning, mayor Valenti, sorry I'm early, but my day is full, and you seemed like you needed this meeting. You appeared quite upset last night! Is everything ok?" Paul asked.

"Come in Paul, thanks for your time. But, please, take a seat."

"Sounds serious mayor, what's up?" Paul walks in and takes a seat at the tiny meeting table. He starts twitching and looking around my office nervously.

"Lincoln came up to me last night, at an event you had no right to invite him to, bragging about the fact that you shared information with him on a new nightclub opening in town!"

"Are you kidding, mayor!" Paul said. "What's the issue? I can invite someone doing so much for the community, like Lincoln, to our city event."

"You must be joking, Paul! It's more about the bloody nightclub for 900 people that I knew nothing about. Lincoln reckons the Press know all about it and will be questioning my judgement on allowing this to go ahead!"

"It's not your fault the nightclub has was approved, mayor. It's not a council issue," Paul explained. "Because of its size, the State Planning Commission has taken over approving anything this large."

"Come on, Paul! This nightclub is a big thing. You should have given me the heads up, so at least I know what is going on in my city." "I don't understand how the council didn't have any say in this matter? Surely something this size should be signed off by the council first? Let's face it; it's our role to protect and look after the concerns of our ratepayers."

"Pity you didn't take the time to read the council minutes when you returned from your relaxing holiday in Bali after your mother passed away! The sitting council approved it then." Paul said.

"I did read the minutes; however, I never received the confidential papers that are normally attached; they were missing. I remember asking for them, and you said there was nothing confidential or of interest to attach. You just said NO to me!" I replied.

"Well, it must have slipped my mind, mayor," scoffed Paul, not caring that I was upset.

"Paul, can I ask that any information you decide to share with Lincoln? I am already fully informed!"

"Mayor Valenti, I can share any information with anyone I choose to, once approved by council. But, if you are not doing your job to read and educate yourself on matters concerning this city, then that is on you. My job is not to babysit you!" Paul said as he got up from the chair and headed towards my office door. "Don't think for one minute that you have the authority to dictate to me who I can and can't talk to. Or what I have to discuss with you. That is my choice, remember, you employ me to be the CEO of this city, so let me do my job. See you later; I have to attend my next, actually, important meeting."

What an asshole, I thought. I am so glad Paul's contract is up in six months!

"Oh, and sorry to dump this on you, basically on your first day back, but the police arrested councillor Donald Geary last week," I said.

"What the fuck? Why are you just mentioning this now! What the hell happened while I was away?"

"Donald came in drunk and saw Wendy on her own and came over and started harassing her; he had been at the pub since lunch. He then started massaging her neck and then slipped his hands down to her breasts for a good squeeze!"

"Bloody hell! How is Wendy? Is she ok?"

"No, Paul, it shook her, more the fact that she didn't react in time than the actual act of Donald grabbing her boobs. Wendy has been on leave since. Tanya has been filling in since and has done an amazing job for a crazy redhead. She is a lot of fun."

"Poor Wendy, I loved that little fitness guru; she made me want to go and grab a smoothie rather than a meat pie! How was the situation handled?"

"Sadly, I spoke with Brian Molloy, who you appointed as acting CEO, and he said it was her fault for being a stupid bitch and wearing the wrong clothes."

"Are you kidding me! I would never have thought that Brian would be like that. You must have picked him on a bad day!"

"No, actually, he bounced into my office in the morning, declaring what a wonderful day it was before I told him about Wendy. So please don't make excuses for him being a total dick!

Wendy pressed charges against Donald for sexual assault. Donald's arrest was in front of the other councillors before last week's meeting. It will not look good for the city. As you said, I can't sack him, but what options do we have?"

"Ok, Liz, I will call the Local Government office later today. I am sure there is something we can do. How ridiculous. I do know that we can dismiss a councillor for serious misconduct, and I believe that we have enough evidence against Donald to have him dismissed as an elected member on this charge."

CHAPTER TWENTY-FIVE

I CALLED MY NEW SECRETARY, TANYA, INTO MY OFFICE. "CAN YOU please get me the minutes, from the council meetings, for the month I was away after my mother died last year?"

"Sure, mayor Valenti, is everything ok? Paul was quite rude when he left your office. I don't mean to dob him in, but he was calling you names under his breath, loud enough for me to hear, and I am pretty sure he did that on purpose!"

"It's not Tanya. I know it's not very professional to bring you into this, as your employment is with the city and not me. But Paul has given information to Lincoln that he hasn't discussed with me. Lincoln seems to know more about what is going on around this city than I do. I'm starting to feel like a mushroom, kept in the dark and fed bullshit!"

"That is awful, mayor. Lincoln is everywhere; I often see him coming into meetings with Paul and other councillors and officers of the city. He has been coming in to see Paul at least once a week, lately," explained Tanya.

"The minutes Paul provided me when I returned from leave were missing the confidential attachments. Would you please source these papers for me?" I said.

"Sure, mayor, I will get straight onto that. You have your radio program in 20 minutes. Have you got your notes? I put a spare copy on your desk in case you forgot them." Tanya said.

"Crap, I had forgotten about the radio show. Thanks, Tanya; I'll head over to the radio station now and spend 10 minutes reading through them and preparing for it. You are amazing in the way you keep me on track. Thanks for doing such a great job."

I quickly ran out of the office, clipboard in hand, and got into my council supplied Lexus. The radio station is only five minutes down the road, so I had plenty of time to relax and read the notes. I carefully checked through them to make sure there were no words that I couldn't pronounce or that I would stutter on, then headed inside.

"Good morning, beautiful mayor Valenti. It is always a pleasure to see you on a Monday morning!" Golfie said.

Golfie is a guy who was a golf professional, doing the whole international touring stuff. Until one day when he was playing in a PGA tournament in South Carolina, Fripp Island Golf Course, this bloody giant Alligator leapt out of the water and bit his foot. The Alligator grabbed and pulled him into the water. His caddie started whacking the Alligator with a seven iron, and the Alligator let go. His caddie saved his life that day, but not his foot. The Alligator crushed every bone in his foot with his massively strong jaw. The doctors couldn't keep his foot and had to amputate it. That ended Golfie's golfing career. His real name is Peter Johansson, but Golfie means so much more.

"Morning, Golfie," I replied as I stepped into the studio and gave him a quick kiss on the cheek.

"We have ten minutes to spare, running a little behind schedule today. Can I grab you a coffee before the next set ends?" Golfie asked.

"Sure, Golfie, I always love your coffee."

Golfie walks out of the studio as I read through my notes again. Nothing too exciting to report on today. Mosquito spraying in progress, Kids painting the skateboard ramp, the city giving free homeless packs to those less fortunate and so on.

Golfie walks back in and places the coffee in front of me. "So, I hear we are about to have the largest nightclub in South Australia on our doorstep! Is that in your notes today?" Golfie asked.

"Argh! No! I only just found out about this the other night. How do you know?"

"Lincoln popped in for a coffee, as he regularly does, and told me. That guy is full of news, gossip, whatever you call it. But he is usually on target!" Golfie said.

"Well, I am feeling a little embarrassed about this, as it was approved when I was away last year after my mother died and was kept secret from me until now!"

"Yeah, I'm sorry, I remember that your mum passed away. It happened quickly, too, from what I remember. You never knew she was sick, and the next fortnight, I heard you can't come in because you are attending your mum's funeral. Then you were in Bali. It felt like forever that you were away!"

"It was only four weeks, Golfie. The only weeks that I had off in the last three years!"

"The nightclub approval was last year Liz, surely someone on council has discussed this with you since? A nightclub of this size could dramatically change this city forever."

"I agree, Golfie, but no! No one has mentioned it to me, especially not the CEO who should be keeping me informed on everything happening in the city."

"I am sorry, Liz," Golfie said, "but I am going to throw you into the firing line! It's what journo's do. Armed with this info, I have to fire!"

"Really, Golfie, I thought we had a better relationship than that. You are truly going to embarrass me on live radio without warning!"

"Consider this warning, Liz, five minutes and counting. You need to come up with a response ASAP!"

Shit! I excused myself and stepped out into the hallway. I rang the media team in the city for help!

"Hi Melanie, thanks for the radio notes; I have just been going through them."

"Everything ok with the notes, mayor? You sound a bit worried." Melanie asked.

"Golfie has just told me he is going to ask me about the bloody 900 person nightclub approved for Wanjup! What do you know about this, and what can I say?"

"Oh crap, we weren't ready to answer questions on that. But, as far as I know, there is no approval by the State Government planning commission." Melanie said.

"That doesn't help Mel! I am about to be asked how it was approved, who approved it, why we would approve it, and all the rest. I am about to sound like a bloody idiot on live radio in five minutes." "You have one minute to reply with an answer, Mel!"

"I will do my best, mayor, stall Golfie for as long as you can, and I will text you my best reply."

It felt like forever, waiting for Melanie's reply. Golfie was sitting across the table from me. Wearing that smug smile, like he was the one who ate the last cookie and no one knows! We both had our headphones on and our monitors in front of us.

"If Mel doesn't come back with an answer for me, Golfie, you will make me look like a dick! Can we leave this question till next week, so I have more time to prepare?"

"Nope! I have one more commercial to play; then we are back on the air."

"Shit! Fine, I am feeling a little crushed right now mate, I thought we had a better understanding!"

"You will be fine, Liz; I have seen you bullshit your way through worse on live air before."

"Not like this, though. I just found out that the CEO told Lincoln about it months ago! The council approved it while I was away on a health retreat in Bali after my mother passed away, and I was never informed about it until two days ago."

"The question I will ask you then, mayor, do you approve of it?"

"No! Absolutely not! I was not part of the sitting council that approved it. It was the State Government that took away our powers to approve it anyway. It will not bring harmony to our city. Any extra increase in economy generated from this nightclub is gone because of the expensive clean up from the night before!"

"Correct answer Mayor," Golfie said. "I knew you had it in you." "Let's go on air!"

The red 'On Air' light came on, and my heart was racing. I was annoyed with Golfie for being set up! We pleasantly talked our way through the first half of the notes, and my phone lit up! Golfie saw it as a trigger to jump in on the next question.

I quickly read the message from Mel, and it said the council approved the use of the premises as a nightclub as it already had approval for a movie theatre that held the same amount of people. They didn't believe that the noise would be an issue.

How useless is that information? Golfie jumped right in! "On another subject that has flown under the radar, mayor, what can you tell us about the new 900 person nightclub opening up in the middle of town?"

I replied, "You are quite correct on the flying under the radar Golfie; I personally only found out about it two days ago. It was passed by council, with deputy mayor Derwent Peabody chairing the meeting when I took leave after my mother's death."

"Are you making excuses, mayor Valenti?" Golfie asked.

"Not Golfie, the minutes I was given, on my return from leave, did not contain any information regarding this proposed nightclub. It was the state government that has final approval over proposed businesses like this."

"Am I picking up on a conspiracy theory here, mayor? Are you confessing to not doing your job?"

"No! I am totally against this proposal. The last thing this city need is a 900-person nightclub. Once they kick everyone out at the closing time, where are the drunk people going to go? I can only assume they will fight, probably vomit or graffiti our beautiful city."

"Interesting that it came to council in your absence! I think we should open a phone poll up on this matter!" Golfie said, "Anyone that doesn't want this nightclub to open in Wanjup, call in now! The lines are open, and we are waiting to take your calls."

We continued our live show; I finished the rest of the information required to report to the public and politely left the building. But, knowing that next week, I had to face the results of today's poll!

CHAPTER TWENTY-SIX

AFTER MY RADIO SHOW, I WENT BACK TO MY OFFICE AND ASKED MY secretary Tanya to get Paul down to my office. "Tell him it's urgent and won't take long."

Paul came into my office, didn't knock or even acknowledge me. "What is so urgent mayor?" Paul said.

"I was just ambushed on live radio about the 900-person nightclub! Lincoln told him last week!"

"How is that my concern, mayor?" Paul asked.

"When the mayor of the city does not receive information on matters as important as this, it is your concern. So consider this a formal warning, Paul. I won't be voting in favour of you continuing your employment with the city in six months. I think you have been here too long."

"You didn't get that part of the council minutes either, then!"

"What are you talking about, Paul? Was there more confidential information that you haven't told me about?" I asked.

"The council renewed my contract for another seven years," Paul said.

"Are you kidding! You can't renew it for that long; five years is the limit. When were you going to tell me this?" I asked.

"I figured you knew; it was in the minutes. Maybe if you took the time to read them, you would know."

"I have read the minutes, Paul, and there was no mention of your employment contract. Another apparent matter was missing from the minutes I received. I have asked Tanya to get me a copy of the missing confidential papers. Is there anything else that has come up that I should know about?" I asked.

"Nope! Now, if that is all that you wanted, I have work to get back to." Paul sneered.

"Thanks for your time, Paul; oh, I nearly forgot, what is going to happen with Donald?"

"That silly bastard has given me a golden ticket to get rid of him for good! I contacted the South Australian local government authority, who agreed that he could lose his position as a city councillor due to serious misconduct. I notified him yesterday. He will be returning the city's assets and his security swipe card today," explained Paul.

"Again, Paul, it would have been nice to have been told about this earlier. When had you planned on actually telling me if I hadn't asked you?" I asked.

"You would have noticed him missing eventually, mayor. I thought you would have been happy. Donald has been a pain in the arse to this council for years!"

"Still not acceptable, Paul. Especially anything to do with my councillors. You must tell me immediately if anything happens. Are we clear?" I asked.

"Yes, mayor Valenti, by the way, Wendy has quit! She had formally filed a sexual assault charge against councillor Donald Geary. So the temp, Tanya, will be staying on as your permanent staff now."

Poor Wendy, she must be going through such a hard time. I must remember to call her to see how she is going.

Have a nice day," snapped Paul as he angrily walked out of my office.

That man makes my skin crawl; I don't trust him one bit.

I called out to my secretary, "Tanya, can you please come in here for a minute!"

"Sure, mayor, what can I do for you?"

"Did you end up getting a new copy of the minutes from the council meeting that I was absent for?" I asked.

"Yes, they are on my desk; I'll grab them for you."

Tanya quickly went back to her desk and collected the minutes for me. I sat there and carefully read the confidential papers at the back of the minutes. These pages were definitely not in the copy I received before.

Sure enough, there is Paul's employment contract, the first item in the confidential section. I was so angry. Now Paul will be 70 and still employed as CEO of the city. He knew I was going to vote against the renewed contract. Paul has no respect for me or any other woman. He speaks to me in such a condescending manner; it makes my blood boil!

I rang the city's corporate lawyer Alan to check on the legalities of Paul extending his contract for seven years. You can only do a five-year extension; however, in Paul's case, the council voted in favour of the seven-year contract, as this will be his final contract!

That topped off my day. I can't believe that he went behind my back and slipped his contract into the minutes while I was away. But, of course, the other councillors never thought to mention it to me either.

The State Government officials confirmed that the contract could not be for more than five years. So I went back to the city's lawyer. "It's not a legal contract; the State Government office just confirmed this with me."

"I am sorry, mayor Valenti but Paul is my boss, and I have to protect my job here. I can't help you fight this. The other councillors all unanimously voted in favour of this contract. You have to respect this. I know how you feel about Paul, but there is nothing you can do." "This is probably a bad time, mayor, but I have Paul's contract on my desk that you need to sign. I have some other paperwork you need to sign as well, so if you are free, I will come to your office now?" Alan asked.

"Ok, Alan, I am free, so please come over now," I replied.

I was so disappointed with the other councillors right now. They all complained about Paul. None of them like him, so why offer him such a long-term contract. They are so weak. Paul is a bully and controlling asshole.

Alan came straight to my office with the paperwork to sign. Most of the signing was tender contracts and certificates for the next Citizenship ceremony. Then I came to Paul's employment contract.

"I am not going to sign this now, Alan. However, if you don't mind, I would like to take my time reading through it."

"Of course, mayor Valenti. Take your time. I'll head back to my office. Let me know if you have any questions with the contract." Alan said as he collected up the other signed documents and went back to his office.

I started reading Paul's contract and was surprised by some of his perks. A new car valued at $100,000 every three years, two international and five interstate conferences per year. A credit card with a $5,000 credit limit per month. Mobile phone, Laptop, clothing allowance and a full gym membership for him and his wife. This is on top of his salary of $300,000 per year. The Prime Minister of Australia doesn't get paid that much.

I took the contract home and got Mike to have a look at it. "Bloody hell Liz!" Mike said. "No wonder he wants to protect his job as CEO. Now I understand why our council rates keep going up so much every year!"

Mike looked through the Key Performance Indicators, "These are a joke, Liz! Who set these KPIs? They should ensure he does his job and keeps everything on target. You need to meet with the councillors and get them changed. Also, why does he need all those conference trips?"

"I agree with you, Mike; I will call the other councillors and set up a meeting with them to discuss it."

On the following Wednesday night, I held the meeting to go over the CEO's contract. There is an executive team on the council, made up of myself, the deputy mayor Derwent Peabody, two other elected members, Sharon Day and Pauline Ashley.

After I thanked them for coming in for the meeting, Paul and Alan burst through the door.

"This is a private meeting, Paul! Why are you and Alan here?"

"You can't discuss my confidential contract with the other councillors. If you have a question, then you have to ask Alan," Paul replied.

"Yes, I can discuss this contract with my fellow councillors. I have already checked with the Local Government authority. Now, if you don't mind, we would like to get on with it."

"If you are going to discuss my contract, I am staying here. You can't make me leave." Paul demanded.

"Can you and Alan please leave the room? I want to discuss your KPI's and a few of your allowances."

"No, I am not leaving this room while you discuss my contract!" demanded Paul as he slammed his fist on the table, making Pauline jump.

"What are you worried about us finding in the contract, Paul! You are acting like a child. Fine, sit down and don't interrupt."

The other councillors had no idea about the spending allowance, the travel allowance etc.

Seeing Paul didn't leave the room, I was able to throw a few questions his way.

"Why do you need so many conference trips per year?" I asked.

"I don't always take that many, but I want them in the contract, in case there are some that I think would benefit the city by me attending," Paul said.

"Ok, I recommend that we cut the international conference to only one per year and the interstate conference to two per year. Paul, you must have my approval before booking any conference."

"This is bullshit, mayor; you have no right to do that!" Paul shouted.

"I do, and I am changing your contract with the approval of the other councillors."

Paul had gone red in the face. Alan just sat there, not saying a word. Then, finally, Paul got up so fast; his chair went flying backwards. "Have fun, mayor, but the contract is not going to change," Paul said as he took off out the room, with Alan hot on his heels.

I and the councillors just looked at each other and shrugged our shoulders. Then, we continued going through the contract and made notes and changes.

The following day, Paul comes flying into my office. "Where's my contract?"

"I am still working my way through it, Paul."

"I need it signed now because I am buying a new car, and governance won't sign off on it until I have my new contract signed," Paul said.

"Sorry, Paul, but I am not finished with it yet. I need to meet with the executive team again to go through the KPIs. I am not happy with the ones currently in your contract."

"I thought you did that last night!" grumbled Paul.

"We ran out of time; there was quite a lot to go through."

Paul barked "What a load of crap; you are doing this on purpose, just to piss me off!"

"I'm not Paul, and I have every right to go through your contract before signing off on it."

Paul stormed out of my office. He is one very angry ant. About two hours later, Alan rings me to see if I had signed it.

"Mayor Valenti, it's Alan. Have you signed Paul's contract yet? Alan asked.

"No, I just told Paul I had to meet with the councillors again to review his KPIs. I am calling a few other mayors to find out what KPIs they are using for their CEO's."

"Sorry to ask, but I just had a fuming CEO in my office, demanding that I get you to sign the contract," Alan said.

"I am meeting with the other councillors tonight, Alan. If we get it finalised tonight, I will discuss the changes with you tomorrow. But nothing is going to happen before then."

"I am just doing my job, mayor, and I have to answer to Paul. Once the variations are complete, I will come to your office to review the contract. I need to make sure that any changes are reasonable and legal."

"Not a problem, Alan; hopefully, I will call you tomorrow."

I met with the executive group, and we finalised Paul's contract. I felt a lot happier with the KPIs and the monetary changes we made to his contract. But, of course, Paul won't like it, but too bad.

I didn't need to call Alan the next day; he was already waiting in my office when I walked in.

"Morning Alan, you are in here early."

"I didn't have a choice, mayor," said Alan. "Paul rang me last night and told me I had to be here waiting for you when you first walk in."

"Wow, he is super protective over this contract! I'll get it out of my briefcase, and let's work through it. Would you like a coffee?"

"Yes, please, white and one sugar, thanks," smiled Alan.

Tanya organised our coffees, and we started working through the contract.

After just over one hour, we finished. Alan took the contract to Paul to then go through it with him. I felt for Alan. Paul bullied him and threatened his job constantly.

There were a few compromises Paul and I had to make, but eventually, Paul got his contract signed. I felt good that I could take a few of his perks away and restrict his travel. That guy has had it too good for too long. And now the unfortunate city has to put up with him as CEO for another seven years.

CHAPTER TWENTY-SEVEN

ANGELO PORCINI IS A TALL, CHARMING MAN, BLACK CURLY HAIR WITH olive skin and the darkest brown eyes. He is always quick to smile with the cutest dimples. His role at the city is the Executive Director, People and Communities. This position, in my opinion, is beneath him. Angelo is a well-educated man. He graduated with honours for his Masters in Psychology and later completed a Bachelor of Commerce.

Being a single man in his early 40's, he was very popular with the female staff, and I think, a few of the councillors. Angelo has made it no secret that he wants the CEO's job. He has the right qualifications and the personality to do a great job.

The councillors would sit in the briefing room, listening to Angelo speak about the report coming up in the next council meeting. We felt able to openly ask questions here without the general public listening. Some items are highly confidential.

Councillor Sharon Day would sit in these meetings just staring at Angelo. I think it was starting to make him feel uncomfortable. She never really asked him many questions, which was strange for her. Sharon always had a lot to say!

The day after the one of the nightly briefings, I saw Sharon walking out of Angelo's office, wearing the biggest smile and the skimpiest skirt. She looked very proud of herself, sharing in a joke and laughing as she walked out.

The next day I bumped into them again at the local coffee shop. They were pondering over another report. Sharon was starting to spend a lot of time harassing poor Angelo over these reports. She noticed me as I walked in, and she pretended to have not seen me and turned her head away.

I ordered my coffee and read the local paper while waiting for my takeaway coffee. I tried to listen to Sharon and Angelo's conversation. There was a lot of laughter coming from them, which made me think it was more of a social coffee than a working one. They pondered over the report before them and slowly sipped at their coffees. I finally got my coffee and walked over to them.

"Hi Angelo, hi Sharon, what are you guys looking at?"

Sharon cut Angelo off as he was about to answer me. "We are looking at the report on the homeless situation in Wanjup that is coming to the next council meeting. I am sure that this is of no interest to you."

How bloody rude! Who does this righteous bitch think she is?

"Sharon, I do care about this terrible, growing situation in Wanjup. Thanks for taking the time to follow it up with Angelo. It shows you are a great councillor."

I knew damn well she was being horrible to me in front of Angelo. Her lack of respect had not gone unnoticed. However, there was no need for me to bite. I thought my response would put her back in her cage.

Angelo gave a little side smirk, and I knew exactly what he was thinking.

"I will leave you two to continue your work. Enjoy your coffee." I said as I left the two of them to finish their coffees.

The next council meeting had a report on a town just out of Canberra that had used old sea containers as homes for the homeless people that lived there. The city hosted delegates from other councils with similar problems to come and look at what they had achieved. Angelo had put the report together and was attending the delegation. The report asked for two councillors to attend.

Sharon was the first to thrust her hand into the air, followed by councillor Pauline Ashley. The whole council approved their request and agreed that they would be joining Angelo on this trip.

This trip would give Sharon direct access to Angelo. Pauline wouldn't even turn up to the delegation; we all know why she is going! She wants a free holiday with free food and drinks. She acts like she is homeless, so I guess she can relate to the conference.

The three of them arrived in Canberra and then were put on a coach for the trip out to Coogong. After arriving at the Holiday Inn, they unpacked and caught up at the bar downstairs for a pre-dinner drink. Pauline had been chatting up the cute young male air hostess on the flight over and managed to wrangle more alcohol from him than she needed. She was already well on her way to passing out.

"I think you need to eat something, Pauline," Sharon stated. "You are slurring your words and should stop drinking."

"Don't tell me what to do, Sharon," Pauline replied. "I can handle a lot more booze than this!" "Who made you the alcohol police anyway?"

"You are representing the city of Wanjup Pauline, and I can see people are looking at us. You need to keep your voice down and eat something now!" Sharon was agitated by Pauline's actions and wanted her to leave her alone with Angelo.

"Fine!" Pauline said. "I'll grab a menu and see what we can eat."

Pauline took off to the bar to get a menu and returned with three of them. "Here, you might as well have a look and order something too. Unless if you want to have a romantic dinner for two?"

"Don't be a dick head!" Sharon sharply replied. "I just want to eat and head up to my room. We have a big day tomorrow."

Angelo just gave one of his gorgeous smiles and looked at the menu. "I'm going to be boring and will just grab a Chicken Parmy; you can't beat crumbed chicken with tomato sauce with lashings of melted cheese."

"That's disgusting, Angelo; I can hear your veins hardening with the fat as you speak!" Sharon teased.

"Give it a rest Sharon," Pauline replied. "You think you know better than everyone. If Angelo wants his Parmy, then let him have it. You're not his mother, or his wife, for that matter!"

"That's ok, Pauline!" Angelo admitted. "I know Sharon is just looking after my welfare. Maybe I should have the Thai Beef salad instead."

"Good choice!" agreed Sharon.

"You're a soft cock!" Pauline replied to Angelo, with her words slurring and dribbling out of her mouth.

Sharon stood up, shaking her head at Pauline. "I don't need to sit here and listen to your foul mouth, Pauline." "I am going to order dinner and have it delivered to my room." "Good night!"

Sharon ordered her food and went straight upstairs to her room without looking back at the table. About ten minutes later, Angelo's phone light upon the table with a text message.

"Who's that checking up on you, Angelo?" Pauline asked.

"No one!" Angelo said as he quickly turned his phone over.

"You can reply, Angelo; you can't keep the women waiting!" Pauline picked up on the way Angelo blushed and turned his phone over so quickly. Pauline thought for sure that it was someone sexting Angelo. However, his reaction gave it away; it certainly wasn't a message from his mum.

"Sure," muttered Angelo. "If you don't mind, I'll quickly reply." He put the phone under the table and sent his reply back. He was cautious that Pauline couldn't see what he was texting or to whom.

Pauline wasn't the sharpest tool and didn't think anything further of Angelo's phone message. She enjoyed her steak burger and chips, downed another wine and then excused herself. Angelo was glad to see her finally leave. He also finished his salad and left the bar.

"Hi Sharon, sorry to call so late, are you still up?" Angelo asked Sharon.

"Yes, Angelo, what took you so long?" Sharon replied.

"I got stuck with Pauline, listening to her crap. God, she has some stupid stories." "Are you still wanting me to come to your room or give it a miss tonight?"

"If you don't get your arse over here now, I am going to explode." Sharon purred seductively.

"I'll be there in five minutes."

Angelo arrived at Sharon's door and quietly knocked. He had grabbed a couple of mini bar wines from his room to bring over to Sharon's. However, he couldn't risk buying a bottle at the bar because Pauline probably would have wanted to share it with him or ask him questions about whom he was going to share it with!

Sharon opened the door, wearing a sexy little white negligée with red bows. Angelo could see her erect nipples pushing through the lace.

"So pleased you could make it, Angelo," Sharon said as she allowed Angelo to walk through the doorway. Angelo was slowly looking at every inch of Sharon's body as he walked past her. He was impressed. For a fifty-year-old, she kept herself quite tidy.

He suddenly realised he was gawking at her and snapped out of it. "I have brought drinks!" Angelo said as he held up the two small bottles of wine. "This is all that was in my minibar. Big choice, red or white?"

"Thanks, Ange, but I have had enough for one night. You can enjoy them both." Sharon said as she sauntered towards the tiny double bed. She pulled back the covers and climbed in.

"Come and join me. We have a big day tomorrow, so we can't have a big night."

Angelo put the wine down and took off his shoes. "Would you like me to turn the lights off?" Angelo asked as he fumbled with his jean zip.

"No! I'm enjoying my strip show. Keep taking it all off slowly."

Angelo blushed and took everything off except his jocks. He then dived under the covers, next to Sharon.

Angelo was like a teenager, about to lose his virginity. "What's wrong, Ange?" Sharon asked. "You are acting strange as you have never done this before."

"Sorry, Sharon," Angelo replied. "It is a bit like my first root! I have never done it with a married woman before, and I keep thinking your husband is going to burst through the door and kill me!"

"I am a grown woman, and I make my own choices; I can fuck who I like. It's my body." Sharon said as she stroked her body slowly, bringing Angelo's focus to her womanly parts.

Angelo started to feel guilty about what he was about to do, but his cock had become so hard that he didn't want to waste it.

"Fuck it!" Angelo shouted and jumped on top of Sharon. They made love all night long. They were exhausted at the end of their marathon and collapsed into a deep sleep.

Sharon's alarm went off at 6 am, and they both woke, startled and a little embarrassed. Sharon had soaked her pillow with dribble; she must have slept the whole night with her mouth wide open. Angelo had blanket marks on his face and arms. He is lucky he didn't suffocate, lying face-first on the bed.

They jumped out of bed, and Angelo took off to the toilet first. He came out and started the search for his clothes. He had flung them around the room in his attempt of a strip show, at Sharon's request. "Can you see my shirt, Sharon?"

"It's over behind the TV." "I remember seeing you toss it that way last night when you were doing your best Chippendale movements."

"Oh my God, Sharon! I am so embarrassed!"

"Don't be!" Sharon said, "I enjoyed the show."

Angelo quickly got dressed and slid quietly from Sharon's room. Sharon jumped in the shower to wash off the sex from last night. Then promptly got dressed and went downstairs to breakfast.

Pauline came down about five minutes after Sharon and joined her table. "I hope you don't mind me sitting here?

"No, Pauline, that's fine," replied Sharon. "Have you seen Angelo this morning?"

"Nope." Replied Pauline. "I think he might be a bit tired after his big night!"

"What are you talking about?" asked Sharon, trying to hide her thoughts.

"Ange got a text message that made him blush! I knew it had to be a hot date. He left shortly after he got it."

Bugger thought Sharon, the last thing she needed was for Pauline to get suspicious.

Angelo then walked around the corner and gave his big smile to Pauline and Sharon. "Morning, guys!" Angelo chirped. "What's for breakfast?"

"Smorgasbord Ange," Pauline said. "Probably a bit like the one you had last night, judging by the smile you have just walked in with."

"No idea what you are talking about, Pauline." "I'm just excited to check out these homeless shelters today." "Let's eat up and head off." Angelo walked over to the buffet and poured himself a well-earned coffee.

"I call bullshit, Ange. You got up to something last night." Pauline teased.

"Stop being crass, Pauline and leave poor Ange alone!" Sharon snapped.

"Yeah, right, Sharon, a married duck like you wouldn't even remember how to do it," Pauline sneered.

Angelo nearly spat his coffee out when Pauline said that. "Wow, Pauline, that's a bit low. It's too early in the morning for comments like that. Apologise to Sharon."

Pauline looked a bit uneasy. She didn't think before she opened her mouth. "Sorry, Sharon, that was a bit cruel. I'm sure you remember how to root!" Pauline said it with a big smirk on her face.

"You're a cheeky shit, Pauline," Angelo said.

They finished their breakfast and headed off to see the homeless storage containers.

The next night Sharon went to Angelo's room and the third night too. On returning home, they continued their coffee catch-ups and were becoming closer by the day.

It was evident that these two were doing the horizontal tango, and I don't think I was the only one who picked up on it.

CHAPTER TWENTY-EIGHT

PAUL RETURNED FROM HIS MONTH-LONG OVERSEAS HOLIDAY AND HAD his regular Monday morning catch up with me.

"Morning, Paul," I asked, trying to be as polite as possible with a man I despised.

"Morning, Liz," Paul grunted.

He put his files down on my table and walked back out to my secretary Tanya. "Can I have a skinny cappuccino, thanks?"

"Sure, Paul," Tanya replied. "Would you like one too, mayor Valenti?"

"Yes, thanks, Tanya," I replied.

"So, Paul, spill the beans! How was your holiday away? I hope you celebrated your wedding anniversary in style?" I asked.

"It was good, thanks." Paul sounded grumpy for a man who had just returned from a fantastic holiday. "Let's go over the council reports that are due for the next meeting."

He didn't want to have any personal chit chat with me today. Something had got his goat, and he was as miserable as shit.

We started going through the paperwork, and Tanya walked in with our coffees. "Thanks, Tanya."

Paul, the grumpy old shit, couldn't even thank Tanya for making him a coffee. She just looked at him, with his head down studying the paperwork, and smiled at me.

After Tanya walked out and closed the door, I had to ask Paul that burning question.

"So, Paul, have you spoken to Sharon? Have you called it off?" I asked.

"I wish you would mind your own business". Paul snapped. "If you must know, Sharon broke it off with me, so you don't need to stick your nose in my business anymore."

I was shocked by this news. But I guess why the cat was away; the mouse did play! I had noticed Sharon and Angelo were getting a little too cosy and making it apparent that something was going on between them.

I carefully asked Paul if he had noticed anything going on.

"Do you think Sharon is seeing someone else, Paul?"

"What do you mean? What do you know? No, she didn't say anything."

Ooh, I had rattled his cage this morning. He must not have considered this option when Sharon broke off their affair.

Being a little cheeky, I thought I would add fuel to the fire. "I have noticed that Angelo and Sharon have been spending a lot of time together. You know they just came back from that Canberra trip together!"

"I wasn't aware of that trip. Angelo hasn't mentioned it to me." Paul said.

"It was all approved by council at the last meeting. Angelo, councillor Sharon Day and councillor Pauline Ashley attended. It was to do with homeless shelters made out of sea containers." I could tell, as I told Paul this, he was getting redder in the face.

He gathered up his files and abruptly left my office. I know I pissed him off telling him about Sharon and Angelo.

Later that day, our conversation started to burn a hole in Paul's head about Sharon and Angelo, so he decided to find out for himself.

"Angelo, it's Paul. Have you got time for a quick chat?"

"Not right now," Angelo responded. "I've got a fair bit on my plate today. I have a deadline I have to meet by this afternoon. Did you want to catch up for a coldie after work?"

"Sounds good, Ange. How about we meet at the pub, on the corner, around 5.30 pm?"

"Perfect, mate! I'll see you then." Angelo said.

After what I had said to Paul this morning, it was stewing in his mind all day, festering away like a putrid abscess. He needed to find out if it was Angelo that had taken his mistress.

Paul arrived at the pub early and got a good seat watching the door. He didn't want to have his back to it. He wanted to know who was entering the pub.

Angelo walked in and spotted Paul. "Hi, Paul," Angelo said as he waved and gave Paul his biggest smile.

I hate that bloody smile! Paul thought to himself. "Hi Angelo, grab a stool. What can I grab for you to drink?"

"That's ok, Paul, I'm on my pins, so I'll grab the first round; what are you having?"

"Just a light beer for me, thanks Ange, I've still got work to do after this."

Angelo returned with the beers and sat down opposite Paul. "So Paul, what did you want to chat about?"

"I found out today that you went on a Canberra delegation to check out homeless accommodation!"

"Yeah, I did. It was actually at Coogong, just out of Canberra. Councillors Day and Ashley came along too."

Paul was trying to hold the steam back that was about to pour out from his ears.

They continued drinking for another hour. Angelo was drinking full-strength beer, then went on to drink Canadian Club and coke. He was getting pissed, and Paul knew he would get more information out of him with every drink.

"Tell me, Ange, being single and all, did you get lucky on your trip to Coogong?" Paul asked as he leant in closer, to give Angelo the impression that he was ready to hear all the juicy bits.

Angelo laughed, "You wouldn't believe who I hooked up with over there?"

Paul knew, all too well, who Angelo 'hooked' up with! "No idea Ange, do tell."

"Councillor Sharon Day." Angelo blurted out. "She has the best tits, and we went hard all night long. God only knows how we survived the three days. I was exhausted!"

Paul was shocked; he thought that Sharon had found someone else but not bloody Angelo. How do you compete with Adonis? He is young, single, well off and can satisfy Sharon all night long!

"Are you going to see her again, Ange?" Paul asked.

"What do you mean by, again, Paul? We haven't stopped screwing since we got back." "Sharon is preparing to leave her husband next week. She is just waiting for her son to finish his high school-leaving exams. Sharon is the best mum, always putting their welfare first."

"Yes, Ange, she is a good mum." "Don't you feel guilty about fucking a married woman?"

"Funny you should say that, Paul that is exactly what went through my mind on our first night together." "I kept thinking her husband was going to come in and catch us out and kill me".

Paul thought to himself; I am ready to bloody kill you!

Angelo went on to share way too much information with Paul. Paul grew enraged because he remembered his and Sharon's Tasmanian disappointing sex romp. Paul thought, on returning from his holiday, he would pick up his relationship with Sharon. Promising her a better effort in the bedroom, Paul even bought a cock ring to prolong his erection.

Angelo and Paul finished their drinks and went their separate ways. Angelo caught a taxi home, and Paul walked back to the office.

Paul was so angry; he couldn't concentrate on work. So he locked his office and headed home for the night to his wife, Sonja.

Sonja picked up on the fact that her husband was out of sorts. "What's wrong?" She asked. "You look like something is troubling you!"

"I've just found out that one of my executive officers is banging one of the married councillors," Paul said as he sat down to enjoy his dinner.

"That's disgusting behaviour by them both! What are you going to do about it? Sonja asked.

"I don't know. I guess they are both adults who can make up their minds. I can't control their behaviour!" Paul said.

"Yes, you can!" Sonja retorted with her hands firmly placed on her hips. I think you should sack the officer. Is it a male or female officer?"

"A male executive officer and a female councillor."

"Can you tell me who they are, Paul?"

"I guess, but please, it doesn't leave this room."

"My lips are sealed, honey!" Sonja was very excited to hear this gossip.

"It is councillor Sharon Day and executive officer Angelo Porcini."

"I never trusted that councillor, especially around you! I reckon she is a proper slut. I almost could have guessed you were going to name her. And Angelo, he is just a young beautiful looking man. So why on earth would he be attracted to someone like Sharon?"

"I know Sonja; no one was as shocked as me." "I think you are right about sacking Angelo. I can't sack Sharon because she is an elected member of the council, but I can remove Angelo".

Sonja was a genius; Paul's mind was so engrossed with rage, he couldn't think straight, and his wife had given him the perfect way to get rid of Angelo. Paul hated Angelo because he was so popular, and he knew, all too well, that Angelo was going for his coveted CEO position.

The following day Paul got into his office early. He needed a reason to sack Angelo. Who Angelo has an affair with is not a sackable offence, neither is stealing your boss's mistress! So he spent the entire morning, locked away in his office, going over different scenarios on ways to get Angelo sacked.

Finally, it came to him. He remembered a conversation he was having with one of the directors in charge of works and services. The staff had uncovered a bag of Methamphetamine hidden in the toilet cistern in the public ablution. Someone contacted the city to report a broken toilet, and the flusher wouldn't work. That is where they found the drugs.

The drugs were locked away in his office safe, waiting for the police to retrieve the drugs. Paul quickly opened the safe to make sure the bag was still there. It weighed about a kilo. Fortunately, no one had weighed it. It was just reported and locked away. This was too good to be true. Like a gift from God had just landed in his lap.

Paul carefully removed nearly a quarter of the Meth and placed it in another bag. He then called Angelo's secretary to find out what appointments he had on that day. Regrettably, Angelo wasn't going to be away from his office for long enough to plant the drugs there.

However, he was aware that the secretary would see him enter the office and ask questions.

As Angelo was a director, he drove a city-issued car. Paul went down to the fleet department and waited until the office that contained the spare car keys was empty. Unfortunately, the office was more like a storeroom than an office and was crammed full of stuff. He quickly used his master key to open the locked cabinet containing the keys. Thankfully the manager in charge of the fleet is meticulous, bordering on OCD, about things being in the correct order. Paul was able to locate Angelo's spare key quickly. He slid it into his pocket and went back to his office.

Paul carefully looked through Angelo's appointments to see when there would be a good opportunity for him to plant the drugs. He had an afternoon appointment at the south side of the building, well away from the car park where his car has a designated car bay.

Paul was feeling very pleased with himself. He took the stash of drugs with him, hidden inside his jacket. Then, striding through the car park, keeping an eye out for anyone watching, Paul reached Angelo's car. He carefully unlocked the vehicle and delicately slid the packet under the driver's seat. Finally, he locked the car and popped the key back into his pocket.

Now he just had to work out how he was going to dob Angelo into the police. This whole process turned out to be a lot easier than he thought. He walked back to his office and felt so much better. Revenge can be so sweet!

As it worked out, Paul was fortunate he planted the drugs when he did. He wouldn't have been back in his office for five minutes when his secretary called him to announce the arrival of two detectives, who had come to collect the drugs. Paul welcomed them into his office, opened the safe in front of them, and then gave them the parcel of drugs.

"Mr Aldman." One of the detectives asked. "We noticed that you are not wearing gloves! How many people have handled this bag?

"I have no idea!" Paul replied. "The staff found it in the Cistern in the main park in town."

"We will need the fingerprints of any staff that may have come into contact with the bag." The detective said. "This includes you, Mr Aldman."

They then took the bag with glove covered hands and produced a fingerprinting kit. Paul obliged and had his fingers pressed into the black ink. Next, they handed him a wet towel to clean his fingers.

"Are you aware of any members of staff that may be using drugs?" asked the detective. "We are asking this because the location of the drugs was a building owned by the city."

What a golden opportunity for Paul to tell the cops about Angelo. "Well, funny, you should ask," said Paul. "I have noticed that one of my directors has been acting rather peculiar lately."

"Can you tell us about his behaviour?" The detective asked. "How is it, peculiar?"

Paul goes straight to the point; he has been so eager to tell them. "This particular director has been going to his car a lot during office hours. Not that this, in itself, is strange, but his mannerisms change as the day gets on. He seems to be very agitated by the afternoon. I have noticed him also wearing expensive clothing and is wearing a new Rolex!"

The detectives seemed very interested in this information and asked to meet with this director. "I checked his appointments with his secretary earlier and knew he would be in his office". Paul didn't want anyone noticing him walking the cops to Angelo's office, so he asked his secretary to bring the detectives to Angelo's secretary; she could then introduce them.

Paul's secretary escorted the detectives to Angelo's secretary's desk, outside Angelo's office, and left them there.

Paul paced up and down his office, waiting to find out what happened. He was like a kid, waiting to open his presents on Christmas Day.

He thought to himself. You fuck with my girl; I will Fuck with you. He was incredibly proud of himself. Then his phone rang. "Mr Aldman, it's Sally." Sally, who was Angelo's secretary, sounded very upset.

"What's the matter, Sally?" Paul asked.

"It's Mr Porcini; the police arrested him for having drugs." Sally continued. "Mr Porcini is adamant that he has never seen them before and someone had planted the drugs in his car."

"I am sorry to hear this, Sally; I am sure that Angelo is innocent, and it has all been a big misunderstanding."

This is gold, Paul thought. So he knocked off early for the night, went down to the florist, and brought his wife a beautiful bouquet. It was Sonja's idea, after all, to sack Angelo. So I now have the perfect reason to dismiss that prick.

Paul arrived home and surprised Sonja with the flowers. "You are not going to believe what happened today, babe!" Paul told Sonja.

"Please tell me you sacked Angelo?" Sonja asked.

"Even better!" Paul announced. He couldn't get the smile off his face. "Funny how things turn out. Two detectives turned up at my office to collect some drugs found in the ablution block in town. Then they arrested Angelo because they found more drugs hidden in his car."

"Really?" said Sonja, "Angelo never came across as a druggy, mind you, he never came across as a cheating son of a bitch either!" "How did the detectives know to look in Angelo's car?"

"I may have mentioned that he had been acting weird lately, and it would be worth checking his car. Can you believe they found a whole bag of drugs under the driver's seat!"

"That makes sense," Sonja replied. "Angelo would have to be drug fucked to find Sharon attractive. Now it has all come together. Wow! What a day! Let's celebrate."

CHAPTER TWENTY-NINE

Now that Paul had Angelo locked away, on false charges, he quickly got about repairing his relationship with Sharon.

"Sharon, I know you have heard about Angelo. Can you meet me at our regular coffee shop for a quick chat? There are a few things you need to know!"

"I can't today, Paul. I'm literally up to my armpits in shit." "The Government has decided to give out free bowel cancer testing tests to every Australian over the age of 50! My workload had quadrupled!"

"It's fairly urgent that we speak. I know that you are not interested in continuing our relationship. You have never told me why! But that is not why I need to speak with you. It is to do with Angelo."

"What!" Sharon said, sounding shocked. "How do you know about Angelo and me?"

"Well, I didn't until you just confirmed it then!"

Shit, Sharon thought; she walked right into that one.

"Nothing is going on Paul, I am just friends with Angelo and am concerned to hear that you need to speak with me about him."

"It's about his drug problem. Do you know anything about this?" Paul candidly said.

"I don't know what you are talking about, Paul, or for what reason you think I would know anything?" Sharon continued. "Fine, I have a lunch break at noon; I'll meet you then."

"Thanks, Sharon; I need to talk to a friend right now. What has happened in the city is just terrible? See you at noon."

Sharon was curious. She knew nothing of Angelo's drug use or what had happened in the city. Nevertheless, she was intrigued and anxious to hear what Paul had to say.

Paul arrived early at the coffee shop, took his regular seat, facing the door, and waited for Sharon to arrive. She came, right at noon, with a big smile, like she was happy to see Paul.

"Hello Paul, you are looking rather spunky today! Got a hot date!" Sharon said.

Paul didn't look amused. "Sharon, you know damn well that I don't."

Sharon looked a little surprised by Paul's response and took the seat next to him.

"What's going on with you, Paul?" "You asked me for a coffee! Remember!"

"Do you know that Angelo was arrested yesterday for the drug haul they found in his car?" Paul said.

"What!" replied Sharon. "You know that is bullshit! There is no way that Ange would be doing drugs."

"How well do you know him, Sharon?" "I believe he has been using and dealing drugs in Wanjup for quite some time."

"No, I haven't heard that." "Are you sure, Paul, it doesn't sound like something Angelo would be involved with?"

"It happened at work. Angelo had the bloody drugs right there in his car. The cops found the stash and arrested him on the spot."

"How did the cops find the stash?" Sharon asked. "I just can't get my head around this. Angelo doesn't seem like that type of guy to be dealing drugs!"

Paul had a smirk on his face and just shrugged his shoulders, "I don't know, I heard someone dobbed him into the cops!"

Sharon sat there for a minute, absorbing this information. Then it occurred to her that Paul knew of her relationship with Angelo.

"How was your Anniversary trip, Paul? I hope you and Sonja had a wonderful holiday."

"Thanks, Sharon, it was a great holiday. And thanks for not saying anything to Sonja; I know you were disappointed when I didn't leave her for you."

"Yes, Paul, you could say I was disappointed, but I have moved on to greener pastures since."

"Oh!" Paul replied. Trying to sound not surprised. "Have you reconciled with your husband?"

"Not exactly!" said Sharon. "But that could still be on the cards!"

Now Paul thought that Sharon wouldn't have a bar of Angelo because he is a low-life drug dealer and will be going back to her husband.

Sharon thought, fuck you, Paul, I will not give you any information about my private life. We are over!!

"Great to hear that Sharon, your husband is a good man."

"Yes, he is Paul, and what we have done must never be said to this, good man! Do we have an understanding?"

"Absolutely Sharon, and of course, the same goes for my wife. She would be devastated if she found out about our Tasmania trip."

"Paul, there wasn't a lot to write home about!" Sharon said with a sneaky smile on her face.

This remark only enraged Paul. He thought, who does this bitch think she is! Belittling me while I am telling her that her low-life lover got arrested for drugs!!

Paul couldn't help himself, so he blurted out, "I told the cops about Angelo's drug use. I could see he was acting different and was going to his car a lot during the day."

"Bullshit!!" Sharon shouted, "You found out about us fucking and wanted to get back at him."

"Oh! Thank you for finally being honest. Probably for the first time in your life." Paul said. "I had nothing to do with Angelo's arrest, and now I know that you were probably involved with his criminal behaviour as well!" "I am sure the detectives that arrested Angelo would love to know that he had an accomplice!"

Sharon stood up, "Now you are ridiculous, Paul. I don't have anything to do with drugs or anyone who deals in them. Good luck proving this bullshit, you asshole."

Sharon marched out of the coffee shop. You could almost see the steam coming out of her ears as she left.

Paul sat there enjoying every sip of his well-earned coffee while he worked out his next move. Life is like a game of chess, he thought.

The next day, Sharon went to the holding centre, where Angelo was waiting for his hearing. She signed in and endured the general body search on her way to the visitor's lounge.

Angelo was so pleased to see a friendly face as she entered the room. "You look like an Angel to me right now."

"And you look like shit Angelo. What the fuck has happened!" "Paul has just informed me of your arrest for having drugs! Is that true?"

"Yes!" Angelo replied. "I know this sounds corny, but someone set me up! I had never seen the drugs found in my car before. And I have never used drugs. The worst I have had is Panadol for a hangover."

"I thought as much," Sharon replied. "Did you know it was Paul that told the cops about your drugs?"

"What the fuck!" "Are you kidding me?" "We shared a drink at the pub, only the night before; he acted like my best friend."

Now Sharon smelt a rat. "Paul didn't happen to mention that we were in a relationship?"

"I did Shaz; I have to admit that I was bragging about the amazing sex we had at our last delegation in Coogong together." "Paul didn't bat an eyelid; he looked pleased for me to have found such a wonderful lady to share a beautiful experience with."

"No, Angelo, you didn't hear me. Not you and me, but Paul and me in a relationship!"

"No!" Angelo blurted. "What! Wait! You and Paul? Yuk, are you serious? You and that old bloke?"

"Well," Sharon snickered. All I can say is that we gave it a go, and he came well before the postman could deliver the mail!"

"He needs to look after his women better than that," Angelo responded. "Now I know why he was so keen to buy me drinks and get me talking."

"You have been set up, babe! Now we just have to be very careful and prove your innocence." Sharon said.

"My hearing is tomorrow Shaz; I'm worried they have real evidence against me, even if planted. How do we prove Paul had something to do with it? They are moving me to the local prison tomorrow to await trial; I need to organise a lawyer."

"Leave it with me, Ange; I will ask around tomorrow. Someone had to see something. How did Paul plant drugs in your car without anyone seeing it? How did he get your car keys to plant the drugs?" "We now have a motive, being me, and him being a dickhead jealous wannabe lover! I will chat to mayor Valanti; she is a lawyer, even if she can't help, she may be able to recommend a good lawyer."

Angelo and Sharon looked at each other in the way that only two people could, who knew that the same person had shafted them.

CHAPTER THIRTY

THE NEXT DAY, LINCOLN CALLED SHARON. "HI SHAZ, I'VE HEARD ABOUT Angelo. I caught up for a coffee with Paul, and he couldn't wait to tell me the gossip!"

"God, Lincoln, you two are becoming quite buddy, buddy, aren't you!" replied Sharon.

"I've needed Paul to keep me in the loop. Since I'm not on council anymore, Paul has become my ears and eyes on everything happening there, but don't sweat it, darling; we are still besties!"

"There is one thing he did tell me, and I am a little concerned because it was about you!"

"What! Me!" Sharon exploded. "What on earth would he be telling you about me?"

"Well, Shazzy, meet me at Roger's Café in 30 minutes, and I will spill my guts."

Sharon jumped in her car and went directly to the café. Her heart was racing, and her mind was full of anger and confusion. Stuff like this didn't happen to her; she was perfect in her eyes. Sharon arrived in 15 minutes and sat at a table in a secluded corner of the café, waiting for Lincoln.

Lincoln arrived five minutes after Sharon and saw her as soon as he entered the café. "Good to see you, honey! Let me order you a soy chai latte." Lincoln said as he approached the counter.

Sharon was about to explode; why was Lincoln taking his time telling her about Angelo, and what did Paul say about her?

Lincoln finally sat down with his table number in hand. "Latte's ordered Shaz!"

"Enough Lincoln, what the hell did Paul say about me?"

"Shaz, way too much!" "You two were in some weird relationship. You were both going to leave your marital partners for each other and then changed your minds! Or something like that."

"Correct Lincoln, but this is none of your bloody business! Why the hell would Paul be telling you that?"

"There isn't a lot that he doesn't tell me. So now you know the reason for my phone call."

"What, Lincoln? What has Paul told you? I am pretty sure he has covered everything by the sounds of it!"

"He told me you were having kinky sex with Angelo from the city. That you dumped him for Angelo, is that true, Shaz?"

"Not exactly; I finished my relationship with Paul when I found out his wife was more important than me. He was only using me and was never going to leave his wife. So the European holiday with her was the clincher for me. Fuck Paul and his wife! Angelo just happened to be there at the right time. We had flirted a bit leading up to our Canberra trip away and then had the most amazing sex while in Canberra. I feel that Angelo is the man I have been waiting for!"

"Well! You have pissed Paul off! When he found out about your relationship from Angelo himself, he saw red and wanted his competition gone!"

"I figured as much Lincoln. But, you do know what he did? Bloody asshole, He set poor Angelo up with the whole drug thing!"

"You know it was Paul? Shit, I thought I had some good gossip to give you," Lincoln said.

"Paul told me himself, Lincoln, so no gossip, just facts." "What I don't know is how he got the drugs in Angelo's car and where did Paul get the drugs. I know he is no druggy, so he must have paid someone for them?"

"This is hilarious, Shaz. The guys working in the parks department found the drugs stashed behind a toilet in the ablution block down the road. They gave the drugs to Paul to put in his office safe until the cops could collect the package. Paul said he couldn't resist this perfect opportunity to set Angelo up!"

"Are you serious, Lincoln? Did Paul tell you this, or are you setting me up?"

"No! It's all true. As I said, Paul tells me everything. He thinks he is the cleverest man on earth right now! It was so easy for him. He got Angelo's car keys from the Fleet department safe, opened up Angelo's car, and slid some of the Meth under the front seat. Just before the cops came in to pick up the drugs."

"What a creep! I don't understand why he would confess this to you?" asked Sharon.

"Paul and I have become very close, Shaz, you know.......very close!"

"Really? I didn't see that coming."

"It's a long story, but I joined this online bondage group. You would love it, and from what I have heard, you are into some kinky shit biatch!" Lincoln said, trying to add a bit of Italian for flare.

"I can see that Paul does tell you everything! Are you telling me that Paul is Bisexual?"

"Shaz, seriously, Paul is a very confused puppy. I don't think he knows what he is," said Lincoln.

Sharon felt sick, the fact that she considered leaving her family for this weirdo! Lincoln was sitting there like he was full of so much self-importance. He loved the fact that he knew this salacious information and shared it with someone who would just eat up every word.

"Lincoln!" Sharon begged. "You must help me prove Angelo's innocence. I do love this guy and can't stand the fact that Paul has set him up and thinks he is getting away with it."

"It's not that hard, sweetheart! But, first, get the security footage of Paul entering Angelo's car. You know that security cameras are everywhere around the city buildings!"

"Thanks, Lincoln, I hadn't thought of that.

"Ok, love, you must fill me in on everything that happens. Life is as boring as watching paint dry around Wanjup."

"I will, Lincoln. Thank you so much for this information. I always knew Angelo was innocent, and now I can prove it. You are the best."

Sharon leaned over and gave Lincoln a kiss on his cheek, which made him blush. "Stop, Shaz! People are watching!"

Sharon went back to the city offices and made her way to Paul's office. She knew he was away at a staff meeting. He held them at the same time every week. Paul's secretary, Rita, was sitting at her desk, outside Paul's office.

"Hi, Rita," said Sharon.

"Hello Sharon, I haven't seen you around here for a while! What's up?"

"Nothing really; I was just walking past and thought I would poke my head in and say hi!"

"You are so lovely, Sharon. I was only thinking of you the other day. I had missed our little chats when you used to come up to see Paul. I am guessing he is not the flavour of the month anymore?"

Sharon was a bit surprised by Rita being so forthright!

"Yes, Rita, like everyone, we all get busy in our lives and somehow don't have time to spend catching up with the people we want to."

"I know Sharon, that is so true. By the way, did you hear about Angelo? That was a real shock. Who knew such a nice man was dealing drugs? Shame on him. Paul was so pleased they caught him."

"I had heard Rita; I also heard that Paul had drugs in his safe?"

"He did Sharon, the cops came on Friday afternoon and collected the bag." "You do know that it wasn't Paul's drugs! The guys from the park's section found the drug parcel containing Meth behind a toilet. They did the right thing and gave it to Paul, who contacted the police."

"Did they weigh the bag, Rita, to see how much was in it?"

"What a strange question, Sharon. No, we don't have a scale in the office. Paul just put it straight in the safe. I watched him do it. He was disgusted to even have it in there."

"I can believe that Rita, Paul is a good man, and to have drugs in his office would have upset him."

"It did, Sharon; I didn't realise until after the police left with the bag how happy Paul was. He had been a bit miserable for a few days before, and by Friday afternoon, it was like a switch turned on to light him up. It was lovely. He even had me order flowers for his wife to pick up on the way home."

"How lovely Rita, Sonja would have loved the flowers!"

Sharon finished her conversation with Rita, full of praise for her wonderful boss Paul.

CHAPTER THIRTY-ONE

ANGELO'S TRIAL WAS FAST APPROACHING, AND SHARON WAS GOING OUT of her mind trying to prove his innocence. However, she was too proud to come and ask me for assistance with the matter, even though I was a criminal lawyer.

Sharon knew that Angelo was caught red-handed with the drugs in his car. But it just didn't make sense. She had never seen Angelo use drugs, and he was not the type of person to inflict drugs on other people and knew he wouldn't be selling drugs.

She went off to the prison to chat with Angelo. Sharon went through the intrusive body search on the way in and waited for her name. "Sharon Day," a very brash voice came across the loudspeaker, "desk two". Sharon got up and nervously walked over to the desk where Angelo was sitting. He looked terrible in that awful green outfit. She sat down and picked up the phone to speak with Angelo, sitting on the other side of the bulletproof glass.

"I hate seeing you in here, Ange! You don't belong in here."

"I don't like being in here, babe," Angelo said, "I have been trying to figure out how the drugs got in my car? Where did they come from, and who told the cops to look there?"

"Rita, Paul's secretary, told me that Paul had meth in his safe" explained Sharon.

"What! meth Shaz? Why would Paul have a stash in his safe?" Angelo asked.

"The city staff found it in the toilet block that they were cleaning. They handed it in to Paul, who reported it to the police. Unfortunately, Paul has had sticky fingers and stole some to set you up." Sharon said.

"Bloody hell! This guy is dangerous and stupid! How do you know all this?" Angelo asked.

"Lincoln couldn't wait to tell me. He was like a kid, excited to see Santa. He was bursting with eagerness to share his knowledge about what Paul had told him."

"Be careful, Shaz; I wouldn't trust Lincoln as far as I could throw the little bastard!"

"Don't be an idiot, Ange; I just can't believe what a fraud Paul is. Lincoln told me that he and Paul have 'caught up' at a few bondage gatherings. Paul swings both ways, and I would keep your cat locked up too!"

"What the fuck! Are you kidding? That guy is one sick, fucked up individual, and to think he is running the city! We are all doomed!" Angelo said.

"True, so true," said Sharon shaking her head.

As Angelo was saying this, Sharon remembered more from her conversation with Paul's secretary. "The cops came in to collect drugs from Paul's office safe on the same day of your arrest for having some in your car. That's a bit of a coincidence, isn't it!" Sharon continued, "The drugs were found in the toilet block in the city's main park the day before your arrest."

"Paul wouldn't do that, Sharon. I know he can be a prick, but to set me up as a drug dealer and ruin my career, no, I can't believe that."

"I wouldn't put it past him, Paul is a jealous shit, and when he found out about us that was his motive to bring you down. Bloody Paul is the one who dobbed you in to the cops. It must have been him who planted the drugs in your car."

Sharon was so angry, "If Paul had access to the drugs that were in his safe, then his fingerprints would be all over the bag. I hope the cops took his fingerprints. It's probably the only thing we will be able to prove your innocence with and be able to pin this on him."

"Hang on, Shaz!" interjected Angelo, "Not only did he have access to the drugs, but he also had access to my car."

"What! How?"

"My car belongs to the city. The city's fleet department has a spare key to my car in a lockbox. Paul has the master key to every lock of anything owned by the city. He could have opened that box to retrieve my spare car key and plant the drugs." Paul said.

"Your right; I am going to the mayor with this information. Hopefully, she can help us out. Proving her worthiness to continue another term as mayor of this city."

"I don't know what your problem is with her, Shaz? She seems smart and nice. You should give her a break; it's like you guys are teaming up against her, so she can't win a motion in council!"

"It's nothing to do with her as a person, but what she stands for. Mayor Valenti has everything anyone could ever want. She has no right to be the mayor. It just shits us that she thinks she can run the city too!"

"Right now, I need her help Shaz, so suck up your pride and get me the hell out of this shit hole. I need to be with you, to hold you, and to smell you," pleaded Angelo.

Sharon left the prison feeling excited that she has a plan to free Angelo and headed back to the council chambers. She went straight to the Security office in the city and asked if she could see the security camera footage of the back car park. She told the staff that her car was broken into and wanted to see if anyone was lurking around the vehicles.

Sharon sat there for over two hours, pawing her way through endless footage, until she recognised this seedy-looking character, peering around cars. He was not very inconspicuous at all! "Ah! That's Paul," she thought. Sharon immediately started copying the footage onto a USB drive. She thanked the staff for allowing her to look through the camera archives and left.

Sharon went to her car for some privacy and called the prison to speak with Angelo.

"Hi Ange, it was Paul that set you up!"

"I knew it, bastard! How do I prove my innocence? This shit is going to ruin my life and my career!"

"I have managed to find footage of Paul going to your car and opening it. You can see him leaning in and taking something out of his pocket. But, here's the kicker, it was one hour before the cops came to pick up the stash of meth he had in his safe," explained Sharon.

"His secretary confirmed that the Meth was in Paul's safe. She also said how happy he was when the police took the Meth. He then went and picked up flowers for his wife. The big Suck!!" continued Sharon.

"Easy girl, you almost sound jealous!" Angelo laughed.

"I have the car park footage of Paul going to your car. I have the confirmation from his secretary and the police that Paul had custody of and accessibility to the Meth in his office. Surely it can't be that hard to pin the blame on Paul and prove you are innocent?"

"Sharon, you are an Angel. Thank you so much for everything you have done. Now let's hope you can convince the cops of my innocence."

"I will Ange, I love you and will do everything I can to get you out of here."

"You know I would do anything for you, Ange, even going to Liz. I hope this will be worth it! Crap! I didn't mean getting you out being worth it, but having to ask Liz for help!"

"Thanks, babe; I appreciate what you are doing for me. Just to sidestep for a minute, how is your separation going. You mentioned that you were moving out of the family home, which I found hard to believe with the kids and everything?"

"Nah! All good; turns out he emotionally moved out years ago, and we were on the same page. I seriously can't remember the last time I had sex with him, and he is happy that I have freed him from the bond of matrimony."

"Fanbloodytastic Shaz!! Now I am as horny as anything, and I have to go back to a bloody cell with only Mrs Palma for company!"

Sharon finished her call with Angelo, feeling excited that she has a plan to free him. She called Pauls' secretary.

"Hi Rita, does Paul have a quick five to chat with me?"

"I am sure I can squeeze you in, Sharon. Let me look at his schedule. Yes, can you be here in 30 minutes?"

"Thanks, so much Rita. I guess I'll see you in thirty!"

Sharon turned up at Paul's office and waited on the soft sofa outside his office. She started to think about the fun times they have had in this chair after the offices had closed for the day.

Paul was saying goodbye to a gentleman from a neighbouring council when he spotted Sharon in the corner of his eye. As he shook the guy's hand, he gently led him away from his secretary's desk. He then turned to Rita, "What is 'she' doing here?"

"Sharon has come to have a quick chat with you. She said it would only take five minutes. You seem upset, Paul. Have I done something wrong? Is everything ok between you two?" Rita asked.

"Everything is just fine, thanks, Rita. I was just a bit surprised to see Sharon here. She hasn't been here in a long time."

"I know, right! That's twice in one day for me!" Rita said.

Paul looked a little unsettled at Rita's last comment. "Give me a minute to tidy my desk, then send her in."

"Ok, Paul, sure, did you want me to ask Sharon if she wants a tea or coffee?" Rita asked.

"No, she won't be here that long."

Rita bought Sharon into Paul's office, and he looked uneasy.

"Hi, Paul." Sharon cheerfully said.

"What do you want?" Paul snapped.

"I had an interesting conversation with Lincoln. About you and drugs and Angelo."

"I have no idea what you are rambling about, girl." "I am swamped and don't have the time to listen to your bullshit about trying to protect your boyfriend," snapped Paul. "You are the biggest slut! I can't believe I even considered you worthy of being my partner. What was I thinking? Now you are doing a greasy wog! Good luck with that drug dealing loser!"

Ignoring Paul's outburst, "Lincoln told me that you planted drugs in Angelo's city car and then told the police where to find it!" Sharon said.

"Lincoln is setting you up; he is just playing his stupid games with you. He knows you and Angelo are fucking because I told him." "He was feeling sorry for me and wanted to get back at you. Don't believe a word he says. Sometimes that guy is like a fish out of water, flipping every way he can to get a breath of excitement in his boring life." Paul said.

"Sorry, Paul, but Lincoln had inside information, which I wouldn't give him credit for making up. I have camera footage of you entering Angelo's car, confirmation from Rita that you had the drugs in your safe, and that the cops took the drugs from you at the same time you dobbed Angelo in for being a drug dealer. So you are going down for this. I hope Sonja enjoys the flowers that Rita organised. They will be the last for a long time!"

Sharon flounced out of Paul's office, feeling very pleased with her efforts. Now to see Liz and hammer the final nail into Paul's coffin. She called Liz's secretary Tanya, to make sure she was in the office.

"Hi Tanya, it's councillor Day, is the mayor in the office?"

"Yes, councillor Day, she is. Would you like to speak with her?"

"Thanks, Tanya; I do want to speak with her, but not on the phone. I am on my way to her office now. Can you ask the mayor to allow me fifteen minutes of her time for a very urgent and private matter?"

"That won't be a problem, councillor Day, mayor Valenti has one hour before her next event that she is preparing for, so I will book you in; how far away are you?"

"Only a couple of minutes away – I am coming over now"

"Ok, I will see you soon."

Tanya walked into my office to tell me of Sharon's arrival. "Mayor Valenti, councillor Day is on her way in to speak with you on a private and urgent matter."

"Thanks, Tanya. Did she give you any indication of what she wanted to talk about?"

"No, she gave nothing away from other than it was of a private matter!"

I cleaned up the paperwork on the desk. Mainly speeches. I hate giving them if not prepared for them.

Sharon turned up at my office breathless, obviously in a hurry to see me.

"Mayor Valenti, councillor Day is here to see you. Can I send her in?" Tanya announced.

"Sure, Tanya, please ask her if she wants a coffee or tea."

"You know I always do, mayor!" Tanya smiled.

Sharon walked into my office like a woman on a mission.

"Thanks for seeing me, Liz!"

"No worries, Sharon, what's up? You said it was urgent."

"You have heard about Angelo's arrest for having drugs found in his car?" Sharon said.

"I have; please take a seat; what can I do to help?"

"I have an excellent reason to believe that Paul has planted the drugs in Angelo's car."

"Wow! I wasn't expecting that. Have you got any proof? What a massive accusation, Sharon."

"You know the drugs the city Parks crew found in the toilet block last week?"

"Yes, I remember that. But what does that have to do with Angelo and Paul?" I asked.

"The city parks guys gave the drugs to the CEO to put in his office safe until the cops could come and collect them; being a weekend, the cops asked if the city could secure them until Monday. So the drugs found in Angelo's car, I believe, are a match to the drugs the cops came and collected from the CEO's safe."

"You are accusing Paul of planting drugs on Angelo?" I asked.

"Yes, I believe Paul did this. And yes, that shit is capable of doing something like this. Please don't defend him, Liz, if only you knew half of what he says behind your back about you. It is disgusting."

"I am aware that Paul is not my biggest fan, but I have to work with him. However, this is an enormously different matter. So, if Paul had access to these drugs, how did he get them into Angelo's car?"

"Paul has a master key that will open any office or lockbox owned by the city. He was able to open the box with the spare fleet car keys in it and open Angelo's car." Sharon said.

"Ok, this sounds plausible; let me just check on one thing!" I asked.

I called Tanya into my office and asked her to get Allen on the phone from the fleet department.

My phone rang, and I answered. "Mayor Valenti, I have Allen on the line for you," Tanya announced.

"Thanks, Tanya, put him through. Hi Allen."

"Hi, mayor Valenti, how can I be of assistance today? Does your Lexus need a service, or have you had a prang?" Allen asked.

"Hi, Allen, no, nothing like that! I just need you to check the lockbox containing the fleets' car keys to see if Angelo's spare car key is in the box."

"No problem, boss, just give me a minute, and I will be right back!"

Allen put the phone on hold and went to check the keys.

"What is your next move, Sharon, if the spare car key is not in the lockbox?" I asked.

"I am sure it's not. You need to call the police to search Paul's house. That prick can't get away with setting Angelo up."

"What has happened, Sharon? I remember that you and Paul were very cosy in Tasmania. Paul even admitted to me that you were having an affair! Do you think that Paul has put drugs in Angelo's car to frame him as a drug user?"

"It is killing me having to tell you this, Liz, but Angelo and I are in a relationship, and Paul found out about it. I broke it off with Paul before he left to go on his wedding anniversary. So Paul found out about Angelo and me somehow! That was his motive to set poor Ange up for being a drug user, and having a safe, full of drugs, must have been too much of a temptation not to take up, as an advantage to get back at poor Angelo."

Just then, Allen came back to the phone. "Are you there, mayor Valenti?"

"Yes, Allen, was Angelo's car keys in the box?"

"No, they are not. Because you asked, which is unusual, I checked out the security camera footage. Unfortunately, the CEO took the keys, so you will have to call him to find out where the spare key is. Also, can you remind him that the policy is to sign out any key taken? I'm pretty sure that was him that made up that policy."

"Thanks, Allen; I am sure Paul has the key and has just forgotten to put it back."

I now believe what Sharon was saying. However, I wasn't surprised that Paul could stoop this low to set up a fantastic guy like Angelo because his mistress chose another lover!

I hung up the phone, and Sharon knew my answer before I delivered it.

"The key is not there; however, Allen has security footage of Paul going to the lockbox on the same day that they found drugs in Angelo's car."

"I have the footage of Paul going into Angelo's car on this USB. What a bastard! Sharon shouted. She was so angry; she was biting her bottom lip. "You have to call the cops now! We need to search Paul's house for the key." Sharon was at the point of explosion.

I grabbed the phone and rang the detective that came to see me when I first became the mayor, the meeting to do with the motorcycle guys! He gave me his card and seemed like a generally lovely guy.

"This is detective Sargreto."

"Hi detective Sargreto, this is mayor Valenti. I need to meet with you fairly urgently about a drug matter, one where I believe someone set up a fellow employee for drug dealing, and time is of the essence. We need you to look at a suspect's property for the clue before he destroys any evidence."

"It will take time to get a search warrant, mayor. However, I am just around the corner from your office, so I will call in to see you in five."

"Great, thanks for that; I will see you soon."

Ok, Sharon, the detective will be here soon. Did you want to sit in on the meeting, or are you happy for me to carry on?

"No, I am out of here; please give me a call and let me know how you get on," Sharon asked.

"This is just a horrible situation Sharon, of course, I will let you know what I find out. Look after yourself."

The detective turned up, and I filled him in on the goings-on at the council.

"Sounds like a bit of a bloody circus mayor, if you don't mind me saying! So let me get this straight, one of your councillors is sleeping with the CEO or was and isn't now! She believes that the CEO has set up one of his employees for drugs because he is jealous of him sleeping with her! Can I ask how he got the drugs and how he planted the drugs on this person?"

The detective looked annoyed that I had dragged him to my office when he was busy.

"Councillor Sharon Day was having an affair with the CEO Paul. They broke off their relationship, and councillor Day began a relationship with Angelo, who was the person they, the police, found drugs in his car."

"This sounds a lot like 'Days of our Life' shit going on here. But, seriously, do you have any proof that the CEO did this?"

"Yes, I have the CCTV footage of Paul removing the key from the lockbox and him accessing Angelo's car, and the fact that the key is still missing is a concern!"

"Also!" I added, "The drugs found in the main city park toilets were collected by the cops from the CEO's office, on the same day that the police found the drugs in Angelo's car. Coincidence or not? I believe that the CEO, Paul, placed the drugs in Angelo's car to frame him for drug use so that he could continue his affair with councillor Sharon Day."

"This is extraordinary evidence, well done. The search warrant will arrive soon. First, I plan to search Paul's house, then to search any other property he owns.

"You have no idea how much I appreciate this. Thank you so much." I handed over the USB that Sharon had given me to detective Sargreto.

The detective notified me shortly from the Wanjup courthouse of the search warrant.

That same afternoon, the boys in blue smashed their way into Paul's home in Wanjup and his Adelaide house. He had a lot of costly things in that small house.

The following day, Tanya came into my office to let me know that detective Sargreto was waiting to see me.

"Send him in, Tanya. This will be an interesting meeting!"

The detective came in and sat down; he looked very pleased with himself.

"Morning, mayor Valenti. I thought I would come and speak to you in person about what we uncovered yesterday."

"Thanks, I appreciate that. Hopefully, you have some good news?"

"After your tip-off, we were able to obtain a search warrant so we could go through Mr Paul Aldman's bank accounts and discovered he has an impressive sum of money tucked away in a term deposit. He also owns five properties without any mortgage against them." The detective said. He then reaches into his top pocket and retrieves a notebook, and flips it open.

"We attended his home here in town and found a Toyota Landcruiser key that does not belong to Mr Aldman. We spoke with a gentleman called Allen from the city's fleet department, who confirmed that he has footage of Mr Aldman taking the car key from the lockbox when they discovered the drugs. So on further investigation, I went to Mr Angelo Porcini's car and opened it with the key that I found at Mr Aldman's home in Wanjup."

"I checked with the detectives who collected the drugs from Mr Aldman's office, on the same day they discovered the drugs in Mr Porcini's car. They informed me that they took Mr Aldman's fingerprints, which did appear on the bag. So it does seem that Mr Porcini is innocent. We are arranging for his release today. We will be arresting Mr Aldman and charging him with possession of drugs, and fabricating evidence. I thought you would like to know the outcome. The fraud team is looking into corruption by Mr Aldman. They believe they have a strong case against him, especially now they have seen his bank accounts."

"Thanks, detective; I am so pleased that Justice prevailed. I appreciate your time and for coming in to let me know in person."

As soon as the detective left my office, I was straight on the phone to call Sharon.

"Hi Sharon, it's Liz."

"Please tell me you have good news, Liz?" Sharon asked.

"You bet! The detective just left. Angelo is innocent, and the cops can prove it. They are releasing Angelo today. The best news is, they are arresting Paul," I said.

"Thank God! I can't wait to tell Angelo. Do you know what time they will release him?" Sharon asked.

"No idea Sharon. Can I ask you something personal?" I asked.

"Sure, Liz, what's up?"

"Do you think Paul committed this crime just because of your affair with Angelo?"

"Yes, Paul found out about us, and that's why he set up Angelo with a fake drug bust," Sharon said.

"That makes sense. Now I understand Paul's motive for planting the drugs on Angelo! What a prick! Have you left your husband then?" I asked with a slight smirk on my face.

"You are a nosy cow now, Liz. Yes, we went our separate way last week. We have been planning on separating for a while; we were just waiting for the right time."

"You have done well with Angelo. He is a spunk. A lot younger than you too! I wish you both all the best. However, you will have to tell Angelo that there is a CEO's position about to become vacant if he wants to consider applying for it."

"Thanks, Liz; I appreciate everything you have done for Angelo and me. I will let Angelo know about the CEO's position. He would be perfect for the job."

I hung up the phone and felt rather pleased with myself. Things around this place are about to get a whole lot better.

CHAPTER THIRTY-TWO

ONE OF THE LAST THINGS MY FATHER SAID TO ME BEFORE HE PASSED AWAY was not to run again for mayor. He could see how much stress I was under, how much weight I had put on, and that I generally wasn't happy. But I still decided to run. So I gathered my friends around, and they helped me start my campaign.

We raised money through various events, and I was everywhere trying to promote myself for the next election. I started campaigning four months out from election day, this time to give myself plenty of time to prepare.

Lincoln's fan club came out in force. They wanted this young guy to be the next mayor. No matter what I did or said. I would have the social media crazies jumping onto their keyboards and writing awful things about me.

One of my friends was looking at running for a seat on the council. He phoned me and asked if I would back him. He just wanted me to go onto his social media and support his campaign. I did help him; then, I received the most significant backlash from three sitting councillors. Even a disgraced ex-councillor jumped in to tear me apart on social media.

Donald started the social media hate campaign with, "It's disgusting that a mayor does not support the councillors who are currently on council and are re-electing to stand again for their seat."

Derwent followed, "Bloody shameful not supporting your current councillors."

Then Pauline Ashley had to put her five cents in, "Now the mayor is trying to load the council with her side of politics. There is no room for politics in this council!"

It was like the flood gates had opened. Every low life that had access to a computer jumped on and started tearing me to strips. It was appalling that people, who don't know me, felt that it was acceptable to write lies and horrible hate messages.

From Donald's original statement, the messages went crazy and totally off the beaten track! Then they accused me of taking credit for the former mayor's hard work. I haven't achieved anything for the city, I am lazy, and I have never attended a school or any other event.

It was the most upsetting thing to read, and it didn't stop there. Random people then attacked my mayoral page. It was like someone organised a group of keyboard warriors to send me hundreds of messages overnight.

I ended up paying someone to answer them because it was making me feel very sad. After the campaign, the young lady I employed told me that she was deleting the hate messages, so I didn't see them. Unfortunately, I also received a few death threats, which, on my behalf, she notified the police about. She took screenshots of those messages before she deleted them.

She told my children and Mike not to comment, reply, discuss or argue with anyone on social media during my campaign. My middle daughter, to this day, refuses to have any social media; she is totally off the grid.

This campaign was so much different from when I ran the first time. Being swamped in my mayoral role didn't leave much time to campaign. So instead, I did the regular press ads and flyers. While Lincoln was driving around with an A-frame billboard on a trailer, with his face plastered all over it.

Lincoln had the support of his political party, who jumped on board and funded his campaign. He also had access to money and political power; meanwhile, I had accusations of using the mayoral role as a stepping stone to launch my political career. I never wanted to go into politics, and after going through this campaign, I never will. I take my hat off to anyone considering it. You need to have thick skin and a lot of family support.

Our family business won a business award, and Mike and I attended a Gala event in Adelaide to receive the trophy. We stayed in Adelaide the night and drove back to Wanjup in the morning. As we drove into town, we could see these large whiteboards with my name on them.

'Vote NO mayor Valenti', 'mayor Valenti is a thief', 'Vote NO mayor Valenti – Liar', and there were more. I couldn't believe it! Mike stopped the car, and he went over to the sign and pulled it down. They were everywhere, and it shattered me. These signs had no authorisation on them; all political advertising must have who authorised them and who printed them.

It stunk of political bullying. It took the city rangers hours to pull them all down. It was the ugliest campaign ever.

I received a lot of unwanted press from these posters. The local paper had front-page news, showing photos of the signs. Great! Just publicise the signs even more. Sometimes I think newspapers are sickening; they will join in to kick someone when they are down. Deputy mayor Derwent Peabody decided he wanted some of this free publicity, too. Hence, he went around to a few of his electoral advertising signs and spray-painted devil's horns on his picture during the night. Derwent then called the local papers to inform them of the terrible damage done to his electoral posters and sent in photos. Then he lied about someone cutting his brakes. So he received the free publicity and sympathy that he wanted. The local car mechanic told me later that no one had cut Derwent's brakes, he didn't take care of his car, and the brake cable had worn through from wear and tear. Never let the truth get in the way of a good story, hey!

About a week later, I was reading to children on stage as part of Children's week. When I arrived home later that night, Mike was sitting in the lounge room, looking very pale. "I am so sorry, Liz! I did what you asked me not to do!"

"What have you done?" I asked Mike as I went over to sit next to him.

"I can't take the crap dished out at you. Someone wrote something tonight, and I couldn't hold myself back. I am sorry, but I have made it worse." Mike said.

"Oh no, you didn't!"

"I was only defending you. That is what a husband does! How dare these people think they can say lies and make up bullshit about you, and no one is holding them to account."

I put my arm around Mike and just held him. He was distraught and outraged by the gross amount of crap written about me.

The next day, the State newspaper wrote about the mayor's husband defending her against online trolls. It was on the news and online everywhere. If you Googled Mike's name, it comes up with, 'mayor's husband defends his wife against online bullying.' Not all the extraordinary achievements, like winning the business awards twice or the massive contracts he has won, etc. My advice to anyone in politics is to ignore the crap people write about you because after the election, it is all forgotten, and people go back to their miserable lives. But poor Mike will have this hanging over his head forever!

The campaign was so nasty; it flowed over into the council chamber. Now that I wanted to kick the sitting council out, which was not true, and councillors, Derwent and Pauline would not speak to me. Sharon would talk to me in private, but her allegiance was with the others.

The director of Sustainability stepped up to the role of CEO until they found Paul's replacement. I didn't want to be a part of this council anymore. It was toxic and unpleasant. Paul's arrest for fabricating evidence against Angelo made minimal conversation amongst the councillors; they were more interested in the election.

I had my mind made up now that I didn't want to be the mayor anymore. However I was not going to concede this and pull out of the election. There was no way Lincoln would get this on a platter; he had to have to work at it.

CHAPTER THIRTY-THREE

THE MAYORAL ELECTION WAS ONLY A FEW MONTHS AWAY NOW, AND I was over campaigning. Mike was not happy that I had given up. Not that he wanted me to continue being the mayor, but that our friends had put a lot of money into my campaign. I at least owed it to them to give Lincoln a challenge and not just roll over.

"What about radio advertising Liz, you sound great on the air now, and I haven't heard Lincoln doing any ads?" asked Mike

"Great idea; I'll call our friend David a call and have a chat with him."

David Sepelt works at the local radio station as a sales rep. I got to know David and all the other staff well during my term as mayor, mainly because I had my regular program on the radio to talk about what was happening in Wanjup. David had the most beautiful, bubbly personality. He could sell ice to the Eskimos, and I enjoyed his company because you always felt happy in his presence.

"Hi David, it's Liz. Have you got time to come over to chat about organising some radio advertising for my mayoral campaign?"

"Sure, love, not today though, I'm really under the pump. I can call around to your place in the morning if that suits you?" David said.

"Fantastic, that would be great, David. I won't keep you; see you tomorrow morning!"

"Can't wait, see you around 9 am!" said David.

David came over the next day as promised. "Morning Darling, how is my Lizzy today?"

"Tired, but great now that you are here!" I smiled as David leaned in and gave my cheek a little kiss.

"Well, let's put the kettle on and get some caffeine into you. Can't have Lizzy falling asleep!" David walked into the kitchen, like he owned the place, and put the kettle on. "Ok, darling, let's get started!"

David had become a close friend, even though he was twenty years my junior, actually not that much older than my daughters. He loved to go shopping with me and had exceptional taste in clothes. A good friend tells you the truth if an outfit looks like shit, or your bum looks too big. David would take clothes off the rack for me to try on, clothes that I would never even consider, but they always looked great.

"What's your advertising budget, honey?" asked David.

"I haven't thought about that! What would you recommend?" I asked.

"Darling! Really! You know I work on commission, right! So, the more you spend, the better for me. I think we start with twenty thousand!" David then jumped up and went to the kitchen to finish making my coffee.

"Wow, I had no idea radio advertising cost so much?"

"Don't worry, it's only money; we will flood the radio, drown out Lincoln's ads. I know he is spending that much! Sarah in the sales team has been bragging that she just signed Lincoln's contract for advertising. So when you called me yesterday, I quickly went into air traffic and booked your time slots. You will need five different commercials, and they are all 30 seconds long. All booked into peak times, you have got this!" said David as he carefully placed my coffee on the table in front of me.

"Twenty thousand dollars it is then David. Now, what do we put in the ads?" I asked.

"I don't bloody know Liz, you are the mayor Darling, you tell me what people need to hear, so they vote for you!" countered David.

I was unprepared for this meeting with David. I felt terrible that I was wasting his time; I should have had some idea of what my radio ads were going to say.

"Sorry, David, my head is a bit fuzzy this morning. I haven't been sleeping very well, and there is so much going on in the city. I haven't had time to even think about my campaign."

"Now, Lizzy, pull up those big girl panties, drink your coffee and get working on your radio campaign. I will head back to the station

194

to draw up your advertising contract and give you a jingle later once completed. I'm thinking a cheeky little lunch in town to sign the contract?"

"Perfect, thanks, David, you're a gem!"

David gave me a quick peck on the cheek and left.

I rang my friend Toni Calmer. Toni used to work for the Australian Football League (AFL) in Melbourne as their marketing Guru. She has a degree in journalism and a fantastic way of putting words together eloquently and professionally.

"Hi Toni, it's Liz; I need your help. I have to come up with five radio ads of 30 seconds each, and I have no idea on where to start?"

"Breathe, Liz, it's ok; I can hear how stressed you are. But, you know I am always happy to help. I am busy today but can call around in the morning before I go to the office. Does 8 am, suit?"

"Yes, thanks, Toni, that's brilliant; thanks so much, I appreciate it." I hung up from Toni, excited to know that help is coming.

Later that morning, David called to say the contract was ready for signing. So I booked us into a restaurant in town for lunch. Eating at restaurants was David's second-best thing to do next to shopping for clothes.

I caught up with David for lunch, signed the contract, and enjoyed a bottle of champagne with him. Champagne would be David's third favourite thing.

During lunch, David asked if Mike and I would sponsor an event he is organising. It was called 'A Rainbow Night to Remember." Held locally; he was very excited to talk about it. There will be Drag Queens, dancing, funky music, and fabulous food. How could I say no? He was raising funds for a great cause.

After lunch, David left a delighted young man, a signed contract, and his fundraiser sponsored. I went back home to start putting some ideas together, so I had something to work on with Toni in the morning. I hated being unorganised, but my heart wasn't in it, and I spent a fortune on the campaign.

Toni arrived an hour late the following day, but that is ok; she was always late. She always squeezes so much into her day and helps so many people.

"Thanks for coming over, Toni. You have no idea how desperate I am to get this right. I have been so used to my media team writing all my stuff that I have lost touch with the real world. So here, these are the notes that I made last night. Mainly just the main points that I want to get across. I need your skills to make them into an interesting ad."

Toni smiled at me. "Give it here; let's start working through the first point."

Toni was with me for nearly three hours, and we finished all five ads. She is a bloody legend.

"I can't believe we completed them, Toni! You are the best. Thank you, thank you, and thank you so much."

"Not a problem, glad I could help, now I have to run, I'm running two hours late for my next appointment," Toni admitted as she grabbed her bag and took off out the front door in a hurry.

I called David, "Hi David, my radio ads finished. Can I come and record them now? I want to get this out of the way so I can concentrate on other things!"

"Wow! You don't muck around, do you, honey? Sure, come on down; Studio two is free today so that we can set you up in there," confirmed David.

I put everything together, hopped in my car, and drove down to the station to catch up with the beautiful David.

The radio station had such a lovely vibe about it. Everyone was happy and friendly. The receptionist welcomed me as I entered, "Hi, mayor Valenti, how are you today?"

"Very well, thanks, June. Is David in?"

"He certainly is, just give me one second, and I will call him," June called David, and he came straight out.

"Well! Hello! If it isn't our favourite mayor!" beamed David as he walked over to me and kissed my cheek. "Come this way; I'll show you to the studio."

I walked into the studio, which reminded me of a padded cell, and pulled out the folder with its scripts. Toni had carefully put together five well-written ads. She does have a talent for writing.

Golfie walked in. "Hello mayor, always a pleasant surprise to see you in here. I heard you have signed up for some commercials! I will be helping you with them today. I will be sitting on the other side of the glass, put the headphones on so we can communicate with each other."

It was very different from my regular radio show, where Golfie would sit across the desk from me in the studio, and it was like we were having a normal chat. He had his soundboard off to the left a bit. I was very comfortable with Golfie; he had a great sense of humour and made me laugh. He was very patient with me when I was learning the whole radio gig. Of course, I had forgiven him for throwing me in the hot coals with the nightclub saga, but that is radio!

I completed my radio advertising recording, thanks to Golfie, Toni, and David. They went to air in two days. I thought they sounded good, and I had terrific feedback from them.

That Saturday night was David's Rainbow event. Mike decided to watch the football with his mates, it was a better option, so I asked Toni to come with me. She had met David and also supported his cause. Mike liked David, but the loud music was just too much for him. He would rather be at home in his recliner with his cold beer.

Toni and I arrived at the very loud event and were surprised to see David's massive effort with the decorations. As soon as we arrived, David came up to us and threw his arms around my neck!

"I am so happy you are here; you are going to love it, and thanks again for sponsoring the night." David took me by the hand and paraded me around to meet his friends; Toni just laughed and followed us.

David introduced me to everyone as, "My best friend, the mayor of Wanjup, my Lizzy."

He is just a sweetie. "David!" I asked, "Can I ask where the money raised tonight goes?"

"Mostly to young men who are struggling for acceptance in society. Whether it's in their heads or not, there is real discrimination out there. Boys aged between ten and twenty are the highest statistic in suicide, and if we can do anything to prevent even just one death, tonight will be worth it. It's also about raising awareness of what is going on. Our charity pays for these young men to attend counselling sessions where they can open up and talk about their feelings."

Just as David was finishing speaking, the music went quiet, as did everyone else in the room. Then the Drag Queens came out dancing, and the music changed to 'I love the nightlife' by Alicia Bridges. They were awesome. Then I realised one of the dancers was Lincoln Harvey!

"David! Is that Lincoln?" I asked.

David laughed, "Yes, Lizzy, that's Lincoln, isn't he wonderful."

I had to admit, Lincoln was an excellent dancer and looked fantastic in drag. I never expected this, though.

"His stage name is Miss Kinky!" David said.

Funny how you think you know someone, and then you are blown away with new information. David seems very fond of Lincoln. I will need to be more careful of what I say to him in our private conversations now!

Overall, I was impressed with David; he had put a lot of thought into tonight's event. The world would be a better place if we had more people like David in it.

Toni and I left shortly after the speeches and headed home. It was a late night for us.

CHAPTER THIRTY-FOUR

THE NEXT DAY, LINCOLN WAS BUSY ORGANISING TEE SHIRTS FOR A GROUP of kids from the local dance school. He had been working out a dance routine with them so they could do a Flash Mob dance as a part of his campaign. Then he received a call from Paul. "Lincoln, it's Paul. Can we catch up for a chat?"

"I heard of your arrest, mate! Where are you?" asked Lincoln.

"I'm at home; Sonja bailed me out. I have just had a brilliant idea, but I don't want to talk about it on the phone. Bloody cops are probably tapping into my calls."

"I'm just down at the dance studio in town. There is no one here. Did you want to come here to catch up?" Lincoln asked.

"Sure, I'll be there in ten." Paul hung up and jumped in his car, and took off to the dance studio.

When he arrived, he made sure he checked the surroundings before entering the studio. Paul had become very suspicious that someone was watching him.

"Morning, Lincoln," Paul announced as he walked in.

"Well, you are a sight for sore eyes, mate! I thought you were going away in the clink for a decade!" Lincoln quipped.

"Nah! They have nothing on me. It's all circumstantial; you'll see, they won't be able to pin anything on me. Remember, they don't call me Teflon Paul for nothing."

"You are too funny, Paul; you are right though, shit doesn't stick to you; you seem always to hand pass it off to someone else. Is that why you are here? Who are you passing your shit to?"

"You want to win this election, don't you?" Paul asked.

"Does a bear shit in the woods? But, of course, I want to bloody win. That position is mine; that bitch stole it from me last time. And to think it was by only a hand full of votes. That shits me."

"Good, as you know, I have had a bit of free time over the past few days. It has given me time to think about how to get rid of mayor Valenti. I couldn't stand having to work one more day with her." Paul growled.

"Are you thinking about killing her? Is that why you wanted to meet me in private? I have got a few ideas that have been playing around in my head. Do you want to hear them?" Lincoln asked.

"No! I don't want to kill her! But I can kill her votes!"

"Now I am intrigued Paul, what do you have in mind."

"I have gone through the list of eligible voters in the area, and there are a lot of deceased people who remain on the electoral roll. I am talking thousands. There are a lot of incarcerated people too, let's face it, if you are in prison, you don't give a flying fuck about what's going on in your local council!"

"I don't understand, Paul? How is this going to help my campaign? How is it going to kill Liz's votes?"

"Simple Lincoln, I am going to apply for the postal voting papers for these incarcerated and deceased people. Then, I will organise for the electoral office to send them directly to the city's administration building."

"Still not getting it, Paul! How will I convince these people to vote?"

"Oh my God! Are you seriously that stupid, Lincoln! You can't convince someone, who is dead, to vote. I will do it for them. I will tell the electoral office that the city's admin will hand out the packages. Once the ballot voting papers arrive in the city, I will get someone to collect them and bring them to my home office. Together we can open them, tick your ballot box and post it back. It's brilliant. You will be guaranteed a win of more than a thousand votes."

"I like the sound of that. You are a sneaky old codger, aren't ya!" Lincoln chuckled.

"How's the campaign trailer working out for you?" Paul asked.

"That was another great idea, Paul. It's been great; I can drive it around and park it anywhere without breaking any election signage rules. I roll up at parks, set my urn up on that small table you gave me, and offer the oldies coffee and tea. I let them tell me all their problems and promise to fix everything. Once I'm mayor, I won't give them a second thought. There are too many older people here. If we make it hard for them, hopefully, they will piss off!"

"Once you are the mayor, Lincoln, I will organise for the city to purchase that trailer, and we can use it in lots of areas. We will continue your campaign right through your term as mayor. Making it even easier for your re-election next time."

"Didn't the city purchase the trailer to start with?" Lincoln asked.

"No one knows that, Lincoln; that's our secret."

"Did you want me to organise a group of friends to help with the ballot papers, Paul? It sounds like there will be a lot to get through."

"No, Lincoln, you don't get it, boy! We can't afford to let anyone else know about this. What we will be doing is illegal. Besides, I have lots of time on my hands; I'm suspended from work until the trial is over."

"Cool, Paul, I understand, secret squirrel shit, right!"

"Yes, Lincoln, correct. Also, please don't call me and mention anything about this conversation. I am sure the cops are tapping my phone. They have even been through my bank accounts and found the money I have extorted from building companies and government tenders. So I have to come up with a bloody good excuse to explain that. But for now, we need to concentrate on getting you elected as mayor so we can get some fun shit done."

"Nothing will leave my lips, Paul; all good here, mate!"

Paul left the dance studio through the back door and quickly slipped into his car.

He loved his idea. He took off back to his house and got straight to work, looking through the list of voters to see who he could use to put in his fake votes for Lincoln.

What Lincoln didn't know was that Paul was setting him up. After Lincoln spilled his guts to Sharon, Paul couldn't can't trust him anymore. Paul kept this secret with him until he needed to get rid of

Lincoln. Paul needed to get Liz Valenti out of the mayor's office first, move Lincoln in and then work out his next move. Like a game of chess.

Sonja walked into Paul's home office and saw that he was happy. "What's going on?" Sonja asked. "You are looking pleased; what have you been up to?"

"I have come up with the perfect plan to ensure Lincoln's success at becoming Wanjup's next mayor," Paul said.

"Ok, what's your plan?" asked Sonja, who was still really pissed off with Paul from what Tracy had told her.

"I'm going through a list of everyone who is dead or incarcerated and is registered still to vote. Then I am going to vote for Lincoln, using their voting papers. Lincoln will be guaranteed at least one thousand more votes than that bitch Liz will get," said Paul

"Interesting concept Paul, you think you will get away with this? said Sonja.

"It's foolproof! Lincoln is the only other person who knows about this, and it's to help him, so he would never tell a soul," said Paul.

At this point, Sonja doesn't give a shit about who the mayor is. Instead, she is trying to work out how to save her marriage to a lying and cheating husband.

CHAPTER THIRTY-FIVE

I HAVE GIVEN SIX YEARS OF MY LIFE TO SERVING THE CITY OF WANJUP. For five years and nine months, I enjoyed nearly all of it. But, for the last three months, it was pure hell! I have seen a side of people; I never wish to encounter again.

During my term as mayor, I was able to meet the most beautiful people. People who volunteer their time to make our city the wonderful place it is to live. They expect nothing back in return for their efforts, except sometimes a thank you. I naturalised thousands of very excited new Australian citizens, attended the end of year ceremonies at our local schools and presented awards to their outstanding students. I learnt to speak confidently on camera, radio and in large crowds. My personal growth was remarkable, and for that, I am eternally thankful.

For the last three months of my mayoral term, I would not wish this on my worst enemy! My entire family received bullying on social media. I had a good friend turn against me over something that wasn't even true, but she believed it, just to use it against me so her husband would have a shot at becoming the mayor.

My team of dedicated, gorgeous friends who were helping me with my campaign worked so hard; I didn't want to let them down and pull out of the election. Instead, I needed to keep going and ignore the bullshit that was hitting me in the face daily.

There was no way I was going to hand over the mayoral position to Lincoln. The other people running for mayor, including my ex-friend Zina's husband, were not close to being a contender.

Mike was breathing down my neck to help out with the due diligence for the sale of our family company, I was working full time as the mayor of the city, and I still had a few legal clients. My family always need my help, and I was being abused on social media every day. Something had to give! Mike asked the American company to hold off on the due diligence until after the election, which they kindly agreed to.

I concentrated on being the best mayor I could be until my term was up. I attended everything humanly possible and conducted all of my meeting commitments for the council. I ignored social media and tried to spend as much time with my family as I could. Family is where my real strength comes from.

Having lost my niece, mother-in-law, mother, and father during my term on council, it is no wonder that I was ready to fall into a hole. Unfortunately, I never had the opportunity to grieve properly. However, my strength allowed me to continue. The love of my husband Mike gave me that strength. Without the support of my family, I never could have achieved everything that I have in my life.

When I first became the mayor of Wanjup, people would call the city's reception and complain about the colour of my jacket. "She wears too much black! Tell her to wear different colours." My hair, "I don't like her hair tied back; I only voted for her because I liked her long hair!" My hair colour, "The mayor, has blonde hair, how come her hair is brown. I don't like it; tell her to change it back!"

People would comment on everything from how I spoke, what I was wearing and how I was wearing it! If I was a man, there is no way people would be commenting on my suit or my hair or my voice. They would be concentrating on what I was doing to make Wanjup a better place.

I was in Melbourne, attending a Bulldogs versus Adelaide Crows game, and I received a phone call from Tanya. "Mayor Valenti, we have just had another fatal shark attack! The press is about to call you. I will have the media team brief you in about ten minutes."

"Thanks, Tanya, you do realise that I am at a football match and have had a couple of wines. Can't the deputy mayor take the call?"

"Sorry, mayor, the deputy mayor said that it is your responsibility and has refused to speak to the media."

"Are you kidding me? I had approved leave, and this is his responsibility. The deputy mayor gets the higher sitting allowance for this very reason!"

"Sorry, mayor, but he won't take the call. This shark attack is such a terrible incident, and you should be the person to take this call.

"Fine! Tell the media team to hurry up because I won't make a call until being fully prepared."

"Fuck!" I yelled. Not appropriate, seeing I was in a corporate box at the MCG.

"What's up?" My friend Frank asked. "You seem a little upset!"

Frank is one of the top detectives in Melbourne. He has been in homicide for five years, a long stint in such a terrible area.

I explained that someone had been taken by a shark and had died because the ambulance couldn't find the victim.

"Are you kidding me! Isn't that their job! How the hell can an ambulance team not find a shark victim?"

I explained to Frank how along our coast, we have names for beaches. Most of these beaches have two, three or even four parking areas. It is a big stretch of land. The ambulance pulled into the first car park, ran down the steps to the beach, and there was nobody there. So they called back to headquarters, who told them to try another car park. So they did, and still, no victim presented. This happened until the last car park assigned to that beach. By this stage, the young man had lost too much blood. The shark had bitten his entire right leg off, and the people trying to save his life couldn't stop the bleeding.

After hearing this, Frank questioned, "Why don't you have an emergency numbering system? It has been in place in Victoria for a long time. Not just beaches but parks, walking and bike tracks, etc."

"I have no idea. Great idea Frank, I will look into it."

I then looked on the internet to check out this emergency system. It was everywhere in Victoria. What a simple and great way to find someone in an emergency. Every sign has a number attached to a GPS code so you can instantly locate the area.

My media team called me and gave me a quick run-down on how the shark attack happened and the trouble the ambulance had locating him. It was unfortunate to hear that this guy was a local man whose girlfriend was expecting their first child; he loved surfing and loved Wanjup. A significant loss to the area.

My mobile rang; I walked outside the corporate box, into the hallway and put my finger in my left ear to hear what the reporter was asking.

"Hello, this is mayor Valenti."

"Oh, good afternoon, mayor Valenti; this is Jill from Wanjup radio. I wanted to ask you a few questions about the shark attack that happened this morning. Are you aware of what has happened? Your office has told me that you are on leave."

"Afternoon Jill, yes, I am aware of what has happened. I can't believe this poor man has lost his life from a shark bite. It is happening too often, and we need it to stop!"

"Are you happy for me to start recording our conversation?"

"Yes, Jill, go ahead."

"Thanks. Mayor Valenti, the terrible shark attack that happened this morning on the coast of Wanjup, could it have been avoided?"

"Good question Jill, but are you asking that no one goes surfing to avoid another shark attack! Or are you asking about the time it took to find the shark attack victim?"

"Thank you, mayor Valenti; I was referring to the delay in finding the shark victim; the report is that the ambulance had to attend four parking lots before they found the young man dying from a shark bite."

"Correct. I have been consulting with a colleague who has informed me about a very successful system in Victoria, which I believe we need to install into our beaches and outside activity areas. It is so basic that I can't believe South Australia hasn't done this before!"

"Is there a system in place now, in other states that could have saved this man's life, and we don't have it?"

"In a simple answer, yes."

"Well, mayor Valenti, can we expect this system in place here, so no one else has to die from a shark attack?"

"Shark attacks are becoming more common because the Government has banned people being able to kill them. Extremely stupid. Now, these creatures are growing to unheard-of lengths; their circumferences are so large they could probably swallow a small boat. They need to be fished like any other fish to keep the ecological system in place."

"Victoria has an emergency numbering system, so any emergency worker, be that ambulance, fire, police, surf rescue etc., can locate the victim in the shortest period possible." I explained.

"What about this system of numbering mayor? How do we get it? This system sounds more important than the size of the sharks."

"The system in itself is simple. However, every location has to have a GPS number attached to it. In addition, every emergency agency needs to be on board with it. I have spoken to the team in the City, and they are all prepared to start work on getting this system in place straight away."

When I returned from Melbourne, I had a meeting with the staff involved in this numbering system. In addition, I met with the brother of the shark attack victim and told him about the same numbering system I was informed about in Melbourne. He mentioned that a fellow surfer had also talked about this system. It is such a simple idea; I can't believe that we didn't have it in place before.

Out of respect to the young surfer, who lost his life to the shark attack, I called the Numbering System after him, for South Australia only.

It has been installed and is now in place across the state. I drive past parks and see the number, at beaches and even remote bike tracks, and I feel proud that I pushed to get this done. I had councillors and city staff push against it, saying it was too hard to bring so many emergency services together to make it work. This Emergency Numbering System is one of the most important things that I can say I did as the mayor of Wanjup. I pushed to make it happen, and the excellent staff at the city did just that.

But now it was time for the election. People forgot about the massive effort I took to get the Emergency Numbering System up and running, and the hate campaign from my opponent had started to ramp up. I was seriously over it. If Lincoln wants this job so bad, he can bloody have it.

CHAPTER THIRTY-SIX

I returned to South Australia after my enjoyable holiday with my amazing Melbourne friends to a fury of hatred thrown my way. If you believe social media, then the poor guy who died from the shark bite was my fault. A woman's child failed year one; it was my fault. A person purchased a rotten apple, and that was somehow my fault! Seriously don't people realise the role of a mayor in local Government in Australia.

People need an education in how the three tiers of Government work. For example, the **Federal** Government controls your taxes, the defence force, immigration, international trade, postal and telecommunications service, banking and insurance, foreign policy, citizenship, pensions, census and statistics, welfare payments, currency, Medicare, marriage and divorce, national employment conditions and immigration.

The state government controls education, public transport, including the railway and roads, electricity and water supply, mining, agriculture, forests, community services, consumer affairs, the police and nurses, prisons and ambulance services.

The local Government only deal with your local roads, foot and cycle paths, signage and lighting. Waste management, parking, recreational facilities such as parks, sporting fields and swimming pools. Libraries, art galleries and museums, sewerage, town planning, building approvals and inspections, land and coast care programs and pest control.

Local councils are not mentioned in the Australian constitution! We exist only because of the income from rates of all local property owners and government grants to spend on local matters. Interesting fact, the

CEO of local level one councils, earn more than the Premier, and I'm sure the Prime Minister of Australia.

There has never been so much interest in a local government election as there was with mine.

Everywhere I went, people questioned about the most random things! "Why are the trains not coming every 10 minutes? It's not right having to wait 15 minutes!" "We are a multicultural country, so why do we still allow ham sandwiches in our schools?" "I missed my plane last week; why aren't you looking after our aviation needs better?"

My head was spinning with how uneducated our citizens were. They have a local member of the state government who was behind my hate campaign. It made sense that he was behind it because I had never had any of these questions or complaints in my whole time as mayor.

I decided to call a meeting with our state member, which, I might add, was a pretty brave thing as I knew he was behind my massive hate campaign.

I walked into his office, and he was outright rude! "Afternoon, mayor, you wanted this meeting, so let's get started!" Fred grunted.

"Thanks for seeing me, Fred. I know this is a busy time for you, and I appreciate that you consider the local Government worthy of my appointment with you today."

"Scrap the bullshit, Liz! What do you want?

Now I knew he was behind this crazy campaign. I have known this man; he has always been as lovely as anyone to me. He has always been accommodating to anything that I needed as the mayor and was happy to support local Government, especially as he is the state minister for Local Government.

"Do you know what is going on with my hate signs? With the constant online bullying? I feel like I have returned from a week break to a collapse of decent human compassion."

"Haven't noticed! You know that I am supporting Lincoln. No secrets there; he is a great young man who wanted to be mayor four years ago. You won't be so lucky this time, Liz; we have pulled out all the big guns for this one. I am planning on retiring after the next election. Now that Lincoln is looking very favourable in the polls to win the mayor's seat, the stepping stone to State Government is in my retirement plan. I am getting too old for this game, and I have a young family that need me. I will do whatever it takes to ensure that you don't become the mayor of Wanjup again. Mark my words, you are finished."

I left that meeting upset and even more disappointed. Fred had always been a friend. Not the type you invite back to your home for a meal, but someone who I confided in and respected their advice. I felt like he had my back. But my hollowed back, covered with stab wounds from horrible people in my life, was not going to recover soon.

I was so tired from my travels and what I had to deal with on my return; I asked my secretary to book me the weekend off. The mayoral election was looming, and I was under constant pressure to attend even the opening of an envelope.

Mike, Nessy and I headed down south to Adelaide; I love this city. We headed to a gorgeous seaside, pet-friendly apartment in Glenelg. I had no idea how much I needed the getaway. We pulled into the car park and walked up to the lockbox outside the front door. I entered the code and retrieved the house keys from the box.

We unpacked the car and let Nessy out on the front lawn for a wee. This place was so beautiful; I felt like it was the best relaxation medicine that I could have had.

It was so close to the ocean; you could hear the waves breaking on the shore.

This was my time to regroup. Mike made a coffee, and we sat outside on the veranda. Nessy jumped up on the couch next to me. It was like she knew I needed some extra love right now.

After we unpacked, we walked down to the beach, and I took my shoes off to feel the sand between my toes. Then, I walked into the water, and every part of my body relaxed. The ocean is the best therapy for anyone who is stressed. I loved the way my body just socked up this experience.

Mike and I just talked for hours on end. We had so much going on in our lives. Our oldest daughter was getting married, our business had an offer of purchase on it, and Mike wanted me back as his wife and not the mayor of Wanjup anymore.

It was a wonderful break, almost like the calm before the storm!

CHAPTER THIRTY-SEVEN

ELECTION DAY HAD FINALLY ARRIVED. I WAS EXHAUSTED AND OVER THE campaign.

"Today's the big day, love!" Mike said as he carefully placed the hot coffee next to me on the bedside table, "It's time for you to get up and face the day. Hopefully, it will be your last day as mayor!"

"I hope so," I agreed as I sat up and grabbed my coffee. "This has been a tough year."

I enjoyed my coffee and got out of bed. After I showered and dressed, Mike and I walked into town to enjoy a quiet breakfast together. We took Nessy with us because the café is dog friendly and she loves her walks. Nessy is such a beautiful dog, keeping me sane during this campaign. She is always happy to see me, never judges me and is the best company.

People wished me all the best for the election during our walk, thanking me for all my hard work and generally being friendly. It filled my heart with happiness to know I was appreciated.

"There you go, Liz, you have done a great job as mayor, but I truly hope you lose today so I get my Liz back and life can go back to normal," Mike remarked.

"Couldn't agree more, Mike. I am looking forward to sleeping in and being able to relax at night with no evening events to attend."

We arrived at the café and sat at an outside table in the morning sun. It was a beautiful warm morning. The waitress came out with a bowl of water for Nessy.

"Morning, mayor and Mike, what can I get for you?"

"Please, just call me Liz," I said with a smile.

We ordered breakfast and enjoyed each other's company.

The waitress returned with our coffees. "Your breakfast will be out soon."

Nessy was starting to play up; she was getting impatient and wanted to keep moving. Finally, Nessy wrapped her paws around my leg and started dry humping it!

"Stop it, Nessy!" I snapped at her.

The waitress walked out with our breakfast and saw Nessy humping my leg under the table. She just laughed as she put the dishes on the table. "I thought your dog was a girl, judging by the pink collar and lead."

"She is." I replied, "She has lost her patience and wants me to keep walking."

"You know your dog is trying to dominate you, mayor, oh sorry, I mean Liz!"

"Yes, she can be very cheeky."

I peeled Nessy off my leg and made her sit next to me.

We finished off our breakfast and walked back home.

Once we were home, I took off Nessy's lead and went to my office to check my emails. Mike walked in. "Come on, Liz! You can't hide in here all day. A lot of people are counting on you to win, so you need to be out and about today."

Mike was my biggest fan. I just love this man so much; he was right; People were expecting to see me out and about today.

"Ok, let's get out of here, last chance to campaign before tonight's vote count."

"Good on you, Liz, that's my girl. Let's head downtown and walk around," encouraged Mike. "Come, Nessy! Let's get that lead back on you; it's time for walkies again."

I put on my hat, sunscreen and my best smile. It was going to be a beautiful day.

Mike took Nessy by the lead, and we all walked out the door and into town.

I turned on my walking app on my watch because I think I'll be walking a few thousand steps today. I am looking forward to having free time to exercise and start looking after myself better. I have so much weight to lose!

We walked through the central park in town and spoke to lots of charming people. One couple approached me, and I thought they would wish me all the best for the election, but no! This lady just started having a go at me. "I think it's disgusting the way you are parading around here like you own the place. I am voting for Lincoln. This place needs someone cool and energetic."

Mike jumped to my defence, "Good on you for voting for Lincoln; he is a great guy. Liz has also done a great job. Thanks for your time."

Mike took the wind out of her sails; she was ramping up to give me a full spate before Mike spoke, and I reckon her partner was going to say his bit too.

Mike lovingly took my hand and led Nessy and me away from this toxic couple.

"I have never wanted you to lose at anything, babe, but I do want you to lose this election. It is killing you," said Mike.

"I want to walk home. I'm done. It's too late now to win over votes."

"No worries, I'm ready for a cuppa anyway; let's go home," agreed Mike.

We walked back home, put the kettle on and enjoyed a lovely cup of tea.

The time finally arrived, the polling booths closed, and the counting of the voting papers began. A close friend was scrutinising the count for me at the Townhall. Her husband rang me after the first hour of counting had passed to give me an update.

"Hi Liz, it's Knobby; it's not looking too good for you. Unfortunately, Lincoln's count is up on yours by around 100 votes. He is doing well; they should be close with the mayoral vote count in about one hour. Are you guys coming down?"

"Thanks, Knobby, for letting me know. Sure, we will be there in ten minutes."

"Mike! It's time to go. Let's get this done. Knobby just rang to say the count is nearly over; they are doing the mayoral vote count first before the ward councillors."

"Did Knobby give you any indication on how it was all going?"

"Yeah, Lincoln's count is around 100 votes up on mine. Let's hope this trend continues."

We drove to the Townhall and Lincoln came straight up to me. He looked very excited to see me. "Liz! So glad you're here; my count is up by 150 votes, not like the bullshit couple of votes last time."

"Fantastic Lincoln, I am so happy for you. I know how bad you want to be the mayor!"

Lincoln turned around and lunged at Mike, giving him the biggest hug! Mike nearly fell over in shock. Then Lincoln wrapped his arm around me like we were best buddies. I think he may have taken a little happy drug before he came out tonight.

You could feel the excitement buzzing out of Lincoln. Thankfully the counting was almost done. I wiggled away from Lincoln's arm and grabbed Mike's hand. "Let's go sit at the front, honey; they are nearly done."

My bum had not even touched the seat when the Returning Officer seized the microphone and said he would announce who the new mayor of Wanjup is soon.

Mike leant into me and whispered in my ear. "Make an effort to look sad when you lose Liz; the photographers are watching you."

The Returning Officer walked into the middle of the Townhall, gripping the microphone. "I am happy to announce that the mayor of Wanjup is......mayor-elect Lincoln Harvey."

Lincoln was so happy he nearly wet himself. He came straight up to me and gave me the biggest kiss on the cheek, then jumped over to Mike and also gave him the biggest kiss on the cheek. Mike instantly started wiping his kiss-off his face.

The cameras were going off. I took Lincoln by the hand to calm him down, "Congratulations, mayor Harvey, you have worked extremely hard for this victory. Wanjup is now in your hands."

We stood together shaking hands for the photographers, with big smiles on our faces. I then threw my arms around Mike's neck and buried my head into his chest. "You have me back, babe! Thank God Lincoln won. Let's go home and open the Champagne!"

Mike just smiled at me; then we thanked everyone on our way out the door. People probably thought we were leaving because I was so sad. But, if I could do cartwheels, I would have cartwheeled out that Townhall door! So, instead, we went with grace and decorum. Said all the right things to all the right people and vanished back to the sanctuary of our beautiful home and little Nessy.

CHAPTER THIRTY-EIGHT

It was 8 am when detective Jamie Ranch from the homicide division received the call.

"Morning detective Ranch, we have a deceased Caucasian male, aged in his late sixties. He was found this morning at 7 am by the Old Railway motel's cleaner." Judy from the coroner's office reported.

"Thanks, Judy, give me 15 minutes, and I will be there. Have the forensic team arrived?" detective Ranch asked.

"Yes, detective Ranch, they arrived as soon as we got the 000 calls. Ann Fletcher is heading up the forensic team," replied Judy. "Just a heads up, the old guy was dressed in leather bondage gear. You know the full get up! So gross that old people still even have sex, but to dress up like that, is just wrong!"

"Thanks, Judy; I will prepare myself for it. Anything else?"

"Yeah, it's suspicious as his hands and feet are bound and attached to the bed by leather straps. There is no way he could have tied himself up like that. The coroner believes the time of death was between 7 pm and midnight last night."

"Ok, can you let forensics know that I am on my way?"

"Sure, detective Ranch, consider it done!"

Detectives Jamie Ranch and Anton Bell headed off to the Old Railway Motel to investigate the suspected crime scene and the death of a man dressed in bondage gear.

They arrived at a media circus. Word spreads fast in a small town.

"Morning detective, can we have a comment about what has happened here this morning?" The reporter asked.

"I have nothing to comment on at this time. I have only just arrived!" Detective Ranch snapped as he pushed his way through the photographers and journalists.

Detectives Ranch and Bell put on their masks, and plastic gloves then slipped the white protective socks over their shoes. They stepped over plastic police tape blocking off the room and carefully made their way over to the forensic team.

"Bloody hell!" blurted detective Bell as he walked past the bed. "This is some pretty fucked up stuff! What on earth is this guy wearing?"

"Leather bondage outfit, Detective." Ann Fletcher replied. Ann had been around the forensic team for many years and had seen a lot. Nothing fazed her now.

"And the smell! God, it's horrible! Did he shit himself or something?" asked detective Bell.

Detective Ranch sniggered at detective Bell's reaction. Detective Bell was new to the detective role, and this was probably his first murder investigation.

"When a person dies detective, their body can release 'poop', but it usually depends on how they died. In the case of anaphylaxis or organophosphate poisoning, the result of the deceased pooping themselves is 80% - 90%." explained Ann.

"Thanks, Ann; I don't know that I needed to know that," retorted detective Bell.

"Ann, what have you come up with so far?" asked detective Ranch.

Ann took out her black light and lit up the bed, and the body perched on top.

"As you can see, detectives, the ultraviolet light is showing you the semen stains location. This man was involved in sexual activity. The semen fluoresces; it absorbs ultraviolet light and then re-emits that energy as visible light."

Detective Bell is listening to every word Ann is telling him. "Ann, if that fluorescent stuff is semen, how come there are darker patches and lighter patches on the bed?"

"Unfortunately, detective, not all motels use water at a high enough temperature to destroy the semen. The lighter stains are not from last night's activity."

"That is bloody disgusting, Ann! I think I will get one of those fancy lights to check out the bed in the next hotel room I stay in," shuddered detective Bell.

Ann smiled and continued. "Judging by the way this man has defecated, I would put his cause of death to be from organophosphate poisoning. I have sent off samples for a forensic toxicology report. We will have the results of this shortly. I have also sent off the contents of the wine glass for testing. The perpetrator may have poisoned him."

"Thanks, Ann," detective Ranch said. "Can you tell us the type of poison used?"

"Until the toxicology report comes back, I can't definitively tell you; however, the most common form of poisoning is with Chloroform or Trichloromethane."

Detective Bell was curious and asked, "I thought Chloroform just put you off to sleep for a bit?"

Ann gave Anton a quick lesson in Chloroform. "Chloroform is colourless, strong-smelling liquid. Its uses include a solvent for lacquers, resins, adhesives and even floor polishes. Did you know that it used to be used as an anaesthetic to reduce pain? It is a carcinogen to humans and, in the presence of oxygen, will convert to phosgene which was a chemical weapon in WW1! It is sweet-tasting and will render a person unconscious.

I am leaning towards Chloroform as the poison because it can asphyxiate or cause heart problems and is readily available. In addition, this body is presenting with organophosphate poisoning."

"What do you mean it's easily available, Ann? I would hate to think people can just go buy Chloroform off the shelf?" asked detective Bell.

"It is easily made from combining simple household products, bleach and acetone. Acetone is in most nail polish removers." Ann explained.

Detective Ranch collected the man's belongings to bring back to the station. The forensics team had finished with the bag; you could tell by all the fingerprint dust on it. It was bagged and tagged, ready for the detectives to do their part.

Detectives Ranch and Bell took a few more notes and left the forensic team to do their job. They headed back to the station and went through the bag.

"I don't think these gloves are thick enough to be touching this guy's stuff, Jamie!" detective Bell complained. "Who knows what kinky crap is going to be in there. But, you are the senior detective on this case, so I think you should shove your hand in first!"

"Stand aside, Anton, watch how a real detective works!" Detective Ranch opened the bag carefully and pulled the items out, one at a time.

Detective Bell took photos and wrote everything down. "Is that a wallet, Jamie?"

Detective Ranch retrieved the wallet from the bag and opened it. "Yep, the driver's licence says that guy is Paul Aldman. There is an office security swipe card in there too. From the city of Wanjep. He lives in Wanjep and is 68 years old."

"I'll check out the city's website now to see if it lists him as an employee." Announced detective Bell.

Detective Bell Googled the internet to find out what he could about the guy they found in a dinghy motel room, covered in shit.

"Bloody hell Jamie, this guy is the top dog! He is the bloody CEO of Wanjep!"

"Brilliant!" exclaimed detective Ranch. "That is our starting point; who is the mayor?"

"Elizabeth Valanti, her office is in the council chambers near the city's office," confirmed detective Bell. "Let's head over there now for a quick chat with the mayor; they usually know everything that is going on in their city."

"I think we should notify the next of kin first, Anton. But I love your enthusiasm. Let's go through the records and find out if he has a wife, girlfriend, boyfriend or relative so we can communicate Paul Aldman's death to them," pointed out detective Ranch.

"Do we need to tell the relatives how we found him? That is going to be a tough one!" detective Bell asked.

"I am sure we can leave out most of it, Anton, but we need to tell them where we located the body and at what time."

Detectives Ranch and Bell searched all their available records and found that Paul was married to Sonja Aldman. So they grabbed a coffee on the way and headed over to Sonja's house. They sat in the car for a few moments outside Sonja's house and worked out how they would tell the poor widow of her husband's passing.

"I can't do this, Jamie; my stomach is still in a knot after seeing his shitty body this morning!"

"I will do the talking Anton; I get it; this is one of the hardest parts of the job."

They headed up to the front door and rang the doorbell. Sonja answered, wearing her gym gear; she was on her way out to a Pilates class. "Hello, can I help you?" Sonja asked.

She had an apprehensive look on her face. Even though these guys weren't in uniform, you could see their badges on their waists. But, of course, no one likes to have a cop knock on their door.

"Morning, are you Mrs Aldman?" Detective Ranch asked.

"Yes, I am Mrs Aldman. Has something happened to Paul?"

"Do you mind if we come in to talk to you?" asked detective Bell.

"Of course, come in!"

Sonja stepped aside so the detectives could enter her home.

"Can I get you a drink, water, coffee?" Sonja asked nervously.

"No, thank you, Mrs Aldman. Can you please take a seat?" invited detective Bell.

Sonja sat down and carefully listened to every word the detectives said.

"At 7 am this morning, a cleaner found your husband's body in a motel room. We have identified him as being Paul Aldman. The time of death has was between 7 pm and midnight last night," informed detective Ranch.

"No! this can't be; Paul said he was going to Adelaide for a conference and would be home later today. Are you sure it's Paul? Maybe someone picked up his bag by accident!"

"His fingerprints match the ones that we have on our system. So, therefore, I can confirm that the deceased is your husband. Would you like me to contact someone for you? We have councillors available to assist you at times like this."

"How do you have his fingerprints? Nothing you are saying makes sense right now! Paul is alive and at a local government conference in Adelaide. I am going to call him; this is crazy!"

Sonja rang Paul's phone. There was no answer. She just sat there, not knowing where to look, where to run, or what to believe. Then, after a few moments, Jamie's phone rang.

"Yes, she did; I will confirm, thank you." Jamie then had to confirm with Sonja that Paul's phone rang at the morgue; it was with his belongings that Jamie and Anton didn't collect.

"I am sorry to confirm that the number you just called was your husband's number; his mobile phone was with him at the motel, which is now at the morgue. The coroner just called to let me know that your number appeared as his wife and knew we would be here with you."

"What was he doing at a motel, here! He could have come home, or I could have picked him up if he had a few drinks!" Sonja wondered aloud.

"There was another person at the motel with him last night. Do you know of anyone who may have asked him to stay there?" Detective Ranch asked.

"No! No way would he be doing anything behind my back. You know we just had the most amazing 20th wedding anniversary holiday trip to Europe!"

"Sorry, Mrs Aldman, I don't know anything about you or your husband, only that we have just found him dead in a motel with very little to go on. I am hoping you can give us names of anyone who may have wanted to hurt him in any way?" Detective Ranch probed.

"Check out that mayor Valenti; she is a right bitch; from what Paul has told me, I wouldn't put anything past her. However, there is another councillor, Pauline Ashley. She is a total psycho, who knows what she is capable of, and I have a weird vibe with one councillor, Sharon Day, who always acts like she is better than me and is always swooning around Paul. I don't like her at all. I am sorry if I sound like I am ranting! I don't believe what you are saying. I need to see Paul!"

"Let me call the morgue now to see if his body is ready for your confirmation of identity." Detective Bell said as he took out his phone and left the room.

Sonja sat in her lounge room, head held in her hands, waiting for approval for her to attend the morgue.

Detective Bell returned and advised, "The morgue has asked that the relative attends in two hours, as there is a fair amount of work to be done to have the body in a recognisable state for identity."

"Was he in some accident? Why is his body not recognisable? You people have not told me anything other than my husband is dead. This is shit! I need answers, and I need to see my husband now!" Sonja screamed. "What are you hiding from me? He is dead; everything is off the table now!"

Detectives Ranch and Bell both agreed and took Sonja in their car to identify the body at the city morgue.

CHAPTER THIRTY-NINE

I CAME IN TO CLEAR OUT MY OFFICE ON MONDAY MORNING AND thought, this will be the last time I will ever have to walk in here.

"Morning, Tanya!" I said as I walked up to her desk.

"Morning, Liz! Wow, that feels weird not calling you mayor! Would you like a coffee while you empty the office?"

"That would be great, Tanya, thanks."

Tanya went off to make me a coffee, and I set about clearing out my things from the cupboards and drawers.

I heard the building front door open and close. As Tanya was away from her desk, making me a coffee, I went out to see who it was.

"Good morning, mayor Valenti, I am Detective Jaime Ranch, and this is Detective Anton Bell; we would like to ask you a few questions."

"Sure, but just call me Liz; as of Saturday night, I am no longer the mayor."

"I am sorry to hear that Liz, you have done a great job as the city's mayor. This shouldn't take long."

"Ok, come into my old office. Excuse the mess; I am in the middle of packing everything up."

I led them through to the mayor's office, and we sat around the small meeting table.

"To jump right in, can you tell us of your whereabouts last night between 7 pm and midnight?" Detective Ranch asked.

"I was at home with my husband, Mike. Why? What has happened?" I asked

"Paul Aldman was found dead this morning, by a cleaner, at the Old Railway Motel. We believe that his time of death is between 7 pm and midnight," Jamie answered.

"Oh my God! This is terrible news. I do know that Paul had a dicky heart; it may have just been a heart attack!"

"It appears that Paul's death was not by natural causes. We are now investigating a homicide."

"Oh! I hope you don't think I had something to do with this?" I asked.

"We are aware that you and Paul had disagreements and hated each other. However, we need to start our investigations with the obvious suspects."

"You are correct, I did not like the man, but I didn't want him killed either!"

"Do you know of anyone who may want to cause harm to Paul?" Detective Ranch probed.

"Paul was not that well-liked by a lot of people. Off the top of my head, I can think of a couple of people who may have wanted to cause Paul harm."

"Can you please provide us with a list of names?"

Detective Bell took out his notepad, ready for me to divulge the suspect's names. He had been sitting there, quietly judging me the whole time. It was like he was looking for apparent body movements to scream out that I was guilty!

"I would have to start with councillor Sharon Day; they were having an affair and went through a nasty break-up. Then there is Angelo Porcini; he was an employee that Paul fired because of a drug bust. I remember how angry he was when he was being cuffed and taken away by the police. He was yelling out that Paul was going to get what was coming to him! Another is Tracy Kardan, who has also been having an affair with Paul. I'm not sure where their relationship is because I haven't spoken to Tracy in a while. Finally, while we are making a list, I wouldn't rule Paul's wife, Sonja, out; if she found out about the affairs, she would certainly have a motive to kill the cheating bastard!"

"Thanks, Liz, that is quite a list. It will give us something to start on while we are waiting for forensics to finish their analysis of the deceased and the motel room."

"One more person of interest would be ex-councillor Donald Geary. He is mentally unstable and has had quite a few run-ins with Paul over his erratic behaviour while representing this city. Paul had him removed as a councillor recently because of his misconduct." I mentioned quickly before they got up to leave. "Can I ask what makes you think it was murder and not by natural causes?"

"It appears that Paul was involved in a relationship with someone he trusted enough to allow them to strap his feet and hands to a bed," disclosed detective Ranch.

"I am not surprised; Tracy was involved in a BDSM group and would meet with different partners in the group and inflict pain on each other. Tracy couldn't wait to tell me all about her sadism and masochism sexual activity with Paul."

"That is interesting, Liz, as Paul was wearing the full black leather bondage outfit. His mouth had a deep throat gag kit in it. His wrists had leather wrist cuffs. He was wearing a five strap Hogtie anchored to the bed with leather straps, with his ankles in sling loops. Oh! And to top it off, the black leather pants had no arse! It was the first thing we saw on entering the room because he was strapped on all fours. A vision that will stay with me for too long!"

"Thanks for sharing detective, I now share that vision and am pretty sure I just had a little vomit in my mouth!"

"The gear that Paul had on is worth thousands, which led us to believe that this is a practice he regularly gets involved in," detective Bell joined in. "This makes Tracy a person of interest."

"The forensic team are with the body now. Hopefully, they will be able to give us a better idea of who was with the victim and what killed him," continued detective Ranch.

"Thanks for your time and your help with this matter" concluded detective Bell.

Tanya walked in with my coffee, "Sorry Liz, I didn't realise you had company, everything ok!"

"Not really, Liz! This is detective Jamie Ranch and detective Anton Bell from the Wanjup Police department. They have just informed me that Paul was found dead this morning."

Tanya slowly and carefully places my coffee down in front of me and steps back. Her face had gone as white as snow.

"What! How?" Tanya asked.

"Not sure yet," I replied.

The two detectives stood up and collected their things. Detective Bell asked Tanya, "Do you know of anyone who may want to harm Mr Aldman?"

"No! Not really. He wasn't very popular with the staff, but I couldn't tell you if they hated him enough to kill him."

"Thank you, Liz and Tanya, for your time. Here is my card, in case you think of anyone else. Please email me any names you consider. Can I have your number, Liz, just in case I have any further questions for you?" Detective Ranch asked.

"I am keeping my mobile number, so here is my 'old mayoral' card with the number. Good luck with your investigation."

The two detectives left the building, and Tanya just stood there in shock, shaking her head.

"I can't believe Paul is dead! Did you have something to do with this?"

"What! Are you kidding, Tanya! No. I had nothing to do with Paul dying. How could you even ask me that?"

"I have heard some pretty heated conversations between you two. Don't forget, I sit right outside your office and hear a lot!"

"I seriously hope you are joking right now, Tanya. I would never take another human's life, even a low life shit like Paul."

Tanya walked back to her desk and sat down to get on with her daily tasks. I now processed what I had just heard. Paul is dead! I needed to pretend that I care publicly or become a person of interest in this investigation. However, I couldn't help but think Tracy must have had some involvement. She is a sick bitch; I reckon something had gone wrong, and she had bolted, leaving Paul in that awful position and dead!

CHAPTER FORTY

THE FORENSIC TEAM, LED BY ANN FLETCHER, THE WANJUP FORENSIC pathologist, was often sought to conduct the autopsies for murder investigations due to her reputation for being meticulous in her work.

She worked through all the evidence collected to identify Paul's killer. First, every inch of Paul's body was carefully examined. Using the state-of-the-art equipment, they could pinpoint a killer just by a simple fingerprint lifted off a murder weapon.

To begin, they carefully undressed the body, or rather, peeled the tight leather suit from his body. They then looked over the suit for any marks, hairs, blood etc., for DNA testing. They were surprised at how clean his leather outfit was. It was like the perpetrator knew how to clean a body, so the forensic team couldn't find anything to examine!

They carefully removed the ball gag from his mouth and placed it in a plastic bag. During the ball gag removal, one of the young forensic scientists, Loretta Brown, noticed a hair caught between Paul's top left canine and incisor tooth. She took her tweezers and gently removed the hair. She then placed it in an evidence bag for testing.

Loretta Brown had only recently joined Ann's team after graduating top of her class from Adelaide University the previous year. She was very excited to be working alongside Ann and was keen to make a good impression on her mentor.

The hair Loretta discovered snapped off between Paul's teeth was pubic hair. Even without DNA testing, it is evident that this pubic hair was from a male because of its thickness. Female pubic hair is often thinner due to excessive waxing. Loretta sent the hair off to Adelaide for DNA testing. It could take at least three days to get the DNA results back, but it will be worth the wait.

Loretta received Paul's blood test results; they came back positive for Chloroform or Trichloromethane. Confirming that Paul had a weak heart, and even a tiny dose of Chloroform could have caused cardiac arrhythmia. A positive result for death by anaphylaxis or organophosphate poisoning.

"Excuse me, Ann, I know you are busy, but I want to show you my findings; I think you will be very interested," announced Loretta. Being was her first big homicide job, she was excited to find something she believed was necessary and vital to the case.

"Well done, Loretta, come over here and show me. I'm elbows deep in human intestines right now, trying to confirm my poisoning theory."

"Well, Ann, Paul's blood results confirm poisoning! It looks like the killer used Chloroform as the poison. Whoever did this must have known that he had a bad heart. So, I am confident that the killer knew the victim," Loretta declared confidently.

"That is interesting Loretta, leave it with me; I will need to contact the detectives in charge of this case. Well done, not bad for your first homicide job!" complimented Ann.

Ann then rang Detectives Jamie Ranch and Anton Bell to tell them what they had uncovered. "Good afternoon Jamie, we are not quite finished on the DNA, but an important thing has arisen that I thought you should know. I believe there may have been two killers, not one. Let me finish my testing, and I will confirm with you what I know. There is one thing you need to consider; the killer appears to have known the victim. Not a random act by a stranger," concluded Ann.

The detectives started a long list on the whiteboard of people known to Paul, persons of interest and motives. Top of their list was Liz Valenti, Sharon Day, Angelo Porcini, Tracy Kardan and Donald Geary. "Let's work out their motives Anton, why would these people want to kill Paul Aldman?" contemplated detective Ranch.

Detective Bell was very keen to catch the killer, "Liz is obvious, she hated Paul, she probably blames him for losing the election and wanted revenge. Sharon Day was having an affair with Paul, and they may have had a falling out, but I don't see Sharon as a real suspect; my money is still on Liz. Angelo Porcini is an interesting one. He lost his job at the city when Paul sacked him, and he is in a relationship with Sharon, who used to be Paul's mistress. Paul had a charge of falsifying evidence to pin a fake drug bust on Angelo; yep, it gives him motive. Paul's wife Sonja bailed him out until his trial in two weeks. Tracy Kardan, we don't have much to go on with her; maybe we should visit Tracy. Lastly, we have Donald Geary; what a loose circuit this guy is. He was an elected council member until Paul had him removed from his seat because of serious misconduct. Being charged with aggravated sexual assault on a staff member, the mayor's private secretary. Donald's life revolved around the council, so being removed by Paul would give him motive."

Detective Ranch affirmed, "Ann mentioned that she believed the killer knew the victim well. So, we need to add to the list people who knew Paul well. So, his wife Sonja would have to be first on the list; Liz did mention that his wife knew about the affairs he was having, nothing like a jilted wife to kill her husband, good motive right there. Next, his young friend Lincoln Harvey, who was just elected mayor of Wanjup, and I have heard from people I have been speaking with that he was very close to Paul. I can't work out a motive for Lincoln's involvement, so maybe let's start with a quick chat with him."

Detectives Ranch and Bell decided to pay a visit to Lincoln. After a few phone calls, they finally located him at the dance studio in town. To their surprise, when they walked in, Lincoln was in a whole drag queen getup and looked pretty good. Anton whispered to Jamie, "That is a beautiful woman if I didn't know it was a man!"

"Are you serious Anton, fuck me, man, that's a bloke? It's all wrong," Jamie hissed.

"Have you been down the local pub lately, Jamie? Women around this town could take some lessons on how to make themselves presentable from this bloke. They should stop wearing exercise leggings as casual wear, especially when the leggings are too small and are transparent because they have stretched too much! Hey, not that I am gay or anything but, just saying!" Anton shut up quickly as he realised he was defending a guy in drag over the local girls.

"Let's just question Lincoln and get the fuck out of here, Anton. This place gives me the creeps!"

The detectives walked over to Lincoln and interrupted him mid-dance. "Sorry to interrupt your dance practice; I am detective Jaime Ranch, and this is detective Anton Bell. Are you Lincoln Harvey?"

"Yes, I am!" confirmed Lincoln, raising his arms in the air like a Spanish dancer. "I am the new mayor of Wanjup; what would you like to know?"

"Excellent, we just have a few questions to ask you about your whereabouts last night between 7 pm and midnight." Detective Ranch asked.

"Why do you need to know that? I haven't done anything wrong. I live a very public life, and my personal life is my business, and not yours to know where I was last night."

"Someone was murdered last night in Wanjup," stated detective Bell.

"Oh! Well, that does change the conversation, doesn't it! I have a private pastime where I am a sex worker, but only in a very close-knit online group. Not your normal group either. Most of the members are very prominent people in Wanjup who want some fun and a bit of release without anyone knowing who they are. The group is mainly involved in BDSM, and I am assuming that our conversation will be kept private?" explained Lincoln.

"Sorry mate, I have no idea what you are talking about; never heard of BDSM?" Detective Bell replied.

"Really! A strapping young man like yourself should know about these things; BDSM means bondage, discipline/domination, sadism/submission and masochism. Sexual activity involves tying up a partner and playing games where one partner controls the other and giving or receiving pain for pleasure. I would be happy to give you a personal demonstration Mr Policeman! So tell me, who did you find pushing up the daisies then?"

"A Mr Paul Aldman. Were you with him last night?" Detective Ranch asked.

"Yes, but he was alive when I left. Shit! How do I prove my innocence? Seriously, why would I kill him? He was my friend and my lover. He paid me very well to do what I do! Maybe you should be asking this one very naughty and cheeky little minx called Tracy in the group. That girl is bad news! You should be checking her out. She always goes that little bit too far. I have seen her with Paul at these gigs too, so I can guarantee she knows him well."

Jaime knew that mayor Valenti mentioned Tracy was a person of interest in this investigation, but there was something about this guy that just didn't sit well.

"Thank you for that descriptive information about BDSM Lincoln, and congratulations on winning the mayoral election. Please don't leave town, as we may have some more questions for you," directed detective Ranch.

"Don't worry, boys! I'll be right here where you can look me up anytime!" Lincoln gushed he blew kisses to the two detectives as they left the dance studio.

As the detectives drove away, detective Jamie turned to Anton, "don't you think it was weird how Lincoln just blurted out that he was a sex worker! Farrk! All he had to say was yes, I was with Paul. So what the hell was he rambling about BDSM. That guy is a freak! A sex worker is the elected mayor. What has happened to this place? The way he was talking was irrational. I have a feeling he knows more about what happened to Paul than he is letting on. He has just gone to the top of the list of suspects in my book."

The detective's visit genuinely rattled Lincoln. "Shit thought Lincoln. I am not going down for Paul's murder, think quick, who can I blame? I know. Liz Valenti. Yes! She is perfect. Everybody knows how much she hated Paul, and she probably blames him for losing the mayoral position.

Lincoln got onto his computer straight away; his heart was racing. He was too pretty to be locked up in prison. He opened up his social media page and started typing. Breaking News! I have just found out that Paul Aldman, CEO of Wanjup, was murdered last night. Then he repeated that same sentence on the Wanjup Community page.

It didn't take long, and people were commenting. Some comments were concerned about Paul's death, and others were just nasty, referring to how much they hated him. Finally, Lincoln replied to someone who hated Paul. "I'm guessing whoever killed Paul must have hated him. Was it you?" They replied, "No! But you are right. Someone must have hated him." Then a flurry of comments naming people who hated him. Then Liz's name popped up on the screen. Perfect, thought Lincoln.

Lincoln wrote, "I have heard that Liz and Paul have had some real doozies in the office. The staff have told me!" People jumped on his post faster than lightning. More than one thousand comments, accusations, hateful and soul-destroying words were all condemning me as Paul's murderer.

Lincoln's post caused a frenzy of people speculating on who murdered Paul. I now found myself vilified by internet trolls as being the murderer. I had taken down my mayoral social media page. But that didn't stop people; they still found a way of reaching out to me. These keyboard warriors were now attacking my friends and family.

Detectives Jamie Ranch and Anton Bell are reading through the community posts when detective Anton piped up, "Wasn't it Liz Valenti that Mrs Aldman mentioned first, as a person of interest in this case? Correct Anton, reading through these posts, she certainly had motive, and it seems like plenty of people knew of her hatred for Paul Aldman. It looks like Liz Valenti is our lead suspect; Ann did say that she believed there could have been two people involved in the murder!" Maybe we should be concentrating our efforts on building a case around her" detective Ranch suggested.

CHAPTER FORTY-ONE

"Good afternoon. Is this Tracy Kardan?" Detective Ranch enquired.

"Yes, who is this?" Tracy replied.

"I am Detective Jamie Ranch of the Wanjup homicide division. I was hoping to ask you a couple of questions."

"Sure, anything to help; I heard on social media that Paul knocked off the porch last night," said Tracy flippantly.

"Detective Anton Bell would like to speak to you about Mr Aldman's death. Are you able to come into the station, or we can come to you?"

"I've got some errands to run around town, so I will pop into the station in about half an hour. Not sure I can help you, but I wouldn't mind checking out the new police station. See you soon!" agreed Tracy.

Tracy came into the Police station. She bounced in, full of self-importance. She walked up to the station desk and announced that she is here to see the detectives.

Detective Bell walked out to escort Tracy into the meeting room where detective Ranch was already sitting with his phone set to record on the desk.

"Afternoon, guys, what can I do to help?" queried Tracy as she sat down in the chair Anton had pulled out for her.

"Thank you for your time, Tracy; this won't take long. Just so you are aware, we record our meetings, and anything said may be used in court as evidence. Do you understand? explained detective Ranch. "We are just trying to figure out the timeline of Mr Aldman's last hours. The new mayor Lincoln Harvey, mentioned that you knew Mr Aldman well and hopefully can shed some light on the matter?"

"That is just too funny! I knew him, hell yeah! We were fuck buddies. I told his wife, but she didn't believe me. The guy was a horny freak; he liked to get funky with the whole bondage getup. We have played around a bit with that, but he scared the crap out of me the last time we did it. He wanted me to strangle him until he passed out, which I did, and he didn't come back quickly enough for my liking. I thought I had killed him. He had a code to tap out for me to stop before it went that far" Tracy informed.

"Can you tell me, Tracy, when did this happen?" asked detective Bell.

"It wasn't bloody last night if that is what you are thinking! It was two weeks ago. I brought in some photos to show you." Tracy then pulled some photos from her bag and showed them to the detectives.

"Yes, that's the gear he was wearing when we found him dead. Where were you last night, Tracy, between the hours of 7 pm and midnight?" asked detective Ranch.

"What! Am I a bloody suspect now because I showed you these photos? Lucky for me, I have an alibi, I was at the same Motel as Paul, but I was playing with someone else. It is like a secret society, so I can't tell you his name."

"I am interested in the reason for you carrying photos of Paul, dressed in bondage gear, around in your handbag?" asked detective Ranch.

"I went to tell Paul's wife Sonja that Paul and I were playing bondage dress up sex games. She wasn't too pleased when I told her. So, I showed her the photos. She had to believe me then. She wasn't a happy camper when I left."

"For what purpose would you have approached Sonja Aldman to give her this news? What were you hoping to achieve from your meeting?" Detective Ranch asked.

"Well, it doesn't matter now, does it! Paul is dead. I threatened her with the photos because Paul freaked me out so much two weeks ago; he had to pay me $50,000 for my trouble. He refused, so I went to see his wife. Sonja is paying me cash; if she didn't pay me, I would take these photos to the newspaper. The papers eat this shit up and would have loved it." Said Tracy.

"To make sure I have this clear, Tracy, you were having an affair with Paul Aldman; you nearly killed him during a sex act and then took photos of him while asphyxiated. You then proceeded to extort money from his wife with the photos you have brought in with you today and have just shown us?" Detective Ranch asked incredulously.

"Yep! That pretty well sums it up," retorted Tracy.

"You will need to give us the name of the person you were with last night to verify your whereabouts during the hours of 7 pm and midnight." Detective Bell told Tracy.

"Why? I told you I can't; it's secret; it's against the group's rules. Am I now a fuckin suspect?" demanded Tracy.

"Correct, you will need to provide that name. Can I ask you to please stand up?" So asked Anton as he also got up and walked around the table to Tracy.

Tracy stood up, looking very confused as to what was happening.

"Tracy Kardan, I am placing you under arrest for extortion; please place your hands behind your back," instructed detective Bell.

"What the fuck, I came in here, out of the goodness of my heart, to give you blokes a hand in Paul's murder, which by the way, I didn't do. Now you are arresting me on a bullshit charge!" yelled Tracy.

"You have the right to speak to a lawyer, is there anyone you would like to call?" asked detective Bell.

"Yes, my lawyer, Chris Johnson. By the way, he was the guy I was fucking last night. So no point holding back now is there!" fumed Tracy. "You might also be interested to know that I saw Lincoln there last night too. He quite often frequents the room with Paul, so you should be checking him out.

Detective Anton Bell led Tracy down the hallway to the holding cell. When he came back to the interview room, detective Ranch had gone. He walked back into his office, and Jamie was at the whiteboard writing down names and scribbling something down next to Tracy's name. Then his mobile rang. "Hi detective Bell, this is detective Sargreto; I won't take up much of your time. I just had the former mayor, Liz Valenti, on the phone. You questioned her about the murder of the city's CEO Paul Aldman?"

"Correct!" answered detective Bell. "We are about to head out to question her again."

"Can I ask why? Have you received new information that vindicates Liz Valenti?" enquired detective Sargreto.

"Um, No! It is just that social media has gone crazy with accusations that she has committed this crime, and I feel that we owe it to the community to be more thorough with our investigation. According to the Wanjup community forum, Liz Valenti is the leading suspect," said, detective Bell.

"Just as I thought, Mrs Valenti has now started receiving death threats; that is why I have become involved. She called me asking how this trial by social media can stop! You boys need to start doing some good detective work and ignore the crap you are reading. Because enough people say something, it doesn't make it real. Do you have any other suspects, or are you focusing on just Liz Valenti?" reprimanded detective Sargreto.

"Well, as it has just happened, we have a new suspect with Tracy Kardan, and she was quick to mention that Lincoln Harvey was at the place we found the victim's body. However, we have already spoken to Lincoln, and he had admitted that Paul was alive when he left him," said detective Bell.

"You need to widen your web Jamie, look further into who would have had a motive to kill the victim. Please do not get dragged into social media bullshit. You guys should do your job, so bloody well get to it and get the job done," detective Sargreto barked.

"I appreciate your feedback, detective Sargreto; we will do our best to find the killer. I will keep you in the loop." Detective Bell replied. As he cancelled the call, he felt a little embarrassed that he got pulled into the social media frenzy naming Liz Valenti as the killer. It's incredible how fast these lies become the truth by people fabricating bullshit.

People just eat it up, take it on board as the truth and repeat and repeat until it has to be the truth. We live in a terrifying world when someone can lie about you, and it is not questioned or quashed. But these lies are put on a pedestal for others to make comments. People who have no idea about who you are as a human being but feel like their keyboard gives them the authority to send you to hell!

CHAPTER FORTY-TWO

Sonja's phone rang, "Hello?"

"Hi Sonja, it's Tracy, don't hang up because I only get one phone call, and I'm gifting it to you."

"Well, you wasted your bloody call then, you Psycho!" Sonja snarled.

"I saw you in the car park at the motel, the night Paul was murdered. I think the cops might like to know that bit of juicy information." Tracy quickly quipped.

"I have no idea what you are saying. I was never there." Sonja retorted.

"Ok, say what you like, but the gentleman that I was with that night also saw you and mentioned it before I did. So you now have two witnesses putting you at the place of your husband's murder. Think about it, darling; you are in the shit right now. I have nothing to lose. I have given the photos I showed you over to the cops" provoked Tracy.

"What do you want from me, Tracy? My husband is dead, I have just found out what a sick bastard he was, and you are asking me for what, seriously! What the fuck do you want from me?" Sonja complained as she wiped the tears off her cheek.

"Then tell me honestly, Sonja, did you kill Paul for being the cheating bastard that he was?" Tracy asked.

"No! I did soak that ball thingy that goes in his mouth in nail polish remover, hoping it would give him a bit of a high, but I never intended it to kill him. Oh my! What have I done? I am not a murderer; I just wanted him to pass out and not enjoy whatever he was doing so much. I wanted him to come home to me and not be with you." Sonja wailed.

"Well, the funny thing is Sonja, he wasn't with me that night; he swung the other way, and not for the first time!" Tracy enjoyed saying this to Sonja; she knew damn well it was cutting deep into her soul to know her husband was with a man.

"Oh my! Are you kidding me? Who the hell was he with?" Sonja begged.

"Lincoln Harvey! Are you kidding me? You never knew those two were doing the tango." Tracy was enjoying torturing Sonja right then, and Sonja was allowing her to do it. The poor woman was still coming to grips with the fact that her husband was dead. Dealing with the fact that he was cheating on her with other women, wearing submissive bondage outfits, and now having sex with men!

"Oh! I don't know what to say! I am going to puke. Sorry I have to go." Sonja hung up from Tracy. Seriously was too much for this woman to take in one day. How do you process this much information on someone you thought you knew for over twenty years?

Sonja knew that Tracy would tell the police that she was at the motel the night of her husband's murder, and it didn't look good for her. So she decided to get on the front foot and call the detective that came to her home to question her and deliver the news that her husband Paul was dead.

"Hello, this is detective Jamie Ranch; how can I assist you?"

"Hi detective Ranch, you came to my house to question me about my husband, Paul Aldman."

"Yes, Mrs Aldman, how are you going? Do you need assistance?"

"Yes, actually I do; I just had a call from your holding cell, from Tracy Kardan. She claims to have seen Lincoln at the property with Paul that night. Do you know if that is true?"

"We have reason to believe that Lincoln was at the property on the night of your husband's murder." Detective Ranch replied.

"Did you know that Paul fixed the vote in favour of Lincoln at the last election?" Sonja disclosed.

"No, I knew nothing of that. It's getting late, how about we meet in the morning, and you can tell me what you know. What time can you come? We open at 8 am."

"I'll be there at 7.50 am," Sonja said.

Detective Ranch called for a late meeting with all the detectives; he even asked detective Sargreto to come along.

They all came into the station, got their evening coffee and took their seats in the meeting room. Jamie now knew he needed to nail this murder or lose face with many of the older detectives.

"Thank you all for being here; I just wanted to go through the evidence we have received to date. The leader of our forensic team, Ann Fletcher, has indicated that there could be two killers. The crime scene consisted of a gentleman in his late sixties, wearing black leather bondage gear, strapped to a bed with semen and hair in his mouth. In addition, there were markings around his neck, indicating strangulation. However, these bruises are not connected with his murder as they appear to be at least a week old." Detective Ranch was extremely nervous delivering to this meeting, but he believed in what he had discovered.

"Social media has pinpointed former mayor Liz Valenti for the crime. However, she was at home with her husband Mike, and they have a solid alibi. The next suspect is Sharon Day, a councillor with the city of Wanjup, and she also has a solid alibi with Angelo Porcini, who also was a person of interest. Next, Donald Geary was a person of interest. However, he was in the hospital that night with a glass injury caused by a Corona beer bottle that became stuck on his penis; not going into that one, guys!

Next on the list is Pauline Ashley; she was found drunk outside the local Irish bar and spent the night in the holding cell to dry out.

Tracy Kardan, we have received confirmation from her lawyer that she spent the night with him at the motel.

The main suspects we are concentrating our attention on are Lincoln Harvey and Sonja Aldman. Any Questions?" Detective Ranch asked.

Detective Sargreto queried, "Why do you only have two suspects now? I thought you had a plethora of suspects, according to social media!"

"As you are all aware, the local community webpage has been giving former mayor Liz Valenti grief as they had her pinned as the murderer. We need to start putting out the truth and stop this. Liz Valenti is not a suspect; we do have reason to believe that the killer could be one of three people or all of them. At this stage, we have Tracy Kardan, the victim's lover, Lincoln Harvey, the victim's lover and close friend, and Sonja Aldman, the victim's wife. All three of them were at the motel on the night Paul was murdered." Detective Jamie continued.

"The victim was wearing a mouth gag, also known as a gag kit. Forensic evidence has come back that soaked in Chloroform. The person who did this had access to Acetone or heavy-duty nail polish remover was the wife, Sonja. Sonja is a nail technician who has access to this chemical, and she was at the motel on the night. Lincoln Harvey had admitted that he was also with the victim but declared that Paul was alive when he left. Sonja has informed me by telephone earlier this evening that Paul fixed the mayoral vote in favour of Lincoln. She is coming in the morning. I will find out more information then. That leaves Tracy Kardan, who has an alibi, conveniently being her lawyer."

"Can someone please call Liz Valenti and let her know she is no longer a suspect. That poor woman has been through enough. I have been watching the social media bullying she received." Detective Sargreto instructed.

"Sure, I will call Liz as soon as we finish the meeting," agreed detective Bell.

Back at the forensics' lab, Loretta had received the DNA results and was excited to tell Ann. "Hi Ann, I just received the results from the pubic hair I sent away for DNA testing, the hair they found in the victim, Paul Aldman's, mouth and found out who it belongs to!" Loretta exclaimed excitedly, as if she had just won the lotto!

"Well done, Loretta; who does the hair belong to?"

"A man called Lincoln Harvey. The hair jammed in Mr Aldman's upper teeth; he must have been receiving the act of fellatio from the victim."

Ann Fletcher rang detective Jamie Ranch about the DNA result on the hair.

Detective Ranch's phone rang. "Excuse me, everyone, it's the forensic expert Ann calling."

"Good evening, detective Ranch; we have just received the DNA test results for the victim Paul Aldman. It is confirmed that the item found on the victim belonged to Lincoln Harvey. Is he a person of interest in this case?"

"Hi Ann, thanks for this information. Yes, Mr Harvey Lincoln is a person of interest. What DNA did you get analysed?" Asked detective Ranch.

"A tiny pubic hair located between Mr Aldman's upper teeth," Ann replied.

"I love modern forensics; how did you get Lincoln's DNA from a small pubic hair?" Detective Ranch asked.

Ann went off on one of her lectures again. She loves talking about what she does and loves to educate anyone who will listen.

"A simple pubic hair can contain a minimal amount of nuclear DNA, but small unique genetic markers in that DNA can pin down a suspect. In this case, they found a perfect match. Lincoln had been caught shoplifting as a kid, and they collected his DNA. Because he was a minor at the time of the offence, there was no criminal charge recorded against his adult record. I hope this explains it, detective?" Ann said.

"Fantastic Ann, I appreciate your call," replied detective Ranch as he hung up.

With this new information, detective Jamie Ranch went back to his meeting. "It has been proven that the DNA found on the victim's body, was in fact, belonging to Lincoln Harvey. We will search any available CCTV around the motel to look for footage that can confirm the time of Lincoln leaving, even if we have to extend our search to all the buildings in the area. A camera must have captured something in the area! Thanks, everyone, for your time tonight. I will inform you of the outcome of the meeting with Mrs Aldman in the morning. Have a good night."

It had been a long day. Detectives Ranch and Bell turned off the lights and left the station for the night, knowing that tomorrow would be another big day. One last thing they had to do, was to call Liz Valenti.

I finally got the phone call from the police and slept for the first time in weeks. I was exhausted and sick of social media. I didn't turn my computer on for a week.

CHAPTER FORTY-THREE

As promised, Sonja Aldman was waiting outside the station when the detectives arrived for work in the morning.

"Morning, Mrs Aldman, please come in and just take a seat. We just need to prepare the office and will come out and get you in a minute," detective Ranch advised.

Sonja sat down in the waiting room. She looked terrible like she never got any sleep the night before. She sat with her head held in her hands.

Detective Bell walked in shortly after and called Mrs Aldman through to the meeting room. She very slowly got up and followed him.

Detectives Ranch and Bell reached out and shook Mrs Aldman's hand in turn.

"Thanks so much for coming in this morning Mrs Aldman." Detective Ranch said.

"Please call me Sonja; I don't deserve the name Mrs Aldman; Paul is dead!" Sonja sniffled as she burst into tears.

Detective Ranch quickly handed her a tissue. She took the tissue and wiped her eyes dry, then blew her nose on the only dry bit left. Jamie took three more tissues out of the box and handed them to Sonja.

Before detective Ranch or Bell could say another word, Sonja yelled out. "I did it! I killed my husband, Paul. I'm a murderer. I didn't mean to do it, but I did. Arrest me now, please!"

Sonja started sobbing uncontrollably and Jamie pulled more tissues out of the box. They certainly didn't see this coming.

"Ok, Sonja, please start from the top. Take your time. You did jump in early; I needed to inform you that we record all interviews. Do you understand, and would you like a glass of water?" questioned detective Bell.

"Yes, I understand, and yes, please to the water," Sonja answered.

Detective Bell quickly went out of the room and returned with the glass of water for Sonja. He placed it down in front of her with a whole box of tissues.

"Tracy Kardan called me to spill the beans on the affairs that my husband Paul has been having. I was distraught to hear that, then the bitch tried to extort money out of me for some photos; she threatened to go to the papers with pictures of Paul half-naked wearing bondage clothes. I went through Paul's private emails, his Google account, his clothing and anything else I could think of. I found an old suitcase in the carport that contained his leather gear.

One piece looked like it went around your head with a large ball attached to it. So I googled bondage gear, and what came up on my screen was bloody disgusting; it's called a Deep throat Gag Kit! I then realised what Tracy was telling me was correct. My husband is, or was, a sick bastard!" Sonja was struggling to speak between the sobbing, but she went on.

"I knew my husband had a week heart, so I thought if I soaked the ball in Acetone and bleach, it would knock him out. I didn't think it would kill him, though!" Sonja started bawling again.

"Please take your time, Sonja; there is no hurry." Detective Bell said.

"I soaked the ball thingy for about an hour then carefully placed it back in his suitcase, with his other disgusting bits and pieces. Later that night, he made up some stupid excuse about an urgent meeting in Adelaide and left the house. I went into the garage, and the suitcase had gone. I knew he had taken it to one of his sick sex romps. I decided to follow to see who he meets. I knew which motel he was going to, thanks to google maps. I sat in the car and waited. I saw Tracy walk into the motel at around 7 pm. There were quite a lot of people going into the old motel around the same time. I had assumed it was Tracy that Paul was with, but she tells me it was Lincoln.

I don't believe a word that bitch says. Anyway, I saw Tracy leave the motel at 10 pm. I never saw Lincoln leave. Most people left around 10 pm; I waited until 10.30 pm, left the motel car park, and went home to wait for Paul. I had quite a few things to say to Paul when he got home, but he never came home, did he!" Sonja starts sobbing again.

"Thank you for your statement, Sonja; we will need to investigate the information you have shared with us today. We are very sorry for your loss. At this stage, we cannot confirm the cause of death. You can't leave South Australia until after we finalise this matter. You are free to return to your home. We are not placing you under arrest at this time," detective Ranch informed.

Sonja looked surprised. She nodded and got up, and left the room.

Detectives Ranch and Bell sat there for a while and went over what Sonja had just admitted. "Something is not right, Jamie," detective Bell noted. "Sonja tried to knock her husband out, not kill him. I think we need to interview Lincoln Harvey again. There is something about that guy that gives me the creeps."

Detective Ranch agreed, and they set up another meeting with mayor Lincoln Harvey. They were lucky enough to get in to see Lincoln that afternoon, giving them time to get their questions prepared.

They both arrived at Lincoln's mayoral office at 1 pm and spoke with the secretary, Tanya. "Good afternoon, I am detective Jamie Ranch, and this is detective Anton Bell. We have a 1 pm meeting scheduled with mayor Lincoln Harvey."

"Yes, that is correct; please take a seat, and I will let the mayor know you are here," Tanya advised.

Tanya walked into Lincoln's office and informed him that the detectives were waiting for him. "Make them wait five minutes, then send them in," Lincoln said with a snigger. He just wanted to have a power play with them.

After five minutes had passed, Tanya walked over to the detectives and informed them that the mayor was ready to see them now. They both got up and walked into Lincoln's office.

Lincoln greeted them with the biggest smile. "Good afternoon guys, you both look dashing today. What can I do for you?" Lincoln asked.

"We would like to ask you a few questions," stated detective Ranch.

"Sure, take a seat. Ask away!"

"We have found your DNA on the victim's body, so we can confirm that you were in fact with Paul Aldman on the night of his murder," detective Ranch explained.

"Yes, I have told you that already; got anything new?" Lincoln sneered.

"Can you tell me what time you left the motel?" continued detective Ranch.

"Yeah, I left at around 10 pm, give or take a few minutes, and Paul was wide awake and laughing when I left."

"How did you arrive and leave the motel, Lincoln?" Detective Ranch asked.

"I drove my mayoral blue Lexus there, and I parked in the main parking area," said Lincoln.

"Did you see Mrs Aldman in her car in the parking area?" Detective Ranch asked.

"No, Oh God, what was she doing there? If she knew about Paul and me, then she probably killed him."

Detective Ranch continued "Can you please tell me what you were wearing with Paul Aldman on Sunday night?"

"Some very kinky leather shorts and leather belted bustier with silver studs. Here I can show you a photo if you like!" Lincoln replied.

"No, thank you Lincoln, I don't need to see a photo. Were you aware that Paul had fixed the votes in your favour to win this last election for mayor?"

"How the hell do you know that? Who told you? Paul told me that it was our secret, nobody knew about that. I haven't told a soul! Bloody idiot, I could lose everything because of that son of a bitch!" snarled Lincoln angrily.

Lincoln's face had gone red; he looked very agitated at the last question from detective Jamie.

"Angry enough to kill him, Lincoln?" asked detective Ranch.

"Don't be ridiculous; I told you already, he was happy, even sharing a joke with me when I left him," Lincoln countered.

"Thank you for your time Lincoln. Please do not leave South Australia until we have finalised this investigation, just in case we have any more questions," instructed detective Ranch.

"Sure thing, I'm not going anywhere. I hope you find out who killed Paul."

The detectives left the mayor's office and went to the forensic lab to speak with Ann Fletcher. The forensic lab is located at the city morgue, as most of Ann Fletcher's cases are homicide. The detectives needed answers about what Paul's state of mind would have been in if he had been poisoned with Chloroform.

Detective Bell asked "Afternoon Ann, how is everything going with the Paul Aldman case?"

"Just about done, thanks, detective. What can I do for you today?"

"Mrs Sonja Aldman has confessed to soaking the ball gag in a mixture of nail polish remover and bleach. The victim was found dead with the ball in his mouth, so can we assume that is what killed him?" queried detective Bell.

"The ball gag would have contributed to his death, but I believe strangulation to be the cause of death," said Ann as she pulled back the sheet to expose Paul's bruised neck.

"You can see some older bruises in the same area, but these were done with much smaller hands and were not as deep. The last person who was with the victim strangled him. I know that asphyxia is a form of sadism, and the victim presented in a position suggesting bondage.

We have been able to lift fingerprints off the victim's body by using a new TRX powder, Ruthenium tetroxide and recovered a positive result that matched Lincoln Harvey" explained Ann.

"As you have confirmed, Paul Aldman was poisoned by the Chloroform on the gag ball in his mouth. Can you tell me if he would have been happy and laughing at jokes three hours after sucking on that ball?" detective Bell asked.

"Absolutely not! He should have been out to it. Sleeping like a baby. There was enough Chloroform on that ball to knock an elephant out."

Detective Bell mused aloud "Interesting, the last person with the victim said they left him happy and laughing".

"Then that person is quite clearly lying to you. It would be impossible for the victim to have been even coherent at that time" Ann said

Detective Bell asked "Could the Chloroform on the ball have killed the victim if not for the added strangulation?"

"No, it could have given him a heart attack, but the Chloroform could not have killed him. It wasn't as strong as we first expected. The person who made the batch of Chloroform didn't use the correct technique to make it."

"Thanks for your time Ann, you have been very helpful," said detective Bell.

"Yes, thanks Ann, I have taken down all the notes that you have said, and I believe we have our killer. There is just one more piece of evidence we need, and we have nailed him," added detective Ranch.

"We should give Mrs Aldman the heads up that she didn't kill her husband," Detective Bell said.

"You are correct; that poor woman has put up with a lot" agreed detective Ranch, "The guy sounded like a total arsehole, and she was married to him. Now that he is dead, she is blaming herself. Let's make the call now".

"Hi Sonja, it's detective Bell here; we have just left the forensic lab and can confirm your husband's cause of death is strangulation and not by Chloroform. Therefore, you are in the clear for his murder. The poisoning charge is a lesser charge as your intention was not to kill your husband; however, you did poison him with the intent of harming him. The police will be contacting you shortly."

"Thank you so much for calling me. I hated thinking Paul was dead because of something I did. Yes, I am willing to accept the poisoning charge. Can you tell me yet who killed my husband?" Sonja asked.

"We have a suspect in mind but can't tell you who that is until we make an arrest. I will contact you as soon as we can. Goodbye." Detective Bell hung up the phone.

They left the forensic lab and headed over to the petrol station across the road from the old motel where they had discovered the victim, Paul Aldman. They had called earlier to ask them for their CCTV footage from the previous Sunday night.

"Good afternoon, I am detective Anton Bell, and this is detective Jamie Ranch. We called earlier to look through your CCTV footage from Sunday night. Do you mind if we take a look now?"

The young girl behind the counter blushed. She was attracted to the young detective Anton Bell and took quite a shine to him. "Sure, the cameras are on the computer in the office. I will show you."

She turned on the computer and waited a minute for it to warm up. She sat down and scrolled back through the footage until she found the previous Sunday night. "What time did you want?"

"That's ok; we can take it from here. You don't mind if we look through the footage?" Detective Bell asked.

"No, not at all. Did you want me to wait here, or can I go back out the front?"

"We are fine thanks, done this a few times before," said detective Bell with a smile.

They scrolled through the footage looking for when Lincoln left the motel. Finally, the detectives found what they were after; it didn't take them long as they worked back from midnight, and they saw Lincoln walking out to his car at 10.35 pm. They took the USB drive they had in their folder and copied the footage as evidence.

"That's the proof we needed. Let's go, Anton and arrest that creep!" said detective Ranch.

They thanked the young attendant for her time and left the petrol station.

They arrived unannounced at the mayor's office and walked up to his secretary's desk.

Detective Ranch said "Afternoon, our apologies for the unannounced visit, but we would like to speak with the mayor if that is possible?"

"I am sorry, but he is not in the office. He left in a hurry after your meeting earlier. He has cancelled his meetings for the rest of the week too," replied Tanya.

"Thanks for letting us know. If the mayor turns up, can you please give us a call? Here is my card," said detective Ranch.

Detective Ranch gave Tanya his card, and they left the office and walked back to their car.

"That bastard has done a runner. Do you think he will try and leave the country?" detective Bell asked.

Detective Ranch agreed, "You're right; let's call it in. Hopefully, we are not too late, and Lincoln hasn't left the country".

It didn't take long, and they received a call from headquarters. "Lincoln Harvey has just checked into the International business lounge. He has brought a one-way ticket to Mexico, and the flight leaves in two hours. We have notified security to keep him in the lounge until you arrive."

"Brilliant, thanks for letting us know. We are on our way," said detective Anton as he reached under his seat and took out the blue flashing light and put his arm out the window to stick the light on the roof, then turned on the siren.

They pulled into the drop off zone, flashed their badges at the parking attendant then ran inside and up the escalator to the business lounge. The staff pointed out where Lincoln was sitting, and the detectives went in and walked up to Lincoln.

The look on Lincoln's face when he saw them was priceless. They were standing in the way of the only exit, and he had nowhere else to run.

"Mr Lincoln Harvey, we are placing you under arrest for the murder of Paul Aldman. Please stand up," commanded detective Bell.

Lincoln stood up, and detective Ranch placed handcuffs on him and firmly led him out of the lounge. Detective Bell collected all of Lincoln's belongings and followed. Lincoln was taken back to the station for processing and was formally charged.

They took Lincoln into the meeting room and sat him down. "Can you take these handcuffs off? I normally get off on wearing handcuffs, but these don't match my outfit and are hurting me" complained Lincoln.

Detective Bell responded "No, just sit there. You can call your lawyer if you like?"

"I don't need a lawyer; I am innocent!"

"Oh, of course, you are. Only an innocent man would be fleeing the country to Mexico, right?" jeered detective Bell.

"I had a sudden urge to travel overseas; I felt like some real chilli con Carne. You don't have any proof that I killed Paul!"

"We are formally charging you with the murder of Paul Aldman. We have your DNA from pubic hair lodged in the victim's teeth and your finger mark bruises on Paul Aldman's neck. Paul Aldman died from strangulation. Sometime between 7 pm and midnight. We have footage of you leaving the motel at 10.45 pm," informed detective Ranch.

"Bullshit, I left the motel at ten; it must have been someone else who looked like me!" Lincoln pleaded.

"Mrs Sonja Aldman was sitting in her car at 10 pm and watched people leaving, and she has sworn that you never came out at that time." Detective Bell said.

"That bitch set me up; maybe it was just after 10 pm!" whined Lincoln, "I do want that phone call to my lawyer now."

Lincoln called his lawyer, "Hi Chris, it's Lincoln Harvey, the cops have charged me with Paul Aldman's murder, and I need your help, now!"

Chris replied "Don't say another word, Lincoln. I am assuming you are in the Wanjup Police station?" Chris Johnson was also Tracy's lawyer; he represented everyone in the bondage group. "I will be there in ten minutes; I am just down the road; hang tight."

Ten minutes later, Lincoln's lawyer Chris walks into the meeting room where Lincoln had been waiting. As he walked in, detectives Bell and Ranch stood up to shake his hand.

"Good afternoon detectives, can I please ask what you charged my client with?" Chris asked.

Detective Ranch replied. "Mr Lincoln Harvey has been charged with first-degree murder."

"What evidence do you have against him for this offence?" Chris asked.

"We have a DNA match to pubic hair found in the victim's mouth. There is also a fingerprint match from the victim's neck; Mr Aldman's cause of death is strangulation. Lincoln Harvey has admitted to being the last person to see the victim alive. We also have CCTV footage of Lincoln Harvey leaving the motel, well after everyone else had left for the night. He also has a motive to silence the victim regarding a fraudulent voting scam that helped him win the mayoral election. Then to top of his guilt, after being instructed not to leave the state, he buys a one-way ticket to Mexico to flee the country" informed Detective Ranch.

"I will apply for bail now, Lincoln and will get you out of here," Chris Johnson said.

"Sorry, Chris, but the judge won't allow bail for Lincoln; the court consider him a flight risk. Which he sealed today when he tried to escape to Mexico," detective Ranch responded.

"What on earth were you thinking, Lincoln, trying to fly to Mexico?" Chris asked.

Lincoln wailed "I was scared, Chris; these guys have it in for me. I was honest and told them that I was with Paul that night, but I swear I never killed him! They have my DNA and fingerprints as well as a motive. I'm fucked!"

"This is a bullshit charge; everything you have is purely coincidental. Don't worry, Lincoln, I will make this charge disappear. These young detectives wouldn't know a killer if it jumped up and bit their arse. The worst detective work I have ever seen. I am going to leave and look into this further." Chris left the room with Lincoln looking like he was about to burst into tears.

"Come on, Lincoln, let's get you comfortable in your holding cell; you will be staying here until the judge has set a date for your trial." Detective Bell helped Lincoln to his feet and walked him down the hall to the holding cells.

EPILOGUE

Tracy Kardan was charged with extortion and is currently serving a three-year prison sentence in the Adelaide Woman's Prison.

Zina Parkin is still pretending she is a wealthy socialite. She has damaged her reputation, is broke, and people are sick of listening to her gossip. Zina will never be my friend again!

Ex Councillor Belinda Stump and her husband Harry were both convicted of Theft and Fraud. They both received a minimal fine and received a spent conviction after Belinda provided a formal submission to the court based on their young family and business. The judge directed them to reimburse their victims and return all vehicles not sold. Additional penalties included the cancellation of their car dealers' licence and Belinda's removal as a sitting councillor due to her criminal activities.

Ex-councillor Donald Geary is currently unemployed. He served three months of a nine-month sentence for his first offence of Sexual Assault. He now has a criminal record and can no longer be admitted to the position of councillor or hold office in any Government position. His penis never fully recovered from being stuck in the Corona bottle. He had an inch removed due to blood loss.

Wendy Hunt left working for the city and got a job straight away at a local, all women lawyer's office. Wendy was disappointed at Donald's light sentence for his sexual assault charge. Still, she knew he wouldn't be doing it again, especially after his 'accident'. Wendy calls it Karma!

After Yanel Winley's forced retirement, she moved, with her husband, into a local retirement village, and she has taken up lawn bowls. They are both thrilled.

Tanya Riser is still working for the city of Wanjup as the mayor's secretary. She is currently working for the acting mayor Sharon Day.

My sister's ex-husband Scott moved in with his girlfriend Veronica, with whom he was cheating on my sister Lisa. He now has a bad case of Herpes, and his kids won't speak to him.

My sister, Lisa, started her own company as a private detective, specialising in catching out cheating husbands. She loves having her own space and being able to bring justice for these women.

Sonja Aldman collected her husband's life insurance and payout from the city. She is currently travelling around the world in a first-class cabin on one of the largest cruise ships. She has never been happier. She also located a few bank accounts in Switzerland that she immediately cashed in, paid off the home mortgages and brought herself a luxury convertible Mercedes Benz. The judge quashed Sonja's criminal attempt to poison her husband due to the lack of intent.

Angelo Porcini is the new CEO of the city of Wanjup, having been acquitted of any crimes and is now engaged to Sharon Day.

Acting mayor, Sharon Day, is genuinely in love with Angelo and is busy planning their wedding in the Barossa Valley. Sharon and I are best friends now, and Sharon has taken up playing tennis with me.

My friend Cornelius (Neils) Smith pursued the city tender process. He believed the CEO was involved in skimming money from the city. That case is currently with the Crime and Corruption Commission, awaiting a hearing date. Even though the CEO is deceased, the commission wants to get to the bottom of how it happened to avoid future corruption.

David Sepelt is in love! He has been promoted to sales manager at the radio station and is CEO of his Rainbow foundation. David is loving life.

Ex-councillor Barney Jones, unfortunately died, losing his life to cancer. He fought it hard for so many years, but in the end, it was quick.

Ex-deputy mayor Derwent Peabody never married again. He left South Australia and moved to Western Australia to start a new job in the mining sector. He has kept well away from being on another council.

Patricia Peabody, I have no idea, and frankly, who cares!

Councillor Pauline Ashley is still standing out the front smoking! Still a waste of space on the council, and people continue to vote her in!

Councillor Jack Piper and his beautiful wife Monique have just had their sixth child; a bouncing baby boy called Phillip. Jack is still on the council.

Councillor Lucy Meadow continues to look after and protect every tree in Wanjup and is still running her fruit and vegetable business in town. She will always be a beautiful person who cares about her city.

Councillor John Driver has just taken four months off council to take his wife on a big holiday through Europe. As a result, he has taken extended service leave from working at the shopping centre.

Councillor Alex Smith is still sailing under the radar. He doesn't cause any grief, speaks when he feels the need and just gets on with his life.

Ex-mayor Lincoln Harvey was charged with first-degree murder and fraud for vote tampering and serving eight years in Yatala Labour Prison. Parole is in four years.

The city of Wanjup continues to be run by dim wits who have just paid landowners to take a portion of their land and widen a new major road heading into town. With all the road works completed and months of traffic closure, only to discover they can't move the power poles. They never got approval from the electricity company before beginning works! So the road remains a two-way street with a huge bike path. Waste of money again, but not my problem, I'm not going back on council.

Well, what is Liz Valenti up to these days! You could say I got away with murder! That's right. I was so angry with Paul for the way he treated me; I had enough. But, I wanted to see what these guys were up to on a Sunday night. I could hear them with their whispers around the council chambers, and my curiosity got the better of me.

I heard mention of this old motel near the railway station in town and guessed that they all meet up there for their secret get-togethers. Mike always goes to bed before me; he doesn't last much past 9 pm. So once I heard Mike turn off the bedroom lights, I quietly went to my car and drove to the motel. I didn't pull into the car park but parked across the road at the rear of the petrol station. So I still had a good view of who was coming and going and was out of sight of any security cameras.

I watched Paul walk into the motel. Then to my surprise, his wife Sonja pulled into the car park. I never saw her leave the car.

I recognised Tracy's car and Lincoln's mayoral blue Lexus in the motel car park. Bloody hell, they are all here. I sat and waited, read a book and drank my coffee.

It would have been around 10 pm when people started to leave the motel. Whatever they were doing in there was finished. In the end, only Lincoln, Paul and Sonja's cars remained in the car park. I got out of my car and walked around the back of the motel; I could just make out that Sonja was still in her car, and she looked like she was getting ready to leave. I slipped on my latex gloves, just in case I found anything I could use against Paul.

I could hear laughter coming from one room and instantly recognised it as Paul's horrendous laugh; he laughs like a Hyena and Lincoln's high-pitched giggle. They were still very busy doing whatever they were doing. I had to take a peek; I couldn't help myself. I tried the door handle, and they hadn't locked it. These guys are very trusting.

As I carefully opened the door, I could see Paul dressed in some God-awful black leather outfit and Lincoln prancing around the room. I quickly shut the door before I heaved. Honestly, my stomach was turning. I hid behind the pillar and waited. Lincoln was the first to leave, and once I knew he was gone, I went back to the room. I had no idea what I would do, but I needed evidence to get rid of my shit CEO.

I crept into the room and saw an old suitcase on the floor near the bed. I couldn't see Paul anywhere. I tiptoed over to the case and opened it. I had to close my eyes for a second as I took in what was before me. The black mouth gag looked interesting, so I removed it and held it as Paul walked in. "What the fuck are you doing here?" he said.

I froze, now realising that I hadn't thought this through. "I was curious to see what you guys have been up to, so I followed you. I had no idea you were into this kinky shit Paul."

Caught out in his leather outfit made Paul as mad as hell. I had to pretend I was somehow into it too. What other reason is there for me being in his room!

"I just saw Lincoln leave. It looks like you had a good time, judging by the smile Lincoln had on his face when he left."

"What do you want, Liz?" Paul asked.

I held up the mouth gag with the black ball attached to it.

"I've always wanted to try this shit out, but Mike is just not into it. I would love to tie him up, shove this ball thingy in his mouth and make him my servant. Isn't that what this is all about?" I asked.

Paul's mood changed; he was now curious to see how far I would go.

"Take off your dress, Liz!" Paul demanded.

I slowly slid my dress off and stood in front of him with my bras and knickers on.

"Now I am going to lay on the bed, and you have to tie my feet and hands to it using these straps. You can take off those ridiculous gloves too!" said Paul.

"I'm keeping the gloves on, Paul. God knows where these things have been; I'm not touching them; I will get my gear one day." I walked over to the bed, picked up the leather straps and tied Paul to the bed.

"Yes, Liz, after tonight, you will be online buying your gear; trust me, it's addictive."

I finished strapping Paul to the bed; he was face down on all fours. Pathetic looking!

"Now that mouth gag you were holding before, you need to wrap it around my head. Then, the ball goes in my mouth, and it ties up at the back," instructed Paul; you could tell he was enjoying this.

As instructed, I did just that. What kind of sycophant enjoys this? Now that he was strapped onto the bed and couldn't move anywhere, he couldn't yell at me or do anything. He started to look very sleepy, and I was trying to work out what he was saying. I could see the fresh bruising on his neck and gathered he wanted more.

"Do you want me to squeeze your neck or something?" I asked Paul, trying to figure what my next move was. Shit, I didn't think this through; here I am in my undies, my CEO strapped to the bed. What if someone walked in right now with a camera? A bit hard to explain my innocence.

Paul nodded, so I carefully leant over him; I didn't want to touch the mattress; there were noticeable wet patches on it. I put my hands on his neck and started to strangle him. I have pretty strong hands from years of boxing, and I knew I was squeezing his throat hard. I never asked for a code or whatever these guys use to stop pressing. On realising this, I immediately removed my grip from his neck and moved away. Paul didn't look too good.

"Paul, Paul, wake up!" Shit, Shit, what am I going to do now? He has passed out! I quickly slipped my dress back on. I double-checked the room, made sure there were no video cameras. Great I haven't left anything behind, and I left the room, carefully closing the door behind me.

I walked back around behind the motel and crossed the road to my car parked at the rear of the petrol station. The motel car park was empty except for Paul's car. Everyone had gone for the night, no vehicles on the road. No one came to this old area anymore since they closed down the railway.

I drove home, disposing of the gloves in the school bin down the road. I walked into my house to my bedroom, put my pyjamas on and climbed into bed where I could hear Mike snoring like a chainsaw.

Yes, you can get away with murder!

Printed in Australia
AUHW010834151021
353723AU00007B/26

9 781982 292195